WHEN
YOU
READ
THIS

WHEN YOU READ THIS

A NOVEL

mary adkins

An Imprint of HarperCollins*Publishers*

WHEN YOU READ THIS. Copyright © 2019 by Mary Adkins. All rights reserved. Printed in the United States of America. No part of this book may be used or reproduced in any manner whatsoever without written permission except in the case of brief quotations embodied in critical articles and reviews. For information, address HarperCollins Publishers, 195 Broadway, New York, NY 10007.

HarperCollins books may be purchased for educational, business, or sales promotional use. For information, please email the Special Markets Department at SPsales@harpercollins.com.

FIRST EDITION

Designed by Bonni Leon-Berman

Title page and openers illustration by James Iacobelli

Library of Congress Cataloging-in-Publication Data has been applied for.

ISBN 978-0-06-283467-6

19 20 21 22 23   LSC   10 9 8 7 6 5 4 3 2 1

For Lucas and Finn

GOOGLING GRIEF

by Jade Massey

All the poems about grief

are wrong.

My grief is the

opposite

of a couplet.

It is not pretty.

It does not make room

for rhymes.

Here is my poem

about grief:

So this is pain.

This is what it was

all along.

SIMONYI BRAND MANAGEMENT
96 Morton Street, 9th Floor
New York, NY 10014

June 18

Dear Mr. Simonyi:

I came upon your company on the Stanford University Employers Forum, on which your firm is listed as a place where Stanford students have had positive internship experiences previously. Grace Wang ('16) wrote that she had a wonderful summer working with you and your colleague Iris. While "wonderful" is rather nebulous and uninformative, her point is well made. I see that you have not posted a fall internship opening, but I am writing to express my interest in interning for you come September.

I am a rising fourth-year with a deep and abiding commitment to public relations and communications work since the wee age of three and a half, at which time I launched my first promotional campaign for a line of children's toys created by my father, Carl Van Snyder Jr. My contribution consisted of conspicuously playing with the toys (which later became the award-winning ToddleGenius™ line) while at day care, in line with my father's at-home demonstrations. ;)

Since that time, I have established a proven track record of promotional success after promotional success. I am the youngest ever member of my fraternity to be elected social chair, and as such, I organized the Palo Alto chapter of the Race Against Alzheimer's this past spring, raising over $100,000 for the organization Don't Forget Us. I am also a Krav Maga black belt, nationally ranked chess player (12–15 age group), and founder of the online magazine *SHAVED*, devoted to topics of personal hygiene and masculinity's fluctuating contours.

I would be thrilled to join Simonyi Brand Management in New York City as a fall intern and am available to begin as early as August 24. Also, I would not require a salary, as this Urban Internship Semester must be in exchange for credit hours only.

My résumé is attached. In an attempt to be thorough, I have declined to be brief. Please let me know if you have a page limit, and I will do my best to trim it down to one (though the font size, of course, may have to decrease, which I'm aware can be a challenge to more mature eyes).

Sincerely,
Carl Van Snyder III

If you want to find out you're dying from a bot, I have a recommendation: Dr. Hsu at New York Presbyterian delivers death
warrants with the empathy of a salamander.

I should have expected nothing less, given that two weeks
ago, he informed me that a CT scan showed lesions on my lungs
by saying "This does not necessarily mean you have cancer."

I explained to Dr. Hsu that telling someone they don't necessarily have cancer is only good news if they already think they
have cancer. For those of us who believe ourselves to be healthy,
the correct phrasing is, "I have some bad news."

He thanked me for the suggestion.

Here's how it happened today. I arrived at the office around
8:30 as usual, before my boss as usual. I was reading news online. NASA reports that 25 million Americans have stockpiled
guns in preparation for doomsday. A man has spent $100,000 on
operations to become a real-life Ken doll. My phone buzzed, and
like that, I have lung cancer.

Dr. Hsu explained that not only are the lesions on my lungs
indicative of cancer, but they also mean that I will probably be
dying soon. He mentioned chemo, trying it, seeing what happens. But my cancer is special. It isn't referred to in stages like
other cancers. It only comes in two varieties: limited and exten-
sive. Mine is the bad kind.

"I want to be honest with you. The prognosis is not good," he
said. I thanked him for his honesty, because that's what you do
when someone bothers to point out they're being honest.

"Death is a fact for us all," he went on, "but yours will most likely come in six months or sooner," like the end of my existence is a gestating baby, or the love of my life. Half a year. Twenty-four weeks. Before summer.

The call was short, just long enough for us to plan for me to go in Wednesday. At some point in the conversation my boss walked in, and I noticed my 98-cent deli coffee had tipped over. The puddle dripped off the desk onto the floor. "WE ARE HERE TO SERVE YOU," the paper cup promised, sideways.

As I told Smith that I have six months to live, I laughed, like it's a joke. Is it?

He hugged me. I can't remember if I hugged back. He smelled like the Ralph Lauren cologne I once bought for Daniel but then gave to him instead, after some fight Daniel and I had, of the dozens or hundreds. *Do you tell ex-fiancés you are dying?* The question flitted through my mind as a matter of etiquette, one my mother would have an answer to. Somewhere, on a shelf in Virginia, there probably is a well-worn book with a paragraph on what courtesy ex-lovers owe one another with regard to announcements of terminal illness.

For Smith's benefit—he looked like he might have a heart attack—I kept talking, explaining the series of increasingly ominous events that led to this morning. First came the chest pains, then the CT scan, the results of which were delayed because of Christmas. Then the biopsy. It felt like someone else was talking about me. The actual Iris had fled. She's already gone.

He asked how long "this" has been going on. I know now that by "this" he was referring to the tests—to my discovery of the disease rather than to the disease, itself. But I misunderstood.

"Who knows?" I said.

I realized on the train home he meant the tests. He meant: *Why didn't you tell me?*

I didn't tell him, of course, because when you tell people things, they treat them as real, and then you have to decide. I had been hoping for the best. I have always been an optimist.

Neither of us knew what one does after being diagnosed with cancer that will probably kill you. Certainly not resume business as usual. So I came back to my apartment, which I'm now regretting. Maybe I'll go back to work. At least then he'd stop texting to ask if I'm okay being alone.

Is that what people do? Avoid being alone with their new cancer? I could call Jade, but I'm sure she's in the kitchen with her cell tucked away in a closet. Using my triannual call to my mom to tell her I have cancer just seems cruel. And I'm not in the mood for the baby mamas (my friends from my early twenties who had babies in our early thirties and then ceased to be capable of talking about anything but their children, so we've drifted. Plus, our friend Sabine, who was the glue keeping us together, moved to California).

Frankly, I'm surprised this site made it to fruition. A year or so ago the founders came to the firm looking for branding assistance in exchange for equity in their "graphic storytelling platform start-up." Todd and . . . Chad? Ethan? According to Ethan/Todd/Chad, both people with terminal illnesses and stay-at-home moms were itching to blog in triangles, arrows, and colorful bar graphs. They had a colorful binder of demographic research on target niches, and Smith had been intrigued, initially (I wasn't—they were both the same shade of too-tan and talked about the future like it was a lottery they'd rigged). They had originally called it a d-log (drawing log, like "vlog"), but that didn't go over well in focus groups. Throughout the presentation,

Smith and I both fought to suppress our laughter. For days afterward, he and I came up with who else might like to make a d-log: geriatric clowns! Racist poets! Disgruntled ghosts!

Now, here I am, a data point come to life. Bravo, Chad. I have a heads-up, a full six-month lead. I get to sit with my impending death over coffee so we can make plans.

Things you don't think about dying, until it's happening: I will break my lease.

I was an assistant while I saved to open a bakery, which never happened. I wanted a family, too, but so much for that. I got skinny then fat then skinny again. I smoked then quit.

She was an admin who got skinny then fat then skinny then died.

Here's the thing I need to figure out. This whole time I thought my real life hadn't started yet. Turns out that was my life. I have six months or so to make that okay, somehow.

COMMENTS (10):

DyingToBlogTeam: Welcome! We see you've already begun sharing. Remember that commenting on other users' Exit Posts will bring more visitors to your own page. Dying to Blog is a community of members facing the same challenge, and we want you to get your Maximum Departure Value™ out of it!

BonnieD: hi I'm Bonnie. I like your blog. u have to use more graphics tho because this is a graphics site and posts that get on the Popular page are never ones like yours. no offense but it looks like a word document. but i stumbled on you and like u so i will follow u anyway.

IrisMassey: Thanks, Bonnie. Do you have a blog on the site?

BonnieD: no. my mom used to be on it.

BonnieD: hers was really good but it moved to the afterlife page.

BonnieD: they have to move them otherwise u'd just have a bunch of corpse blogs and that would be depressing lol

IrisMassey: I'm sorry.

BonnieD: it happens

IrisMassey: Thanks for the tip.

Jan10101010101: buy Viagra buy romaine penis large buy not here thank u for your excellent content

EIGHT MONTHS LATER

Friday, August 28 | Simonyi Brand Management

---

from: smith@simonyi.com
to: rosylady101@yahoo.com
date: Fri, Aug 28 at 10:55 AM
subject: Vandalism of your posters

Dear Rosita,

I got your message. I understand your concern, especially after, as you note, we spent so much time perfecting the subway ad, and I remain grateful for your patience and gracious spirit during the photo shoot—agreed, he wasn't the most professional photographer around (apologies again for the fingernail clipping on-site), and I know you weren't thrilled to learn that I plucked him off of Craigslist, but that says nothing of how much I value you both as a client and as my dentist.

Remember that a year ago, no one knew who you were, because no one knew Paula Abdul had a ghastly mouth as a child. But then we all learned, thanks to that intrepid *Post* reporter, that you built Paula's mouth chair-side. You *made* Paula. It is a phenomenal feat, and one for which I'm glad you're finally receiving the recognition you deserve. Since the news broke, we have done an outstanding job (if I say so myself) harnessing your initial publicity to develop a personal brand. The interviews, the book deal, the additional celeb endorsements. Now that the book's coming out, and our campaign targeting commuters in the region has finally launched, I need to warn you about something:

fame comes at a price. You will have haters. It is inevitable. My clients don't read the comments, don't read the blogs, don't read the tabloids. And in your case, they don't pay attention to a little graffiti on a few subway ads.

We knew (or at least I did, and perhaps should have made more clear) when we decided to place the posters in New York subway stations that they would be vandalized. If you spend much time riding New York City transit, you will notice that no advertisement is immune from the occasional mustache or profane smear. These interactions with the ads, I would suggest, aren't something to bemoan. On the contrary, they enhance the likelihood of people noticing and remembering your smoldering, shimmering grin! Rosita de Santiago, DDS!

This is the time to welcome attention in any form.

You reference with loathing the estimable Dr. Zizmor, New York City's first medical professional to take to in-motion, 2-D campaigning on the trains. Sure, his posters about getting rid of pimples rendered him the target of ridicule. He also now owns a yacht and three houses on two different coasts.

Relatively speaking, I think T-E-E-F-S neatly penned across your five front incisors is fairly innocuous.

Warmly,

Smith S. Simonyi

President

Simonyi Brand Management

from:	YOPLAY <philgergel@gmail.com>
to:	smith@simonyi.com
date:	Fri, Aug 28 at 11:34 AM
subject:	YOU WILL NOT BELIEVE THIS B AS IN BULL + S AS IN SATIRE

NOPE.

NOPE NOPE NOPE.

NOT AGAIN.

YES *AGAIN*.

GO TO YOUTUBE

SEARCH MY NAME PLUS RAPPER SO YOU DON'T GET THAT YOYO TRICK MAN

CLICK ON "IT'S NOT EASY HAVING GREEN—ORIGINAL VIDEO"

SURPRISE!

IT IS NOT MY ORIGINAL VIDEO *after all*. THE LADIES HAVE BEEN REPLACED WITH MUPPETS, AKA I HAVE A BEAST FETISH APPARENTLY WHEREIN THE BEASTS ARE MADE OUT OF CLOTH

NOTE, FURTHERMORE: THE MUPPETS I "KISS" IN THIS "PARODY" OF MY RAP ARE ALL "MALE," BUT DUMMY DIDN'T EVEN USE KERMIT

FOOL

SO WHAT ARE THEY TRYING TO SAY NOW—THAT I AM A SINGER *FOR CHILDREN?*

SMITH, I AM DONE. WITH. THIS. DRAMZ.

AFTER "RAIN ON ME, SIR JESUS"—ok GOSPEL WAS A BAD IDEA, NOT MY FORTÉ SO MUCH AS not my forté—I HAVE STRUGGLED TO ESTABLISH MYSELF AS AN ARTIST WITH RANGE DESPITE PRESSURE FROM THE MASSES

WHO NEED ME TO FIT INTO A NEAT AND APPROVED CATEGORY OF MUSIC. I SUPPOSE MY RECENT DIP INTO COUNTRY DIDN'T HELP. DO PEOPLE THINK I CAN'T MAKE UP MY MIND ABOUT TO WHAT GENRE I BELONG?

BUT I AM AN ARTIST, AND ARTISTS:

A. EXPERIMENT
B. UNDERSTAND THAT JUST BECAUSE YOU EXPERIMENT DOES NOT PLACE YOU INTO A CATEGORY
C. ARE SUBJECT TO SO MUCH SCRUTINY WE OCCASIONALLY OFF OURSELVES

I'M NOT GOING TO OFF MYSELF, BUT I do EXPERIMENT, AND AT THIS POINT IN MY CAREER, I DO NOT HAVE ANY INTEREST IN PRETENDING ONLY TO BE INTERESTED IN ONE FORM OF SELF-EXPRESSION JUST TO PROTECT MY "brand" LEST I BE ABANDONED BY MY FANS, AND MY CAREER END BEFORE I AM DECREPIT AND USELESS, SUCH AS AT AGE 45.

I AM A VERNAL 32 YEARS OF AGE. BUT AS A WHITE RAP ARTIST OF SHORTER STATURE CLIMBING AN UP-HILL HILL, I AM FATIGUED.

I AM SLEEPY.

EVER SINCE I WON *SARAN WRAP'S FREESTYLE SHOWDOWN* AND GOT MY FIRST RECORD DEAL FOR "DON'T WHIZ ON ME" FOUR YEARS AGO, I HAVE BEEN THE TARGET OF THOSE WHO WOULD WISH TO SEE ME SHRIVEL UP LIKE A MAN'S JUNK IN THE SNOW.

IT IS TIME TO END THESE JUVENILE ATTACKS ON MY

MUSICAL GENRE EXPLORATION ONCE AND FOR ALL.
HOW DO WE FIGHT BACK?
AS THEY SAY: D.I.Y.D.D.Y.O.
DO IT YOURSELF
DON'T DO
YOURSELF
OFF
PLEASE ADVISE,
YO-PLAY/Phil

---

from: smith@simonyi.com
to: YOPLAY <philgergel@gmail.com>
date: Fri, Aug 28 at 12:04 PM
subject: re: YOU WILL NOT BELIEVE THIS B AS IN BULL + S AS
           IN SATIRE

I understand your frustration. I truly do. You are my most valued client, and I give you my true opinion, always.

I think we should ignore this video. It's nothing. "Fighting back" or responding in some way could be seen as thin skinned. You want to be perceived as having a sense of humor, right? Being playful, like your music?

Finally, remember what they say about all press?

SS

from:	carl@simonyi.com
to:	smith@simonyi.com
date:	Fri, Aug 28 at 12:09 PM
subject:	Today's Agenda

Good morning Boss!

Today's schedule:

~~10—Leah Rollins-Loebel (Prospective Client), Nutritionist to the Stars~~ (sorry—already passed)

1—Call with Phil Gergel (aka Yo-Play)

3:30—Proposed meeting with Carl, me, on the following action items:

A. The possibility of assigning me more tasks that utilize my strengths rather than tasks that a chimp could do

B. How one schedules a book tour when one doesn't agree with the premise of the book

Also, I took the liberty of cleaning out my desk a bit, as there were a few drawers on the bottom with contents, and I will be needing the storage space for my gym clothes, etc. I imagine these items belonged to your former employee who predated my tenure here at Simonyi Brand Management. Much of it appears to be trash (receipts, scraps, to-do lists), but I didn't toss anything, as there were some other items as well—a straightening iron, lip gloss, a few self-help books, an article torn from a magazine titled "Becoming Your Best Self" (what a bleak testament to the pressures of womanhood, this assortment—I might have to use it in a short story).

I have placed it all in crates I found in the lobby of the building, so if the super comes a-knocking, guilty as charged. They are stowed behind the conference table.

Oh, and there was also what appears to be a printout of a blog. It is titled "My Life's First Draft: A Blog Turned into a Book by Iris Massey." She seems to want you to publish it. (Side note: Based on this Post-it, I have inferred that this woman who last sat at my desk *died*? How recently?? Because fyi *that* is something I'm going to need some time to process . . .)

Off to lunch,

Carl Van Snyder

Associate

Simonyi Brand Management

---

from:	smith@simonyi.com
to:	carl@simonyi.com
date:	Fri, Aug 28 at 12:11 PM
subject:	re: Today's Agenda

Carl,

Thank you, but an agenda would be much more helpful if you would send it at the beginning, rather than the middle, of the workday.

Also, you are not an associate so please remove that from your email signature.

And what is this about Iris and a blog? I don't see it on your desk . . .

Thx,

SS

from: smith@simonyi.com
to: iris.a.massey@gmail.com
date: Fri, Aug 28 at 12:58 PM
subject: no subject

I wonder how many people continue to email other people after they die. That'd be an interesting radio story. Or just a depressing one.

I have a new intern who started this week, Carl. He fell out of the sky in June, and Richie convinced me to hire him since it's going on four months and I haven't been able to bring myself to look for your replacement. He is twenty-one and full of pep. I figure it might be nice to have someone around.

Meanwhile, a month after his spectacular "rap funeral," Phil—the one client making me any money at this point—has decided to return to rap, having discovered that country requires more of a "singing voice" than he's capable of. And of course the transition from "Yo-Play" to "Phil Gergel" did not go unnoticed by the tabloids. Now that he's done with country, he's pretending that he never left the hip-hop world, and we are continuing to pretend that he's straight.

His "funeral," your cannabis-induced brainchild (I am tempted to make a joke about how your death spared you from having to endure the execution of it), rivaled your original vision in its spectacle. Webster Hall was packed. His coffin was ushered in by six bodybuilding pallbearers in white tuxes as a gospel choir sang a funeral march. Dwarves in party hats distributed folded paper unicorns that looked more like horses wearing KKK gear, since the paper didn't take well to the horns. He retained your idea of being "reborn," emerging from the coffin via suspension cords, just like the best part of a community theater production of *Peter Pan*, and the crowd was delighted. It was exhausting, and far less amusing than if you had been around.

I am shocked by how much I miss you.

Every day, I knew you'd be here when I walked in, and every day, we would make fun of this absurd field we are in.

When I offered you the job, I was sure you'd leave it within six months, tops. I think we both did. This job was your bridge to your future.

But then a year went by, then two . . . should I have pushed you to leave? I didn't because I liked having you here. I was selfish.

Iris, I have no clue why you stuck around this place so long. But dammit, the best part of every day was making you laugh. I wasn't conscious of it as my goal, but it was.

The last time you and I spoke, it was about Richie, how happy you were with him. You sounded downright giddy about it. Then, you said that the night before, your sister had taken you dancing. To me these seemed like good signs.

I asked if you needed anything.

"Tell me something funny," you said, so I told you how Phil had adopted a guinea pig and named it Abraham Lincoln. Your laugh turned into coughing. And then we hung up, but first I made myself say that I missed you. You said it back. I think we both wondered if it was our good-bye, since you wouldn't let me come see you, but I told myself that that didn't make sense. You were dating my friend! And going dancing!

I waited for you to come back. And you didn't.

I'm in deep, Iris. I got in deep.

from:	smith@simonyi.com
to:	carl@simonyi.com
date:	Fri, Aug 28 at 1:12 PM
subject:	re: Today's Agenda

Carl,

Please be reminded that lunch is an hour. And what Post-it? Thx,

SS

from:	smith@simonyi.com
to:	carl@simonyi.com
date:	Fri, Aug 28 at 2:29 PM
subject:	re: Today's Agenda

Carl,

I have looked everywhere and do not see a printout of anything. I know we haven't spoken explicitly about this, but it seems like a good opportunity to say that all files and other documents that are work-related should remain here at the office.

Additionally, assuming you haven't skipped town due to the monotonous tasks you feel you've been assigned, do let me know if you plan to be gone for more than three hours in the middle of a workday.

Thank you for so neatly packing away her things, by the way.

from:	wally@homilypines.com
to:	smith@simonyi.com
date:	Fri, Aug 28 at 2:51 PM
subject:	Checking in

Hiya Smith!

Hope all is well in the big apple. You are missing the start of a beautiful fall out here! Took your mom on a walk yesterday to enjoy the sunshine. She's not so much into leaving her room these days, so it was quite a feat to convince her to let me get her in the chair. I swear it feels like she stiffens up like a toddler resisting sleep when I try to move her (though I know that's impossible). I've taken to letting her have her way more times than not, lest I get verbally accosted. Calls it her "jail cell." You know how she can be. What a sense of humor she has!

I was thinking if you came for a visit that might give her some reason to smile. But I know you're busy.

Jillian asked me to remind you that your August bill is outstanding. I told her I was sure you didn't need reminding and it'll come in with your September payment. Your mom says hi.

Wally

from:	smith@simonyi.com
to:	richierich1000@gmail.com
date:	Fri, Aug 28 at 3:08 PM
subject:	Loan

Hey Richie,

Any chance I could borrow like two grand to help me make my mom's rent this month? I hate to ask given what I already owe you, but I lost two clients to a bigger firm in July, one of those corporate giants, and I haven't signed anyone in about six months. I'm working on it. Every time I sit down to write an email to a prospective client, it feels like I'm inhaling sand, but I'm working on it. If you are up for adding it to my tab, I'll pay you back as soon as I can. Beer later?

I was also wondering if you'd be down for putting me in touch with any of your smaller clients, like the guy downtown who got all of that attention for selling the quiche that induces labor? I forget the name of his café.

You know I wouldn't come to you unless I'd already tried everything I can think of.

Beer later?

Thanks man,

Smith

---

from: Airbnb
to: smith@simonyi.com
date: Fri, Aug 28 at 3:12 PM
subject: Your listing is UN-SNOOZED!

Hi Smith,

Congratulations, you have successfully un-snoozed your listing **Beautiful One Bedroom with Balcony on Upper West Side**. It is set to go live again tomorrow, Sat, Aug 29. This means that your listing will show up in search results, and guests can reach out to you to book.

Your date availability is listed as **all dates**, and your termination date is set to **no termination date**. To change the visibility of your listing, or to snooze again, go to Manage Listing.

Thanks,

The Airbnb Team

---

from: smith@simonyi.com
to: richierich1000@gmail.com
date: Fri, Aug 28 at 3:42 PM
subject: Thanks

Just saw the bank transfer. Thanks for handling that so fast.

Beer? When is good?

---

from: carl@simonyi.com
to: smith@simonyi.com
date: Fri, Aug 28 at 4:21 PM
subject: re: Today's Agenda

Dear Smith,

Of course I understand that lunch is not three hours!

And LOL re the skipping town. Don't worry, I'm not that easy to get rid of. ;)

Typing on my phone here—almost back to the office.

The reason I was gone so long is that I intercepted the thieving of a lady's cell phone and found myself dozens of blocks north in pursuit of the thief. Fortunately, one of us (him) hasn't spent four years running Varsity track at the state level (gold medals in 2011, 2012, 2013). Still, he ran like a Kenyan. When I eventually managed to catch up, he had stopped to rest against the wall of a Spanish deli. I stealthily informed an unoccupied cop munching on a hoagie, who abandoned his sandwich to retrieve the phone with little fanfare. Of course I wasn't going to leave a person of color alone with a cop, perp though he was. I remained to legally observe.

I have some internal conflict over the experience, to be honest. The owner of the phone hardly even thanked me. She seemed to think the officer had more to do with the recovery of her phone, never mind that I was the one who hurdled from the West Village to Midtown. Maybe she wanted a new phone anyway.

Gah. It's almost 5. Rats. I have to run to make my 6p hot yoga class because the 8p is canceled. The train takes longer than I expected from our office to my sublet in Brooklyn, where I'm living with three NYU students (*inventing* their own majors—give me a break) who literally don't believe in cleaning. I am not allowed to use Lysol lest they be poisoned from the noxious fumes. But, you know, dust mites and rat pellets I'm sure are fine.

I'll leave the book/blog/whatever on my desk for you because I just walked in, and you seem to be very focused working on something in there. I inadvertently took it with me to "lunch" (as if I had time to eat). In my altruistic lurching, I accidentally knocked over my Arnold Palmer, spilling it on the sticky note she put on top. It is . . . kind of legible still? Hmm. Maybe not. In case, here's what it said:

Smith,
    If you think this is any good, feel free to publish it. No pressure just because I'm dead.
    Iris

I thought that was cute! No pressure just because I'm dead!

I must go so not to get a shitty spot next to the smelly, hairy guy (good for him doing yoga, though), and/or miss Pranayama deep breathing.
Namaste,
Carl

from: UWinNao
to: smithsimonyi@gmail.com
date: Fri, Aug 28 at 5:11 PM
subject: Hey, it's okay!

We heard you had a rough go of it just now!

We get it. It stinks to lose. On the other hand, as Thomas Edison wisely said, "Many of life's failures are people who did not realize how close they were to success when they gave up."

To get you back in the game, we're rewarding you with **25,000 naoPoints**. Remember, you can use naoPoints to unlock new games or uncover strategy tips!

from: gamblersanon.org
to: smithsimonyi@gmail.com
date: Fri, Aug 28 at 5:29 PM
subject: We miss you at Gamblers Anonymous.

Psychiatrist Leonard Higgenbottom, MD, says that one reason we gamble is because we believe that we can, will, and probably should lose.

Is this you?

Come back to Gamblers Anonymous Online, where our fellowship of men and women faces our common problem, one day at a time. Together we can accomplish what we cannot alone.

BEFORE

http://dyingtoblog.com/irismassey

December 30 | 1:32 AM

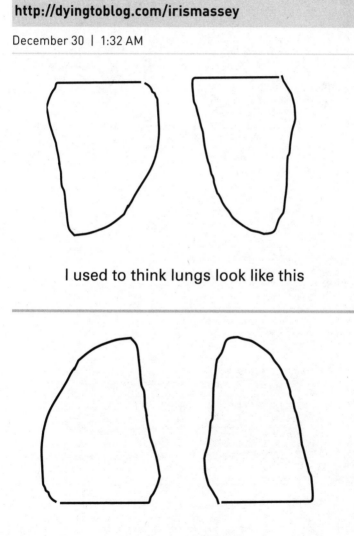

I used to think lungs look like this

but they're flipped

Mine look like

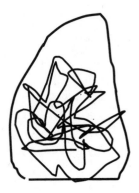

Actually

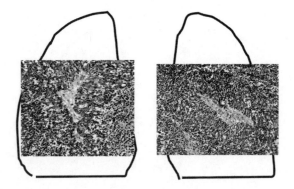

(If you google pictures of your cancer,

beware of the ads.)

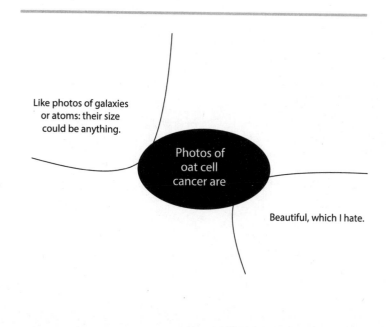

Like photos of galaxies or atoms: their size could be anything.

Photos of oat cell cancer are

Beautiful, which I hate.

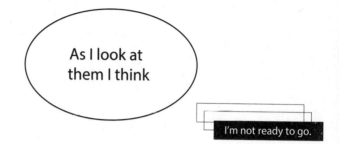

COMMENTS (10):

BonnieD: :-O!

ArduousArdvark: LOL that is fucking hilarious photos warehouse

BonnieD: hey arduous there are kids on this site, plz keep it klean

ArduousArdvark: like me u mean? i'm thirteen bitch

BonnieD: so. i'm 16.

ArduousArdvark: hot

BonnieD: watch ur mouth plz, thank u

ArduousArdvark: so I'm like dying too? so i think i won't? but thank YOU.

IrisMassey: Hey. Support each other, guys?

ArduousArdvark: LOL right

FRIDAY, AUGUST 28: JADE

AMAZON Review (1 of 141) of iRelaxx 100% Authentic Satin Bathrobe in Frisky Lavender
August 28, 4:40 a.m.
Jade R Massey: 4 Stars

I am a bit thick through the hips and bought this in a M.

Unlike other reviewers, I did not have a problem with the ripped seams or missing loops. It's a fucking bathrobe for $17.99. There are going to be some problems. Also it has the inner tie to make sure it doesn't come loose, so it's not like the outside belt is doing that much work, anyway. The knot holds if I tie it in a bow. If I loop it once it comes loose. To me this is common sense, however, so I disagree with Sharon M. that this is a fault of the robe. I believe it to be physics.

Finally, the material is indeed thinner than I expected, as most of the 140 people who have also reviewed this item note. Unlike many of you, however, I am not currently interested in seduction. Still, it's good for lying around in and doesn't feel too sticky on my skin.

from: kwaters@rmpofnewyork.com
to: jademassey@yahoo.com
date: Fri, Aug 28 at 5:30 AM
subject: How EGG-cited are we about your future?!

Dear Jade,

It's been nine months since you attended EGG FREEZING 101: TAKING CONTROL OF YOUR FERTILITY. We would love to hear where you are in the process of planning your future.

Let me know if you'd like to set up a follow-up appointment with our IVF coordinator.

Sincerely,

Karen Waterson

Marketing Director

Reproductive Medical Partners of New York

---

from: mail@rmpofnewyork.com
to: jademassey@yahoo.com
date: Fri, Aug 28 at 5:37 AM
subject: Your email preferences have been updated

You have been unsubscribed from our listserv.

We are always looking for ways to improve our service! If you are willing to share your reasons for unsubscribing, simply reply to this email.

from:	jademassey@yahoo.com
to:	mail@rmpofnewyork.com
date:	Fri, Aug 28 at 5:46 AM
subject:	re: Your email preferences have been updated

I'm dealing with a death in the family and not thinking about freezing my eggs right now.

Free tip—women who come to your seminar have not forgotten that our reproductive systems are aging. I am as aware that my eggs are thirty-seven as I was last year that they were thirty-six, when I attended your seminar. If I don't contact you it's because I have shit going on, or because I can't deal with trying to prolong my fertility window at the moment.

Please treat the women who are your prospective clients with a bit more respect. We are adults capable of contacting you when we're ready to move forward.

from:	jade@barntherestaurant.com
to:	marcus@barntherestaurant.com
date:	Fri, Aug 28 at 7:28 AM
subject:	Course 11

Dear Marcus,

During my time away I had an opportunity to reflect on our menu, and having now returned to work following my leave of absence, I've had some ideas. Please humor me.

The move to the tasting menu was difficult for me. You know my strong feelings about how undemocratic I find tasting menus. But I cooperated and threw the full weight of my support behind it, and of course early reviews seem to indicate that you were right. It was a positive move for us.

But especially after an encounter I had with a patron last night, I feel that if we are going to stick with the tasting menu, the final course must be cut. A tasting menu has an arc; it must. It tells a story. Otherwise, why does it exist?

The Dog Days theme that you created in my absence is lovely. For the most part. The silky Vermont curds. The fluke: A+. My favorite is the disguised balut, but of course it is—that's the greatest achievement of my career, I think. But at the conclusion of this harmonious succession of pure delight and surprise, guests are presented with . . . *an ice cream sandwich?*

Now, we both saw how many of those melted puddles of goo came back to the kitchen last night. And I haven't been around to know for sure, but I'll bet that has been the trend over these last couple of weeks that Dog Days has been live. You are probably working on a plan to retire the sandwich as we speak. But the sandwich itself is not the problem, and a replacement is not the solution. The problem is sugar.

I don't know if you know this about my sister, but the woman was baking up a storm until she could no longer stand upright. Sugar is fertilizer for cancer. And heart disease, and obesity. I realize we don't cook so people can eat. I realize that we are not Burger King, and our mission is not to feed or nourish but to pleasure. Still, there is gravity to every other dish on our menu; it has had a life. It is derived from the organic energy of the living. Ending a tasting menu with a course of refined sugar is blasphemy. It's tacky. It's unnecessary. And it discredits us with guests who may otherwise find that they both are thrilled during *as well as* after the meal, as it doesn't leave them bloated balls of gas one breath closer to a diabetes diagnosis.

I know you believe that we must at least give people the option of a sweet course at the end because that is what people expect. That without the option they will sense something missing, like a phantom limb. I just disagree. I think concluding with the seaweed mole pudding is classy, narratively intelligent, and most importantly, respectful to the guts of our patrons.

You are probably shaking your head, but I ask you only to consider it. I am happy to be the one to respond to pushback, though I doubt it will amount to much.

Finally—a reminder that I'll be in Virginia Monday and Tuesday next week, back Wednesday morning.

See you shortly,

Jade

---

from:	jade@barntherestaurant.com
to:	bernardhsu@newyorkpresbyterian.com
date:	Fri, Aug 28 at 8:14 AM
subject:	Concerning the treatment of your former patient Iris P. Massey

---

Dear Dr. Hsu,

Good morning. I am the elder sister of your former patient Iris Pamela Massey, who underwent chemotherapy in your office from January 6th to March 31st of this year. I am writing to express my deep concern over the treatment she received under your care. If my records are correct, her chemotherapy treatment consisted of Platibon and Topovesin. According to my research (see attached paper by Dr. Peter J. Lachow, MD, PhD, at the University of San Diego), the drug Avazumab has been found to increase the effectiveness of the cocktail when added to the mix. Was it not possible to adjust my sister's treatment in accordance with this up-to-date research?

Sincerely,

Jade R. Massey

Chef

Barn—"2 Michelin Stars for 5 Years and Counting"

from:	jademassey@yahoo.com
to:	winsomebeautydorothy@hotmail.com
date:	Fri, Aug 28 at 8:43 AM
subject:	Flight info

Mom,

I've changed my flight to Monday as you suggested, since you'll be at Bible study Sunday night. See below—I arrive at 8:40 Monday morning and leave at 6:30 Wednesday morning so I can get straight to the restaurant.

Things we'll need to get done while I'm there:

Monday

- Grocery shopping. Last I checked, all you had in your fridge was some brown asparagus and an expired carton of Greek yogurt. I know you don't believe in cooking, but we can at least get you some healthy snacks that you can munch on between cartons of pad thai. (Speaking of which, remind me to talk to you about MSG. There are a million reasons to request it without MSG, and your digestive tract will thank you.)
- Cleaning out the garage. The tower of Winsome products gathering dust is teetering on the brink of a full-blown avalanche. I worry you're going to hit it with your car one day, and then we'll really have a mess. I think we should just send them back. After 30+ years with the company, you are more than entitled to a refund on a few bottles of face serum and BB cream. And if or when you decide to resume selling, you can just reorder new product.

Tuesday

- Doctor's appt. I called Dr. Greenbaum and scheduled you for a physical. I know you don't trust doctors, but I don't think the pain you're describing in your neck and shoulder is normal. Nor do I think it's good to be taking Ambien every single night. According to drugs.com: *Ambien is for* <u>short-term use only</u> . . . <u>Do not take this medicine for longer than 4 or 5 weeks without your doctor's advice</u>.

· Oil change for the Buick.

Tuesday night I'll cook us dinner. I'm thinking either cauli-flower bánh mì bowls or whatever the fresh catch is at the Publix. If neither sounds good we can do meatballs.

Love,

Jade

---

from: bernardhsu@newyorkpresbyterian.com
to: jade@barntherestaurant.com
date: Fri, Aug 28 at 11:40 AM
subject: DRAFT re: Concerning the treatment of your former patient Iris P. Massey

---

Dear Ms. Massey,

I appreciate your patience as this is my first week in the office of Dr. Hsu, and I am still familiarizing myself with office proto-col and processes. In order to remain HIPAA compliant, I must ask that you please have your sister fill out the attached autho-rization form and return it to our office before I may release any details about her medical care to you.

Best,

Anna Truong

Office Assistant

from: jade@barntherestaurant.com
to: bernardhsu@newyorkpresbyterian.com
date: Fri, Aug 28 at 11:48 AM
subject: DRAFT re: Concerning the treatment of your former patient Iris P.
          Massey

Dear Ms. Truong,

How on earth am I supposed to do that given that my sister is

from: iris.a.massey@gmail.com
to: bernardhsu@newyorkpresbyterian.com
date: Fri, Aug 28 at 11:54 AM
subject: re: Concerning the treatment of your former patient Iris P.
          Massey

Dear Ms. Truong,

Please find attached authorization to discuss my medical treatment with my sister, Jade Massey.

Sincerely,

Iris Massey

from: bernardhsu@newyorkpresbyterian.com
to: jademassey@yahoo.com
date: Fri, Aug 28 at 2:50 PM
subject: re: Concerning the treatment of your former patient Iris P.
          Massey

Ms. Massey:

As your sister completed the release I am permitted to respond to your question.

I see in your sister's file that she declined the Avazumab on

January 2. I don't have any further notes. It is possible it was not covered by her insurance. Perhaps you should ask her directly?
Anna

Friday, August 28
TherapistAwayNetwork™
Patient Name: Jade Renee Massey
AUTO PROMPT: **What small change can you make today?**

Dr. Zarchikoff,

I totally understand your decision to hike Machu Picchu on the eve of your 70th birthday. In fact, I'm inspired and awed by it. Good for you. Seriously.

I do, naturally, wish it wasn't happening the same week as I'm going back to work after my leave of absence. Regarding "a small change I can make," that certainly seems like a big enough one for the moment, given that (as you know) I've spent the last several months nocturnal, living on kale chips, red wine, and the home shopping networks. Tech from 8 to 10 is a drag, but beauty from 10 onward is calming. I appreciate that colors, regardless of the item and material, are named after food—licorice, mocha, tangerine. Sometimes I actually place an order—online, not by phone. (God, I'm not that far gone.) I wake up around four under green crumbs (green, the exception, is "grass"). I may or may not brush the maroon (actual Cabernet) stains off my teeth before getting into bed as the sky lightens behind my blinds.

Not anymore. Time to get my life back. I have *finally* finished sorting through Iris's things, and apart from the box of stuff I presume belongs to her Queens boyfriend, it all has a destination—

Virginia to my mom's, or Goodwill. Given that I lost my contacts when I dropped my phone in the toilet last month, I don't know how to find him. Do I even know his last name? Richie...Martin? No, that's a singer. I suppose I could go back into her email (I had to today...long story).

I also emailed Marcus my idea for cutting the dessert course. You will be glad to hear I'm trying to be more vocal about my needs there.

One thing that's bugging me—I learned today that Iris chose not to take the more effective chemo drug she was offered. Why would she do that? It could not have been cost. You know I got her savings. According to Google, Avazumab is pricey. That's apparently why some people don't take it. But that can't be the case for Iris. She had plenty to cover it out of pocket, even at the high end. It makes no sense, unless her doctor did not clarify for her the relative effectiveness of the drug. That would seem to be the only reasonable explanation. I imagine you're going to counsel me to "let it go," but truthfully I think this could be a claim for malpractice.

How long are you gone again? Two weeks? I fly to Virginia on Monday. Lord knows I'll be selected for extra screening at TSA with this case of turmeric. I figure it might relieve my mother's osteoporotic pain. (At your age, you should probably look into taking it, too.) Who knew it was possible for a person's health to deteriorate so rapidly in three months? That sounds callous. I'm just surprised by the physical and emotional toll this has taken on my mother given that she and Iris hardly spoke. Or maybe that's *why* it's so hard for her. Listen to me, I sound like you.

I hope you are enjoying your hike.

Dear JADE,

Thank you for your submission to TAN™. We will make sure your provider receives this message.

"Change" can be traced back to the Latin *cambire*, meaning "to barter." Often, the idea of changing sounds daunting to us, as if we are being asked to uproot our identities and start over from scratch. But most changes, even significant ones, need not be approached with such grandiosity. The simplest changes are like barters, decisions to forgo one thing in exchange for another. These small acts are, cumulatively, more significant than they often feel in a given moment.

TAN™ is not to be used in case of emergency. If you are in crisis, call 9-1-1.

Sincerely,

Your friends at TAN

SATURDAY, AUGUST 29

from:	smith@simonyi.com
to:	jademassey@yahoo.com
date:	Sat, Aug 29 at 11:08 AM
subject:	Hello

Dear Jade,

You and I met briefly at Iris's funeral. I hope you are doing well under the circumstances.

Are you still at Barn? Congratulations on the new Michelin star—saw the write-up in the *Times* last weekend. One of these days when normal folks like me can get a reservation, I look forward to making a visit.

I have some of your sister's things (the stuff she left behind in her desk). Barn isn't too far from my office at 96 Morton Street, 9th floor. Would you be able to swing by sometime?

Sincerely,

Smith S. Simonyi

President

Simonyi Brand Management

---

from: jademassey@yahoo.com
to: smith@simonyi.com
date: Sat, Aug 29 at 11:33 AM
subject: re: Hello

You can mail my sister's things to:
  Jade Massey
  93 Underhill Ave., Apt. 14
  Jersey City, NJ 07306
JM

---

from: smith@simonyi.com
to: jademassey@yahoo.com
date: Sat, Aug 29 at 11:35 AM
subject: re: Hello

Dear Jade,

I figured you could sort through her stuff to see what you wanted to take and what you wanted to leave. There are four crates of items, much of which I believe is trash.

Sincerely,

Smith

---

from: jademassey@yahoo.com
to: smith@simonyi.com
date: Sat, Aug 29 at 11:37 AM
subject: re: Hello

I prefer to go through it in my own home rather than at your office with you standing over me. Please mail them, thanks.

JM

from:	smith@simonyi.com
to:	jademassey@yahoo.com
date:	Sat, Aug 29 at 11:41 AM
subject:	re: Hello

Tone can be difficult to decipher over email, but I am pretty sure I detect hostility in yours. I apologize if I offended you in some way by asking you to come by. I am trying to be helpful. I'll get the boxes in the mail to you as soon as I can.

I don't know if you were aware, but your sister was writing a blog at the time of her death. In boxing up her things, my intern came across a copy she left for me. Iris asked me to try to publish it. I figured you'd want to know about it if you didn't already. I'll put a copy in the mail along with the boxes.

from:	jademassey@yahoo.com
to:	smith@simonyi.com
date:	Sat, Aug 29 at 11:48 AM
subject:	re: Hello

So she wants you to publish her "secret blog."

Not to stomp on your publishing dreams, but thirty-something with cancer writes about her life as a secretary being cut short by the same thing everyone else dies of, too? That is not going to sell. And if it does, it will be to sentimental barbarians who want to read about someone else's illness so they can feel better about their own pathetic lives. She died so young! Before she ever even made anything of herself! Before she even got married! Thank my lucky stars I'm not her! I'M SO #BLESSED!

It's cancer porn.

Here, I'll give you the back cover: "She reminds us to act on our dreams before it's too late." Or how about "#YOLO."

You leave her funeral early like you have somewhere better to be, and now you want to make her blog into a book you can sell? Big celebrity-brand guy, or whatever it is you do? Show a little decency.

JM

---

from: smith@simonyi.com
to: jademassey@yahoo.com
date: Sat, Aug 29 at 11:49 AM
subject: re: Hello

So there's your beef with me.

I left the funeral early because I got a call from my mother's retirement home. My "something better to do" was seeing the area code 608 flashing on my cell, which tells me the call is from Homily Pines in Sun Prairie, Wisconsin, an institution with 24/7 medical professional care of the kind my mother requires. She is disabled over ten years now, and her prognosis was six. That week she'd had an adverse reaction to her medication and spent a couple of days in the hospital. I was afraid she had died, which is my fear every time I see that damn area code. But I am glad you feel like you know me well enough to assume I'm an asshole.

I haven't yet read beyond the first several pages of her blog, so I can't counter your assertion of what it contains. Still, despite apparent appearances to the contrary, I respected your sister. If she wanted to share what she wrote with a wider audience than only those who followed her blog back in the spring, my default response is going to be to honor that. Call me crazy.

And lest you think I am one of those people who treats the

dead as if they stick around as ghosts or spirits, dwelling just over our heads, surveying our actions, let me assure you that I'm not attempting to please some phantasmal version of her corpse. I don't believe Iris is watching, or that she is going to be angry at me if I *don't* publish it. Whatever energy moved in her has dispersed into a universe that is blind to our concocted narratives of "purpose." We are not special. We do not survive death. We only think we are, and do.

If I am wrong and she is assuming gold-tipped wings from a cherub as we speak, no matter. The nature of my interest is principle. She requested it. I'd like to honor that.
Smith

PS—The copy about the dreams isn't too bad (if clichéd), but "YOLO" is just tasteless. And she wasn't my secretary. She was my assistant, and would have been my associate if she'd ever been willing to accept the title.

---

from:	jademassey@yahoo.com
to:	smith@simonyi.com
date:	Sat, Aug 29 at 1:19 PM
subject:	re: Hello

Let me try again: my sister was very ill. As the person present in the weeks leading up to her death, I will assure you that cancer does indeed affect the mind as well as the body. So does chemo.

You may know that I took a leave of absence at Barn so I could stay with her for those last couple of months. I observed that as she was proceeding through the stages of grief, she took to writing to process. Apart from that fling she had with the heavyset man from Queens whom I believe was a friend of yours, her days were spent baking sweets and then throwing them away—muffins, cupcakes, peanut brittle toppling out of the trash can. She said she was making things for people, but she never seemed to give any of it away. It all ended up in the garbage. Do you see what I am saying?

I am not insulting Iris. If she'd written something while she was healthy and alive that you happened upon—perhaps a novel?—that'd be different. This is not that. Lord knows if I was in her position, I'd likely deal with the situation in unhealthier ways than oversharing with strangers on the Internet and obsessive cookie baking. But I think you will find there is little in her blog by way of literary merit or commercial appeal. It was a diary, for fuck's sake. Of a sick woman on the decline.

Speaking of God, if your unsolicited atheistic diatribe was to goad me after my sister has just died, well done. It must feel good to be so much smarter than everyone else because you don't believe in an afterlife. Want to lecture me about evolution, too? Go ahead and start quoting Darwin to me like I don't know who he is. Give me a lecture on religion and be sure to use the words "opiate" and "Richard Dawkins."

You have made your views loud and clear. Here are mine: I'm not okay with you publishing, or seeking to publish, my sister's cancer blog. So no need to send it—I don't have to read it to feel entirely, unflinchingly certain of this.

I'm sorry about your mother.

JM

What the fuck is your problem? Were you raised to

---

from: jademassey@yahoo.com
to: smith@simonyi.com
date: Sat, Aug 29 at 1:22 PM
subject: re: Hello

I apologize for the text I inadvertently forgot to delete at the bottom of my email. Please disregard that part only.

---

from: smith@simonyi.com
to: carl@simonyi.com
date: Sat, Aug 29 at 1:25 PM
subject: Fwd: Hello

Carl,

See below. On Monday, please ship the boxes to her. Use the cheapest means—USPS ground or whatever.

And do include a copy of the manuscript, please. I'll leave one on your desk.

Thx,

SS

---

from: carl@simonyi.com
to: smith@simonyi.com
date: Sat, Aug 29 at 2:04 PM
subject: re: Fwd: Hello

Dear Boss,

In regard to your email just now, I am trying not to work weekends. It is important for boundary-setting for both my immediate and distant future, as studies show that if you start drawing boundaries early, you retain the skill throughout life—and if you don't, well. I'm not sure I'm to that chapter yet.

However, since we are now effectively in communication on a Saturday and the boundary has been crossed, I would like to use this opportunity to express my concern over the conversation in the email chain below. You might want to be a little nicer to her, because while I am not formally a lawyer, last spring I did audit an IP class at Stanford Law (ranked no. 1 in *US News*, tied with unnamed school that rhymes with "tail"). If you indeed decide to pursue publication of the book, I imagine you are going to need the sister, or at least the next of kin, on board as heir of the copyright. Should I email my professor to confirm? I don't mind. I have to keep in touch with him anyway so he will write me a LOR—that is, if I succumb to my parents' pressure and decide to go to law school after all. Lulz.

Now get off the computer and enjoy your weekend!

Carl

---

from: smith@simonyi.com
to: carl@simonyi.com
date: Sat, Aug 29 at 2:05 PM
subject: re: Fwd: Hello

Even if she left it for me, asking me to publish it?

What is an LOR?

---

from: carl@simonyi.com
to: smith@simonyi.com
date: Sat, Aug 29 at 2:06 PM
subject: re: Fwd: Hello

Letter of Recommendation.

¯_(ツ)_/¯

from:	smith@simonyi.com
to:	carl@simonyi.com
date:	Sat, Aug 29 at 2:07 PM
subject:	re: Fwd: Hello

I don't know what that thing means either.

from:	carl@simonyi.com
to:	smith@simonyi.com
date:	Sat, Aug 29 at 2:09 PM
subject:	re: Fwd: Hello

It's a shrugging guy!!!!!

Also remember that the words on the Post-it are smudged due to the Arnold Palmer, so that particular document probably wouldn't hold up in court. Sorry/not sorry. In the pursuit of justice spills will occur.

from:	smith@simonyi.com
to:	iris.a.massey@gmail.com
date:	Sat, Aug 29 at 6:17 PM
subject:	no subject

It's funny, you're gone, but reading your manuscript makes it seem like you're not.

You know, I think you're selling yourself short in this thing.

My dad, as you know, was not the greatest guy, especially toward my mom. If there is a person who died full of regrets, and probably hating himself, it was my father.

Whenever he pulled up to the house after being on the road for a while, and my mom came outside to greet him, he couldn't move fast enough. Not a small man, he would more or less fall out of the cab and jog over to her with so much effort that it was awkward to watch. He was like a giant kid, the clasps of his overalls jangling until they embraced. In those moments, they always looked in love. There were times when she actually squealed. It was a scene I came to associate with returns. Of course, returns require departures.

The year I turned nine was the first time she kicked him out that I remember, and the next few months were the most peaceful of my childhood. She started cleaning houses, and I'd occasionally go along to sit on other people's sofas and watch *The Price Is Right*. She'd flip the mops upside-down to transform them into mop creatures, and we'd crack up. I stopped being afraid to come home from school. We ordered a lot of pizza. But there was also something missing—him. She wasn't getting a boot thrown in her face or yelling so loudly I'd crawl in the shower and turn on the water, but she also didn't smile as much. She definitely didn't squeal.

When they eventually got back together, the happiness didn't last, of course. The next eight years went about the way I've described to you before. And I didn't understand that we were a stereotype. It felt like we were the first people to suffer, in secret, the confounding cycles of a rageful alcoholic who gets clean once in a while.

The spring I turned seventeen, she left a handful of times, disappearing with both her summer and winter clothes, leaving a big open space in the hall closet to make a point. But every time, she would return, and there was a moment when they looked in love again. For just a day, or even only a few hours, this fleeting euphoria would exist between them. Eventually I realized they were probably both trying to get that feeling back all the time. It was why she had to keep going, and why he had to keep giving her a reason to go: so that she could come back.

Even for him, a miserable asshole, there were still these kind of . . . redemptive, I guess, flashes that squeaked through the expanse of shit. There was joy in the crevices. I witnessed it.

I find myself hoping as I turn the pages that you came to this understanding about your own life, that for any regrets you may have had, you recognized there were joyous parts. You certainly created them for others.

I don't care what your sister wants. You wanted this manuscript published, so that's what I'm going to do.

---

from:	smith@simonyi.com
to:	sheryl@berringerpress.com
date:	Sat, Aug 29 at 6:49 PM
subject:	Congratulations! And a question

Hi Sheryl,

What a delight to receive your wedding announcement! I had no idea that you and Steve were even a couple!

I have a half-baked idea for Berringer to throw your way. I know you'll be frank with me because you always are, in that college-roommate's-college-girlfriend way. It concerns my former colleague, who tragically passed in May at the age of thirty-three. During the last six months of her life, she authored a blog that received considerable attention online. My office is currently working to determine the copyright situation with this "manuscript," so to speak, but as a preliminary matter, I'm just curious—what do you think of it? In terms of its publishability, assuming the copyright is a nonissue? As you may recall, she and I were close, and I find myself wanting it to be more widely available, but I don't know what that would look like.

Linking to it below.

Congrats again,

Smith

---

from: jillian@homilypines.com
to: smith@simonyi.com
date: Sat, Aug 29 at 7:02 PM
subject: Aug + Sept Rent

Dear Smith,

    We still have not received payment from you for either August or September. Please remit payment at your earliest convenience.
Jillian

---

from: smith@simonyi.com
to: richierich1000@gmail.com
date: Sat, Aug 29 at 7:14 PM
subject: re: Loan

Hey Richie,

    You around? Thanks again for helping me out. Want to get a beer?

---

from: UWinNao
to: smithsimonyi@gmail.com
date: Sat, Aug 29 at 8:19 PM
subject: YOU WON!

Congratulations! You just won **$1,740** at UWinNao! For being one of our favorite players, we are rewarding you with **50,000 naoPoints**.

    Visit us again soon . . . how about *nao*?!

---

from: Bro-vado
to: smithsimonyi@gmail.com
date: Sat, Aug 29 at 9:21 PM
subject: Your account has been deactivated

To reactivate, simply log back in.

Please complete the following brief survey to help us better serve you. You have chosen to deactivate your account because:

A. You prefer a competitor site
B. You are taking a break from gaming
C. You had a specific problem arise with Bro-vado

Come back and we'll start you off with a courtesy **$25** deposit to jump-start your winning!

---

from: Bro-vado
to: smithsimonyi@gmail.com
date: Sat, Aug 29 at 10:14 PM
subject: Your account has been reactivated

If your account was reactivated in error, please contact customer service at the number below. It will now be 7 days before you can deactivate again.

How to find out you're about to die

Answer the
phone.

How to find out you're about to die

Answer the
phone.

Everything and
nothing changes.

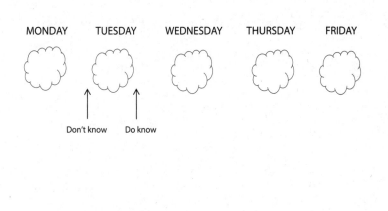

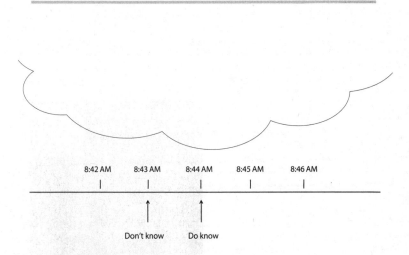

How to face death

X Try to imagine eternity

☒ Read books on dying

"We die as we lived,"
some guy wrote.

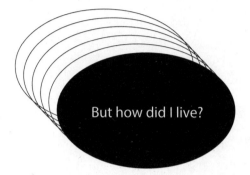

I estimate

But probably more like

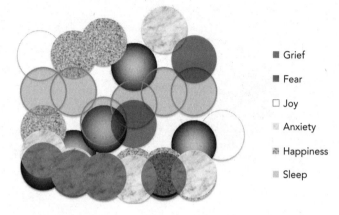

- ■ Grief
- ■ Fear
- □ Joy
- ▨ Anxiety
- ▨ Happiness
- ▨ Sleep

what is happening
on top of
what happened
on top of
what happened
on top of
what else is happening

There wasn't an arc

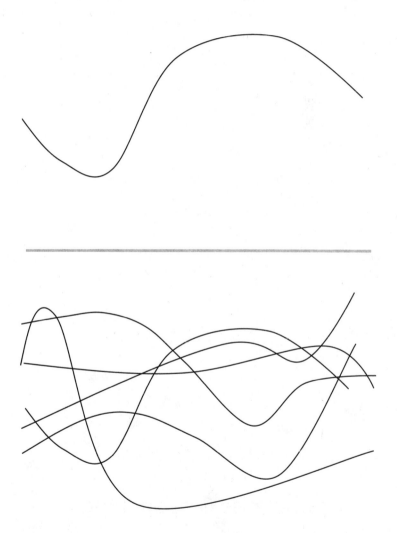

Or a bunch

It was more

dots

The dots look different close up

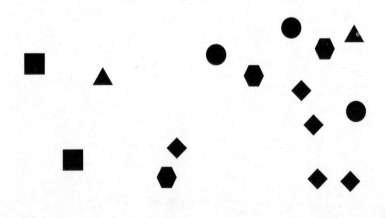

NONE OF IT
MATTERS AND I

Wearing red
boots today

Overheard a
toddler say
"when I was
a child"

NEVER WANT IT
TO END

My bagel's
warm cream
cheese

COMMENTS (12):

BonnieD: S

ArduousArdvark: since when is a triangle a dot

ArduousArdvark: or a square

ArduousArdvark: it's called geometry

BonnieD: I know what she means.

BonnieD: don't worry, Iris

ArduousArdvark: what

BonnieD: some experiences feel like circles and some feel pointy. and some have extra sides

ArduousArdvark: a circle doesn't have sides

BonnieD: sigh

ArduousArdvark: what

BonnieD: you're tedious

MONDAY, AUGUST 31

Monday, August 31
TherapistAwayNetwork™
Patient Name: Jade Renee Massey
AUTO PROMPT: **What have you lost?**

My mind.

It is 5:00 a.m. My flight leaves in three hours, and I just received an email from Marcus, which he must have sent on his way home (could he have bothered to give me more notice?). He says I can't go to Virginia. I quote:

You just returned from a month leave, which turned into a two-month leave, which turned into a five-month leave. The only reason you still have a job is that you're competent. I can't keep finding ways to cover for your absence. You are a chef, and you work in a restaurant that is not an average restaurant. It is a restaurant where chefs all over the world dream of working. The fact that I even granted you a leave of absence would shock people. Now that you're back, I need you around. Your call.

Maybe I shouldn't be blindsided, but I am. Sure, it was a startling act of kindness that he allowed me time off in the first place.

I did not expect that kind of generosity from Herr Marcus. And that's why I have thanked him a zillion times. But to threaten me like this—yes, Barn is *the* Barn, but does he remember why Barn is the Barn? He needs me, and he knows it. If I leave, it will be his loss, not mine. Who is he going to run recipes by—Enar, the Nordic dishwasher? He's extremely ripped, but come on.

Which is why I don't think he'd do it. Fire me. He's all talk.

But what if he does? Fuck.

What do I do.

My mom needs me. That much is clear. And there's more. Last night, I logged into my sister's email again. I just wanted to know why she didn't go with the better chemo. I only searched for "cancer," "chemo," and "treatment." (Okay, yes, I searched "Jade," but then I logged out before I saw anything. And I did discover that her old boss is still emailing her, which makes me feel bad for being so rude to him as he's clearly in love with her.) Though I found nothing on the chemo, I did learn she was on weed. She was ordering "Cannabis Tincture" from some distillery in Seattle. Lord knows how that might have impacted the efficacy of the chemo. So now I have more work cut out for me if I'm going to pursue this possible malpractice claim, which I think I owe it to her to look into.

It appears I know what I have to do. But I will not give Marcus the satisfaction of firing me. I may have lost my sister, but I haven't lost my goddamn dignity.

Dear JADE,

Thank you for your submission to TAN™. We will make sure your provider receives this message.

Did you know "loss" is of Germanic origin, derived from *los*, meaning "destruction of an army?" As you move through your day, consider what army you are mourning the destruction of. What officers were in its ranks? What were they defending you against?

TAN™ is not to be used in case of emergency. If you are in crisis, call 9-1-1.

Sincerely,

Your friends at TAN

---

from: smith@simonyi.com
to: rosylady101@yahoo.com
date: Mon, Aug 31 at 8:43 AM
subject: re: Vandalism of your posters

Dear Rosita,

I assure you with utmost sincerity that in none of the graffitied ads, despite the black markings concealing your teeth, do you appear toothless. Dashing, yes. Glowing, yes. Professional, yes. Toothless, no. If you do not see a spike in bookings this month, I will eat my words, but I would put money on it. Hang tight!

Best,

SS

---

from: smith@simonyi.com
to: mdublin@forwardchartersairline.com
date: Mon, Aug 31 at 9:10 AM
subject: Great to meet you

Michael,

Fantastic to meet you the other night. I am, as promised, writing to introduce myself more formally. I am aware that Forward Charters has had a challenging last year, what with the missing bridal party, the charred wedding dress, and the rumors about the pilot's drinking. I invite you to view this as an opportunity to create a revitalized face for the airline. Four years ago I assisted Tiny Planet Airlines in rebranding in the wake of its public image crisis after it crashed into that pile of medieval ruins outside of Budapest. Today, its ridership is at a peak since the early '00s.

I'd love to chat further.

Best,
Smith S. Simonyi
President
Simonyi Brand Management

---

from: mdublin@forwardchartersairline.com
to: smith@simonyi.com
date: Mon, Aug 31 at 9:12 AM
subject: re: Great to meet you

Who put you up to this? Listen, my wife is not the president of the airline. *I* am. You can tell her that. Actually, you can tell her I said to go to hell, because I *did* sleep with that agent in Chicago, and it was hot as fuck!

---

from: smith@simonyi.com
to: mdublin@forwardchartersairline.com
date: Mon, Aug 31 at 9:15 AM
subject: re: Great to meet you

I see you've got it covered. Thanks for getting back to me!

from: smith@simonyi.com
to: contact@lassimariset.com
date: Mon, Aug 31 at 9:30 AM
subject: Congratulations!

Dear Lassi,

I first want to congratulate you on your incredible achievement this weekend at the Continental Cup! You are a regular Olaf Rye (the first ski jumper!), and at only thirteen!

I was so pleased to come upon the news of your win in the International Skiing Federation journal online.

Lassi, as the youngest winner in a decade and a competitor for the World Cup later this fall, you are going to be acting on the world stage from this moment on. Are you ready?

I am a celebrity brand manager with a background working with athletes competing at the international level, as well as other stars and thought leaders. If you are interested in ensuring that your remarkable success and talent open as many doors as possible, not only for promotion of your brand but for engagement across media platforms (the sky's the limit!), please give me a call.
Sincerely,
Smith S. Simonyi
President
Simonyi Brand Management

from: sheryl@beringerpress.com
to: smith@simonyi.com
date: Mon, Aug 31 at 9:55 AM
subject: re: Congratulations! And a question

S—

Where is MS? Attached? Yes okay.

College roommate's college girlfriend! Ha! Indeed! What memories we share. My, time. My, time, time, time.

You had no idea about Steve and me, right? You and everyone else we were in school with. It's a huge surprise to many of our colleagues, as well, but we've actually been fucking for years. HR knew, of course.

Here's the other thing that will knock your socks off: we're hyphenating our names. Gritten-Barrett! Like grin and bear it! Ha! I know! With names like those, how could we not?

That's my go-to.

I will have my intern Brutus review. That's a girl. I thought it was a boy till she came in for the interview. Females are now named Brutus in the world and girls are boys and boys are girls. I cannot keep up, nor do I give a fuck.

And I'm glad to hear from you, actually, because I have an author for you. Memoirist with a DISGUSTING rags-to-riches story. I mean it's DISGUSTING. Literally born in the trunk of a taxi, went to Yale, and wound up in the goddamn Musée d'Orsay. People fucking love art. Also her art isn't even about her shitty homeless childhood. How transcendent is that? The most beautiful goddamn thing ever. Her name is Zahara Ferringbottom. Let me know and I'll put you in touch.

xSheryl

---

from: YOPLAY <philgergel@gmail.com>
to: smith@simonyi.com
date: Mon, Aug 31 at 9:59 AM
subject: re: YOU WILL NOT BELIEVE THIS B AS IN BULL + S AS IN SATIRE

IT CAME TO ME.
A PARODY OF THAT PARROT-Y

SHOW THEM I AM TRULY A MAN OF PLAY

WE REPLACE MY FACE WITH MISS PIGGY'S FACE

GET IT? SHE IS CHEATING ON KERMIE WITH ALL THOSE CLOTH BETAS

DO YOU THINK THAT'S FUNNY OR IS IT JUST CALLING MYSELF A LADY PIG?

PS—I WAS READING IN THE AIRPLANE MAGAZINE THE OTHER DAY ABOUT RETIREMENT, WHICH IS WHEN YOU HAVE TO STOP WORKING BECAUSE YOU GET SO DAMN OLD NO ONE WANTS TO PAY YOU TO HEAVE YOUR WRINKLED ASS OUT OF BED. WHAT AM I SUPPOSED TO DO IF I HAVE NOT SAVED ENOUGH MONEY TO SUSTAIN MY LIFESTYLE, COME SUCH A DAY?

I GOT AN ACCOUNTANT SO I DON'T GO BROKE PRIOR TO THESE ALLEGED "GOLDEN YEARS." I TOLD HIM HOW WE WORK IS THAT YOU JUST HOLD MONEY AND THEN TAKE IT OUT WHEN YOU EARN IT. HE SAID THAT IS UNUSUAL BUT I SAID THAT'S HOW WE'VE DONE IT SINCE THE BEGINNING SO. HOW MUCH IS IN MY ACCOUNT? TWO GRAND? EIGHTY? I HAVE NO CLUE. AS I HAVE, IN HIS WORDS, "NOT BEEN ATTUNED" TO MY SPENDING. PLEASE SEND HIM RECORDS SO HE CAN FIX WHAT MY INNER CHILD HAS DAMAGED

THANKS MUCH AS ALWAYS YOURS,

YO-PLAY/Phil

---

from: smith@simonyi.com
to: YOPLAY <philgergel@gmail.com>
date: Mon, Aug 31 at 10:03 AM
subject: re: YOU WILL NOT BELIEVE THIS B AS IN BULL + S AS IN
           SATIRE

Phil:

I can have my intern get on the video right away.

What exactly does your accountant need from the account, what sort of records? He must mean invoices. I can send those over now.

---

from: YOPLAY <philgergel@gmail.com>
to: smith@simonyi.com
date: Mon, Aug 31 at 10:05 AM
subject: re: YOU WILL NOT BELIEVE THIS B AS IN BULL + S AS IN
           SATIRE

HE IS RIGHT HERE. HE SAYS NOT JUST INVOICES, ALL RECORDS, SUCH AS BANK STATEMENTS

HE SAYS I AM AN EMOTIONAL SPENDER.

BUT I DON'T KNOW WHY THAT IS A BAD THING WHEN IT SOUNDS SO GOOD

WHEN CAN THE VIDEO BE READY?

---

from: smith@simonyi.com
to: YOPLAY <philgergel@gmail.com>
date: Mon, Aug 31 at 10:06 AM
subject: re: YOU WILL NOT BELIEVE THIS B AS IN BULL + S AS IN
           SATIRE

I'm swamped today, but I'll get the documents over to you as soon as I can, and I will make the video a priority.

from: carl@simonyi.com
to: smith@simonyi.com
date: Mon, Aug 31 at 10:06 AM
subject: Paging Benjamin Franklin!

Call me crazy, but I think I just had a very good idea for the United States Postal Service. They need to do pickups where they actually come in and box up your stuff for you. Because while I do believe in patronizing the USPS, figuring out how to pack and transport this much stuff is *not* a strength of mine. On a scale of 1 to 10, I am a zero.

You know, it probably makes most sense if I just call a courier company that does this sort of thing and have them come do it.

from: smith@simonyi.com
to: carl@simonyi.com
date: Mon, Aug 31 at 10:08 AM
subject: re: Paging Benjamin Franklin!

Carl,

I recall from your résumé that you're adept at video editing, correct? Please see the request below from Phil and get started right away. Instructions for what he wants should be clear. We can talk more in a bit if you have questions, but right now I have to run an errand.

Set aside the packing and whatever else you're working on in order to get started on this video project. Phil is a very important client.

---

from: smith@simonyi.com
to: richierich1000@gmail.com
date: Mon, Aug 31 at 10:10 AM
subject: re: Emergency

Just left you a message—it's an emergency. I need to borrow some money. And I may need a lawyer. I'm on my way to your office to see if I can catch you in person.

---

from: carl@simonyi.com
to: smith@simonyi.com
date: Mon, Aug 31 at 10:11 AM
subject: re: Paging Benjamin Franklin!

No problem at all! I love comedy, videos, and creating comedic videos. I look forward to reading what he has in mind, but first, since it sounds like you're in a hurry—does this mean I'm merely *postponing* packing up all this crap to send to Jade Massey of Jersey City, or am I allowed to outsource it?

---

from: smith@simonyi.com
to: carl@simonyi.com
date: Mon, Aug 31 at 10:12 PM
subject: re: Paging Benjamin Franklin!

Just set everything else aside and focus on this.

from: smithsimonyi@gmail.com
to: richierich1000@gmail.com
date: Mon, Aug 31 at 10:33 AM
subject: re: Emergency

Me again. Just left you another message. Call when you can?

from: YOPLAY <philgergel@gmail.com>
to: smith@simonyi.com
date: Mon, Aug 31 at 10:37 AM
subject: re: YOU WILL NOT BELIEVE THIS B AS IN BULL + S AS IN SATIRE

WE ARE WAITING FOR RECORDS. PLEASE SEND SO HE'LL LEAVE ME ALONE. I TOLD HIM I WANT TO GET IT OVER WITH now SO I DON'T HAVE TO COME BACK AGAIN
   HE IS SO MEAN
   SO I BOUGHT SOME GOATS ONCE SO WHAT??

from: smith@simonyi.com
to: richierich1000@gmail.com
date: Mon, Aug 31 at 10:56 AM
subject: re: Emergency

You here? Ringing your buzzer.

---

from: carl@simonyi.com
to: smith@simonyi.com
date: Mon, Aug 31 at 10:57 AM
subject: re: Paging Benjamin Franklin!

Good news! I know you said to set it aside, but Deshi from GiveUsYourWork is on his way to pack up the boxes, and he's only charging $10 plus shipping costs. (How does he even make ends meet? I'm really beginning to see what my Social Contracts in the Modern Age professor meant when he bemoaned the booming freelancer economy. Still, for our immediate purposes, #worthit.) (Omg, how quickly I became #partoftheproblem . . . so many feelings . . .)

But BACK TO IT (banality of evil, ugh)—fastest method, you said, right? I'll tell him FedEx Overnight.

Oh, he's already here!

---

from: smith@simonyi.com
to: richierich1000@gmail.com
date: Mon, Aug 31 at 11:05 AM
subject: re: Emergency

At coffee shop across the street. Your office light isn't on.

Are you getting my texts? Will wait here till you're back.

from: carl@simonyi.com
to: smith@simonyi.com; YOPLAY <philgergel@gmail.com>
date: Mon, Aug 31 at 11:29 AM
subject: Regarding the video assignment

Dear Smith and Phil,

As a (relatively) straight man, I have long been troubled by my possible role in perpetuating homophobia. This current assignment raises ethical concerns for me. I have been charged with creating a video in which I replace male-to-male amorous activity with female-to-male amorous activity. Yes, they are Muppets. But as Muppets, they are gendered. The goal of this video is, apparently, to dial back the suggestion that Phil is gay. But the underlying message of this project is homophobia.

After a thoughtful twenty minutes of self-struggle, I have determined that I cannot complete this project while maintaining my integrity. I am, however, attaching an article on the historically disproportionate distribution of male vs. female characters among the Muppets, which began to be remedied in the 1990s and yet remains unequal even today.

Sincerely,

Carl Van Snyder III

Senior Intern

Simonyi Brand Management

from:	smith@simonyi.com
to:	carl@simonyi.com; YOPLAY <philgergel@gmail.com>
date:	Mon, Aug 31 at 11:32 AM
subject:	re: Regarding the video assignment

Carl (and Phil),

While I understand your concern, we can deal with homophobia another time. This is important to Phil.

Thx to both of you,

Smith

from:	smith@simonyi.com
to:	carl@simonyi.com
date:	Mon, Aug 31 at 11:33 AM
subject:	re: Regarding the video assignment

Carl,

(Took Phil off) Please *do not* communicate with clients without my permission apart from scheduling appointments. This is very important.

from:	carl@simonyi.com
to:	smith@simonyi.com
date:	Mon, Aug 31 at 11:44 AM
subject:	re: Paging Benjamin Franklin!

Boss,

It's fine! He already wrote back, and you won't believe it, but he had *no idea* the video was speculation about his sexual orientation! In fact, he seems to be completely in the dark re: all those memes about him being closeted. What bliss, to be so naïve! I almost hated to tell him.

But he took it like a true ally. He is not upset, and he agrees that we should abandon the video, as he does not want to be affiliated with bigotry. What a relief—that Phil Gergel is so decent!

Honestly, there's another reason it's best to forgo projects like this one for the time being. Did you know Mercury is in retrograde, so it's a dangerous time to be technologically innovative? Things made of technology tend to break down out of nowhere. Last night my roommate broke his phone by dropping it onto his *own face.* Probably his head didn't give way much due to the fact that his pillow is memory foam. (Those make me sweat, do they you??)

By the way, Phil also asked me to send over some bank records. So he gives you an account and you can just access it as needed? How convenient. Looks like the log-in is saved on this computer, too! Consider it done.

PS—Did you sleep in the office last night? Just wondering because when I arrived there was a blanket bunched up on the bottom of the lobby couch. And if that's an option, I'm definitely interested. My roommates are now into assigning chores to one another and policing the hell out of the chore sheet. I just don't have it in me, not this summer.

---

from: smith@simonyi.com
to: carl@simonyi.com
date: Mon, Aug 31 at 11:45 AM
subject: re: Paging Benjamin Franklin!

Carl,

Wait.

Do not send any financial files or information until I return.

---

from: YOPLAY <philgergel@gmail.com>
to: smith@simonyi.com
date: Mon, Aug 31 at 11:53 AM
subject: re: YOU WILL NOT BELIEVE THIS B AS IN BULL + S AS IN SATIRE

DID YOU KNOW PEOPLE THINK I'M GAY?????

---

from: YOPLAY <philgergel@gmail.com>
to: smith@simonyi.com
date: Mon, Aug 31 at 11:55 AM
subject: re: YOU WILL NOT BELIEVE THIS B AS IN BULL + S AS IN SATIRE

I SPEND BECAUSE I CARE
I HOPE
NO I DO
I DO
I LOVE THAT CARL BY THE WAY
HE SAYS YOU ARE OUT N ABOUT SO HE IS GOING TO SEND THE FILES

---

from: carl@simonyi.com
to: smith@simonyi.com
date: Mon, Aug 31 at 12:00 PM
subject: re: Paging Benjamin Franklin!

Uh-oh. Did I do something wrong? Was just trying to be helpful . . .

from: YOPLAY <philgergel@gmail.com>
to: smith@simonyi.com
date: Mon, Aug 31 at 12:06 PM
subject: re: YOU WILL NOT BELIEVE THIS B AS IN BULL + S AS IN SATIRE

SMITH WHAT IS BARRY SAYING TO ME RIGHT NOW
  I CANNOT BELIEVE MY EARS AND HEARING

---

from: smith@simonyi.com
to: YOPLAY <philgergel@gmail.com>
date: Mon, Aug 31 at 12:09 PM
subject: re: YOU WILL NOT BELIEVE THIS B AS IN BULL + S AS IN SATIRE

I am going to pay it back. I can explain. I am very sorry, but it isn't what it looks like.

---

from: YOPLAY <philgergel@gmail.com>
to: smith@simonyi.com
date: Mon, Aug 31 at 12:12 PM
subject: re: YOU WILL NOT BELIEVE THIS B AS IN BULL + S AS IN SATIRE

YOU STOLE FROM ME?
  ET TU, BRUTE?

---

from: YOPLAY <philgergel@gmail.com>
to: smith@simonyi.com
date: Mon, Aug 31 at 12:13 PM
subject: re: YOU WILL NOT BELIEVE THIS B AS IN BULL + S AS IN SATIRE

STOP CALLING MY PHONE I CANNOT FACE YOU IN THIS MOMENT

---

from: smith@simonyi.com
to: YOPLAY <philgergel@gmail.com>
date: Mon, Aug 31 at 12:16 PM
subject: re: YOU WILL NOT BELIEVE THIS B AS IN BULL + S AS IN SATIRE

I did have to move some money around to cover my mother's rent. I am going to pay you back right away. Today if possible. I have a new prospective client—huge—an author—I just need a day or so to sign her. I promise it will work out if you'll just trust me.

---

from: YOPLAY <philgergel@gmail.com>
to: smith@simonyi.com
date: Mon, Aug 31 at 12:34 PM
subject: re: YOU WILL NOT BELIEVE THIS B AS IN BULL + S AS IN SATIRE

WITHDRAWALS WITH NO FEES INVOICED, BARRY SAYS
    SUMS MISSING, GONE
    FOR MONTHS NOW
        AND YOU BLAME IT ON YOUR MOTHER? ISN'T SHE A
CRIPPLE?

so

low

A CRIPPLE

YOUR ASS SHOULD BE IN A MANILA FOLDER ON THE DESK OF A KHAKI DETECTIVE THIS INSTANT

MY ACCOUNTANT WANTS ME TO PRESS CHARGES!!!

BARRY SAYS WHAT YOU DID IS CRIMINAL.

AGAINST THE LAW.

HOW CAN YOU STEAL FROM ME AFTER ALL THIS TIME? I AM IN GOOD MIND TO SUE BUT AM WILLING TO TALK FIRST TO HEAR YOUR SIDE OF THE STORY, MOSTLY CAUSE I NEED THE KARMA

HOWEVER YOU AND I ARE THROUGH

FOR GOOD

JUDAS

I only tried to see the good in you.

---

from:	smith@simonyi.com
to:	YOPLAY <philgergel@gmail.com>
date:	Mon, Aug 31 at 12:35 PM
subject:	re: YOU WILL NOT BELIEVE THIS B AS IN BULL + S AS IN SATIRE

I'm sorry. I don't know what else to say.

---

from:	carl@simonyi.com
to:	smith@simonyi.com
date:	Mon, Aug 31 at 12:44 PM
subject:	re: Paging Benjamin Franklin!

Oh no. What have I done. Am I fired?

from:	jade@barntherestaurant.com
to:	marcus@barntherestaurant.com
date:	Mon, Aug 31 at 12:49 PM
subject:	Goodbye, Marcus

Marcus,

Thank you for the clarity of your email this morning.

Please consider this email my resignation.

Jade

from:	richierich1000@gmail.com
to:	smith@simonyi.com
date:	Mon, Aug 31 at 12:53 PM
subject:	re: Emergency

dude I was at the gym. u ok? whats going on

I did a little research into how memory works. Turns out when you remember something, what you're remembering is the last time you remembered it. So every time you do, it's different.

Happens.

New layer of detail

When you remember it

Then you remember it again

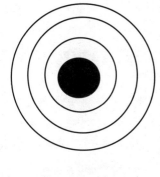

And again

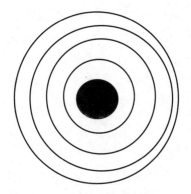

And again

And if you don't remember it

It shrinks up

Like a muscle

—————————————————

·

Or old love

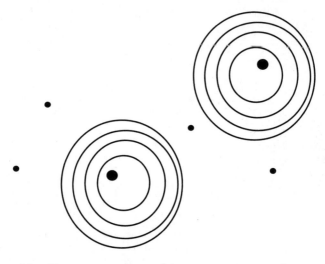

Until eventually what you remember

is pretty much all memories of memories.

I am writing down dots

The mangled dots.

COMMENTS (49):

BonnieD: Told u pics get u on the popular page, congrats! now watch out u are famous lol

HarryBeastMan: tits tits titties tits tits titties

GloriaGlowing: @moderator see above

HarryBeastMan: u want me glowbird u know it

Moderator: User has been removed. Apologies for the insensitive remarks. As you were!

Click to see 43 more . . .

BigJessBarbs: This blog reminds me of my knitting days!

TUESDAY, SEPTEMBER 1

from: Bro-vado
to: smithsimonyi@gmail.com
date: Tue, Sep 1 at 4:49 AM
subject: WHO'S THE MAN?

YOU ARE! Here's a breakdown of your most recent session:

High: $32,319

Low: $0

Walkaway: $0

ProTip: End your session while you're up . . . then come back with more to play with the next time.

from:	smith@simonyi.com
to:	iris a massey@gmail.com
date:	Tue, Sep 1 at 7:50 AM
subject:	no subject

It's ruining me, and yet I go to it. I go to it because . . . what was the email I received the other day? I believe that I "can, will, and probably should lose."

I don't know if that's true. But when I read it, I think of something Clementine said to me once.

Clementine was hung up on one thing that happened early in our relationship, long before we were married. We met on a Monday, and ten days later, on a Thursday, my dad died. I was twenty-eight, and she and I had been on two dates when I got the call. I told her I was going home for a bit but left out the details—that I was going to bury my dad, and that my mom was in the hospital. As I later tried to explain to Clementine, I didn't know how bad my mom's injuries were when I left. No one did, not even the doctors.

I flew to Wisconsin and handled everything—buried him, got her set up in a long-term care unit . . . Then I came back to New York, and Clementine and I continued to date. But still I didn't tell her what had happened. What was the point? So she could comfort me? We hadn't even had sex yet. Of course, she found out eventually that he was dead, and that my mom was disabled. And at that point, fine, I did sort of lie—I claimed the "accident" had happened earlier in the year, and that my mom had *fallen* down the stairs. I implied that these were separate incidents.

But we'd been dating for four months. I was supposed to bare my soul?

The problem was, I suppose, that I never corrected either of these white lies. The night before we were getting married, she learned the real story from Richie, who inadvertently filled her in on the true version of events after she interrogated him. The way she looked at me—like I was a con.

Over the two years we managed to stay married, she would lob comments at me here and there, like, "I shouldn't be surprised to feel invisible to you. Men always end up treating their wives like they treat their moms."

"You mean how I support you both?" I only said once.

"You really think that's what love is?" she said back. It wasn't a question. It was an accusation. Like whatever respect for me she'd maintained was now gone. Like she understood me better than I did myself, and was disgusted by what she knew.

That is how I feel now. That low.

---

from: jademassey@yahoo.com
to: smith@simonyi.com
date: Tue, Sep 1 at 8:08 AM
subject: Apology

Dear Smith,

I'm sorry for my attitude last week. I was unnecessarily rude to you. Thank you for mailing my sister's things. I appreciate you reaching out about them, and for taking care to get them to me.

I hope your week is going well.

Sincerely,

Jade

PS—Speaking of things that need returning—am I remembering correctly that you're a friend of Richie, whom my sister was seeing this spring? Might you have his contact info? I lost it.

---

from: smith@simonyi.com
to: jademassey@yahoo.com
date: Tue, Sep 1 at 8:20 AM
subject: re: Apology

No worries. I apologize, too. I got a bit defensive when you implied that I didn't care enough about your sister to stay through her funeral.

The boxes should arrive today. My intern sent them overnight delivery yesterday afternoon via FedEx.

Richie's email is richierich1000@gmail.com. If he doesn't respond right away, don't be surprised. He's really busy at the moment.

---

from: jademassey@yahoo.com
to: smith@simonyi.com
date: Tue, Sep 1 at 9:23 AM
subject: re: Apology

I'm in Virginia. But I'll be back later this week and can let you know that they made it.

And he's already written back, thanks!

---

from: smith@simonyi.com
to: jademassey@yahoo.com
date: Tue, Sep 1 at 9:26 AM
subject: re: Apology

What's in Virginia? No pressure to respond.

from:	jademassey@yahoo.com
to:	smith@simonyi.com
date:	Tue, Sep 1 at 9:29 AM
subject:	re: Apology

My mother. She's struggling.

from:	smith@simonyi.com
to:	jademassey@yahoo.com
date:	Tue, Sep 1 at 9:40 AM
subject:	re: Apology

Ah.

from:	jademassey@yahoo.com
to:	smith@simonyi.com
date:	Tue, Sep 1 at 9:58 AM
subject:	re: Apology

She's doing better than she was. Right after Iris died, she disappeared for ten hours, which may not sound like very long, but was long enough to freak me out. I found her in the freezer section of Costco in Queens, with no idea how she'd gotten there from the hospital. After the funeral, she headed back to Virginia. I came down a month or so later to check on her.

My mother, a proud Baptist all of her life, joined her local church choir when she moved to Virgina years ago and has been super active at the church since. Well, after Iris died, she quit going. To Sunday services or choir practice. It was a concern for all of us since singing is her favorite thing these days (she's also been director of her local social club's "Gray Lady" chorus of geriatric women for several years). In July, the choir director and

I convinced her to go back. But apparently she showed up and started telling everyone that God doesn't exist. He said it was like she wanted someone to correct or stop her, but no one did. This happened a few weeks in a row. Finally, one week, they were rehearsing some song, a mass—and I'm not sure what happened. She didn't give me details. But when the song was over, she believed again.

The choir leader and I were relieved for different reasons. He was glad she wouldn't be showing up lecturing everyone on God's nonexistence any longer. I was glad because she had her community back.

So now she's at church regularly again, and that's good since the people there seem to take care of her. But between the Costco situation and the 360 on God, I'm nervous. The disappearing and not remembering it especially freaked me out.

Sorry. Don't have many people to talk to down here. I'm rattling on.

---

from: smith@simonyi.com
to: jademassey@yahoo.com
date: Tue, Sep 1 at 10:32 AM
subject: re: Apology

When my dad died, I would sit for hours staring into space, unaware that I was doing nothing, or that time was even passing. I fantasized about how it happened, and how I might have stopped it had I been there. But mostly I just stared.

Maybe the Costco situation doesn't need to be concerning. It sounds pretty normal.

I'm sure she's grateful to have you there. And it's good you're able to take time off work!

---

from: jademassey@yahoo.com
to: smith@simonyi.com
date: Tue, Sep 1 at 10:40 AM
subject: re: Apology

Well, I quit. Or was fired for wanting time off. Guess it depends on how you look at it.

Let me know if you know of anyone hiring!

---

from: smith@simonyi.com
to: jademassey@yahoo.com
date: Tue, Sep 1 at 10:42 AM
subject: re: Apology

That's too bad. Okay, I'll keep an ear out. On? Out.

---

from: jademassey@yahoo.com
to: smith@simonyi.com
date: Tue, Sep 1 at 10:44 AM
subject: re: Apology

You mean an eye out? Thanks.

Oh, and—I am a bit embarrassed to tell you this, but I shouldn't be, because I had a good reason. I needed to log into my sister's email earlier in order to check something about her medication, and I saw that you had emailed her. I didn't read anything, don't worry. I'm not a snoop. But I think you should know that I saw it, and I may have to get back in there as needed.

---

from: smith@simonyi.com
to: jademassey@yahoo.com
date: Tue, Sep 1 at 10:47 AM
subject: re: Apology

Talk about embarrassed.

---

from: jademassey@yahoo.com
to: smith@simonyi.com
date: Tue, Sep 1 at 10:53 AM
subject: re: Apology

Don't be.

So that you don't think less of me—I am trying to figure out if her doctor has perhaps committed malpractice by not putting her on the more effective chemo drug, or by not telling her that it was the more effective drug. I did learn from her email history that she was taking weed this spring, unbeknownst to me, and, I imagine, unbeknownst to her doctors. I have no idea if it was for pain or what. At least now I know.

---

from: smith@simonyi.com
to: jademassey@yahoo.com
date: Tue, Sep 1 at 11:14 AM
subject: re: Apology

She was on a cannabis-based regimen she found online. It wasn't for pain though. She was convinced it could cure her cancer. It was why she acted so loopy sometimes. Our client—former client, rather, who you may know as Yo-Play—decided in the spring that he was going to leave rap in order to become a country music artist. Terrible decision. But Iris, high on her "tincture," wrote out a fantastical "rap funeral" plan for him, which she didn't run by me before emailing to him. The cosmic joke was that I had to go through with it in June.

At least those were some fun days. In a relative sense. You know what I mean. If she was going to be at work with cancer, at least she was laughing.

"Taking" weed, ha. Aren't you in the restaurant business?

---

from: jademassey@yahoo.com
to: smith@simonyi.com
date: Tue, Sep 1 at 11:27 AM
subject: re: Apology

Oh. Well, she never told me about it.

People in my industry, at least in the back of the house, aren't big drug users. Front of house is another story. But in the kitchen we stick to cigarettes (not me). I have never even tried marijuana. I don't plan to. I have no interest. And I'm certain, without even having looked into it, that it doesn't cure fucking cancer. Good grief, I could have told Iris that much if she'd bothered asking. I used to be married to a doctor for pete's sake.

I have to go. Thanks for sending the stuff.

Jade

---

from: carl@simonyi.com
to: smith@simonyi.com
date: Tue, Sep 1 at 11:32 AM
subject: An idea

Hi Boss,

I woke up in the middle of the night last night with two ideas to run by you.

First, while the name Simonyi Brand Management has its own . . . special quality, I am wondering if you've considered a more current moniker for the firm, something fresh like BRAND-AID, or BRAND CENTRAL (since we're in New York!). Lately when I tell people where I work, they (a) don't understand what "Simonyi" is ("a Hungarian soup?"), and (b) don't understand how to pronounce it. They spend all their time focused on your last name when what they *should* be asking is what the firm can do for them!

Two, Iris's book—I've finally gotten a chance to read it. Defining audience is so important. Who are we selling it to? Who actually has an interest in this stuff? Thus, I can see it being repurposed as a children's book (what with all the illustrations), à la GOODNIGHT MOON: **GOODNIGHT, IRIS.**

What do you think?

Carl

---

from: smith@simonyi.com
to: carl@simonyi.com
date: Tue, Sep 1 at 12:01 PM
subject: re: An idea

I don't think a pun is the way to go with firm name. And a children's book feels off.

---

from: smithsimonyi@gmail.com
to: horn@horncriminaldefense.com
date: Tue, Sep 1 at 12:56 PM
subject: Inquiry

Dear Mr. Horn,

I came across your ad online and am reaching out because I find myself in a position in which I may need an attorney. This is a somewhat humiliating and delicate situation, thus I prefer not to reach out to any of the attorneys I know socially—you understand, I hope.

I left you a voicemail a few minutes ago with the details.

Is this the kind of thing you could help me with?

Best,

Smith

---

from: horn@horncriminaldefense.com
to: smithsimonyi@gmail.com
date: Tue, Sep 1 at 1:10 PM
subject: re: Inquiry

Don't talk to anybody about anything. Don't say what you said on this voicemail for fuck's sake. Can you come in on Friday? First hour is $525. $10K cash retainer.

---

from: smithsimonyi@gmail.com
to: horn@horncriminaldefense.com
date: Tue, Sep 1 at 1:14 PM
subject: re: Inquiry

Well, that makes sense except that I've already admitted to all of it.

---

from: horn@horncriminaldefense.com
to: smithsimonyi@gmail.com
date: Tue, Sep 1 at 1:15 PM
subject: re: Inquiry

---

how? where? in person? phone?

---

from: smithsimonyi@gmail.com
to: horn@horncriminaldefense.com
date: Tue, Sep 1 at 1:17 PM
subject: re: Inquiry

Over email. He wouldn't answer my calls.

---

from: horn@horncriminaldefense.com
to: smithsimonyi@gmail.com
date: Tue, Sep 1 at 1:19 PM
subject: re: Inquiry

---

of course. fucker wanted it in writing. can you do Friday or not

---

from: smithsimonyi@gmail.com
to: horn@horncriminaldefense.com
date: Tue, Sep 1 at 1:22 PM
subject: re: Inquiry

I don't have $10K right now.

from: horn@horncriminaldefense.com
to: smithsimonyi@gmail.com
date: Tue, Sep 1 at 1:26 PM
subject: re: Inquiry

well when you do, you have my number. no more talking to anyone about this. And no talking to your former client at all. Got it?

I've been thinking about love lately. When did I first experience it?

It was my second week of public school, and Jade and I were
on the bus in the town in Alabama where we'd just moved, the
last town we'd ever live in for more than a few months, though of
course I didn't know that at the time. I was six and she was ten.
My shoe had come untied, and I was standing in the aisle of the
bus tying it. Because I was looking down, I didn't see that I was
blocking the path of a giant fifth-grader named Lance. Everyone
was scared of Lance. He terrorized the school bus so viciously
from the back that kids scrambled to sit at the front. Sometimes
we squeezed three to a row up there, risking reprimand by the
driver, just to avoid him.

Lance had just boarded, but I was tying my shoe.

"Move, fatty!" he yelled, and his friends all laughed. My Polly Pocket backpack suddenly felt really stupid, as did everything else about me: my ponytail, the ribbon in it, my shorts with the orange zebras. As I started to cry, crawling into the seat with Jade, she looked up at this bully, who was a full year older than her, and said, "Real brave to pick on a first-grader. You must feel super proud."

No one had ever stood up to Lance before. No one until Jade. He didn't know what to say back. He muttered something about me being in his way and walked away.

Over the years, when I hear the term "tough love," I think of my sister. That's her. Love in Teflon form.

COMMENTS (1):

DyingToBlogTeam: Here's a friendly tip from your friends at DyingToBlog! Try posting at the same time every day. When users know when to expect your post, they're more likely to pay you a visit!

FRIDAY, SEPTEMBER 4

---

from: jademassey@yahoo.com
to: smith@simonyi.com
date: Fri, Sep 4 at 11:49 AM
subject: no subject

Are you sure all of this is hers?

---

from: smith@simonyi.com
to: jademassey@yahoo.com
date: Fri, Sep 4 at 12:16 PM
subject: re: no subject

It should be. Why?

---

from: jademassey@yahoo.com
to: smith@simonyi.com
date: Fri, Sep 4 at 12:17 PM
subject: re: no subject

It's just a lot of entrepreneurial books and stuff. It doesn't seem like her.

---

from: smith@simonyi.com
to: jademassey@yahoo.com
date: Fri, Sep 4 at 12:19 PM
subject: re: no subject

Because of the bakery.

---

from: jademassey@yahoo.com
to: smith@simonyi.com
date: Fri, Sep 4 at 12:20 PM
subject: re: no subject

Bakery?

---

from: smith@simonyi.com
to: jademassey@yahoo.com
date: Fri, Sep 4 at 12:28 PM
subject: re: no subject

BAKED. Or HYBRID. She went back and forth on the name. When I met her at the incubator at Tufts four years ago it was HYBRID. Back then all the items were going to be hybrids. But the restriction of only selling cross-breed pastries (à la the cronut) eventually felt stifling to her, plus the name is not very appetizing, so BAKED became the leading contender until she realized it was taken.

We came up with a bunch of marketing copy like: What happens to a cream deferred?

I'll be here all week.

---

from: jademassey@yahoo.com
to: smith@simonyi.com
date: Fri, Sep 4 at 12:33 PM
subject: re: no subject

Cream deferred? I don't get it.

---

from: smith@simonyi.com
to: jademassey@yahoo.com
date: Fri, Sep 4 at 12:36 PM
subject: re: no subject

Cream, like dream. The Langston Hughes poem?

---

from: smith@simonyi.com
to: jademassey@yahoo.com
date: Fri, Sep 4 at 12:40 PM
subject: re: no subject

Shit. I just realized that joke is just sad under the circumstances.

---

from: jademassey@yahoo.com
to: smith@simonyi.com
date: Fri, Sep 4 at 12:43 PM
subject: re: no subject

What is an incubator?

from: smith@simonyi.com
to: jademassey@yahoo.com
date: Fri, Sep 4 at 12:48 PM
subject: re: no subject

Boot camp for entrepreneurs. Four days of lectures and work-shops. I was there to restructure my business because I was spread thin and needed to make a conscious decision about my focus. Iris had come up with the idea for her bakery, but once she got there she decided she wasn't ready. She had just left her retail job—a makeup store or something? Anyway, she needed some-thing to tide her over. And I needed an assistant.

from: jademassey@yahoo.com
to: smith@simonyi.com
date: Fri, Sep 4 at 12:58 PM
subject: re: no subject

I see.

Friday, September 4
TherapistAwayNetwork™
Patient Name: Jade Renee Massey
AUTO PROMPT: **What is difficult for you to talk about?**

Iris was planning to open a bakery and didn't tell me, her chef sister. I worked five blocks away from her for crying out loud.
I am in the restaurant business.
She hoarded piles of cutouts of cakes and pies stapled to reci-pes stapled to seasonal theme ideas stapled to sketches of store-fronts and interior layouts. She and Smith Simonyi met at some

"incubator" she never mentioned. They wrote business plans. She told him and not me. Just like she left this online journal for him and not me.

Did she think I'd be overbearing? Take over?

Is it the same reason she didn't tell me about her blog or the weed?

I suppose I did sort of know about the blog. There was a day last spring. I had been living there for three weeks, ever since she called to ask if I'd stay a night or two in case she needed help getting to the bathroom. She had entered a phase in which she loathed any comment or expression that resembled pity.

"Act normal," she begged. "*Please* act normal."

But what was normal about the two of us living together in her one-bedroom apartment as adults? What was normal about her being so sick she had trouble standing on her own at times? Every so often she'd take out her laptop and type. I assumed she was emailing someone. I wondered if maybe it could be Daniel, her ex.

I asked.

"It's a blog," she said. "Dying people write about dying on it," she said.

"Sounds uplifting," I said.

She shrugged. "It's the only place I feel understood now."

I started to tear up.

"Dammit, Jade," she yelled, "stop it!" Then she went to her room to take a nap, leaving me crying alone like an asshole, the one who *wasn't* dying of cancer.

So I take it back: she did tell me about her blog.

Dear JADE,

Thank you for your submission to TAN™. We will make sure your provider receives this message.

Did you know "difficulty" is derived from the Latin *dis*, meaning "reversal," and *facultas*, meaning "ability or opportunity." When we think of a difficulty as a reversal in opportunity, it becomes possible to see it in a new light. Difficulties are about shifting the frame of reference from old abilities to new opportunities. Today, ask: What is my difficulty inviting me to experience?

TAN™ is not to be used in case of emergency. If you are in crisis, call 9-1-1.

Sincerely,

Your friends at TAN

---

from: wally@homilypines.com
to: smith@simonyi.com
date: Fri, Sep 4 at 3:22 PM
subject: Checking in

Hiya Smith,

So sorry about this but we got your check and can't cash it. I got the rates off! I knew they went up but I was thinking they'd gone up $200, to $7,185. Turns out it's a $400 increase for residents with single rooms, so that's $7,385. I don't know if you want to consider moving your mom in with a roommate. I don't know if she would like that or not, to be honest. On one hand I think the company could be good for her, and on the other she's kind of an introvert and likes her shows the same every day so sharing the TV with another person might make her pretty unhappy, since that's the thing she looks forward to. I think it'd be good if you were able to come up with the $200 extra, I guess is what I'm saying.

Let me know. Apparently energy costs went way up because the local energy company changed ownership and we were all underpaying or some hogwash.

Hey, you know what, I'll go ahead and cash this check and just front the $200 for now and you can pay me back.

Holler when you can make it out for a visit! We'd love to see you.

Wally

---

from:	Airbnb
to:	smith@simonyi.com
date:	Fri, Sep 4 at 3:40 PM
subject:	BOOKING INQUIRY for "Beautiful One Bedroom with Balcony on Upper West Side" for Sat, Sept 5—Thurs, Sept 10

Hi,

My name is TRAVEL MAN2,

I am looking for a house to stay in right away starting tomorrow with my girl for five nights and five days after those nights.

We will use very cleanly. Actually we are students. So we don't have enough budget. Could you make it cheaper????

If this message makes you feel bad, please disregard!

Many thanks!

from: sheryl@berringerpress.com
to: smith@simonyi.com
date: Fri, Sep 4 at 4:12 PM
subject: no go

S—

Just got a chance to discuss your colleague's blog with my interns. Brutus was ambivalent. Willow's assessment is that no way should you attempt to do anything with this. "Plenty of people die with books or poems or drawings lying around in some drawer. It's sad, but it doesn't mean we should publish them. The work has got to stand on its own."

A little jaded for a twenty-year-old, I thought. But given that this thing has a millennial feel, I take her point.

Glad you want to take on Zahara Ferringbottom. She is truly a remarkable person, and you will thank me.

xSheryl

from: smith@simonyi.com
to: cfournier@treblepublishing.com
date: Fri, Sep 4 at 4:38 PM
subject: Manuscript of note

Dear Christian,

I hope you are enjoying the final days of summer.

I am writing to let you know about a manuscript authored by a colleague who passed in May. During the last six months of her life, Iris wrote a blog that I can see working as a Treble self-help title. I am linking to it below.

I look forward to hearing your thoughts!

Let's get Campari soon,

Smith

A symptom of cancer appears to be insomnia. Unless insomnia is just a symptom of dying. Here's how I always felt about the chicken vs. egg conundrum: who cares? They come as a pair.

I am sort of dating someone. Richie. He makes coffee sleeves for coffee shops. Everyone loves his coffee sleeves because they have quotes on them, like "The only thing we have to fear is fear itself." And they're made out of recycled litter he finds around New York City.

Our first date was New Year's Eve, right after I got my diagnosis. Smith had set us up. At the end of November, he gave my number to Richie and let me know I might receive a text or call, but it took us another four weeks to get a date on the calendar. We thought it would be funny, and maybe fun, to have our first date on New Year's Eve. This, of course, was before I'd gotten the news. I gave him an out due to my suddenly having cancer, but he ignored it. We met at the office to watch the fireworks from the window because it's a great view of the Hudson, and he brought pizza and wine. I wasn't sure if his nonchalance about my cancer was charming, or just bizarre, but now I find it refreshing not to be coddled.

Even though I've only known I'm dying for two weeks, Jade has already taken to policing my intake of all things, as well as monitoring my daily schedule, medical plan, and "questions list" for my doctor, which she keeps telling me needs to "remain living." I know she means I need to add to it as I think of things, but it sounds like it's the list we're trying to keep alive, not me.

Jade is also not happy that I haven't yet told our mom that I have cancer. I think I'm still hoping I won't have to. I've started chemo. If the cancer goes away, it'll be a conversation we never have to have. I know it's wishful. But I'm in the wishful thinking business. This is what I've spent four years doing for people— dreaming big, or "DB," as Smith my boss calls it. I have seen how it can work for others. Now it's time for it to work on my fucking cancer.

COMMENTS (13):

ArduousArdvark: DB = lame

ArduousArdvark: DB = dying 2 blog lol

BonnieD: my mom didn't tell me for a long time and when I found out I was mad

BonnieD: I found it patronizing

BonnieD: also if I had known I could have cheered her up and stuff

IrisMassey: what would you do to cheer her up?

BonnieD: tell jokes about skinny women who used to be fat

BonnieD: she loved making fun of those women because their per-
sonalities always changed once they got skinny.

BonnieD: she was fat and fine with it

IrisMassey: what kind of jokes?

BonnieD: like walk around and be like, "this lettuce juice that I made
in a blender is even more delicious than French fries, I have
soooooo much energy! I looooove cucumber juice"

IrisMassey: Haha. Get some sleep! It's late no matter where you are.

BonnieD: Colorado. it's 3 in the morning here but I don't really
sleep. ok nite

SATURDAY, SEPTEMBER 5

---

from: smith@simonyi.com
to: cfournier@treblepublishing.com
date: Sat, Sep 5 at 9:02 AM
subject: re: Manuscript of Note

Dear Christian,

I'm so thrilled to hear that you're interested in my former assistant's manuscript. In response to your question, I am in the process of ensuring we're clear on the copyright front.

I'll be in touch soon.

Best,

Smith

---

from: smith@simonyi.com
to: carl@simonyi.com
date: Sat, Sep 5 at 9:10 AM
subject: Copyright

Carl,

Please check out Dying to Blog and suss out if, as a contributor, Iris signed away the copyright to her posts.

And would you begin Monday researching imprints that might be appropriate for her manuscript? At the moment, I'm drawn to self-help, but there could be other takes on it I'm sure. I mean frankly, we aren't even strapped into publishing. Given the interest you've expressed in alternative approaches to presenting her blog, perhaps you'd like to explore various platforms on which we might distribute it. Something tech-y? An app? Feel free to think creatively.

I know this past week was a difficult one for both of us. I am glad to have you as an intern, and I hope we can find a way to work together in a way that makes use of your skills and caters to your interests. But, of course, as we spoke about on Tuesday—it is very important that you check with me *before* sharing any materials with clients.

Have a good weekend.

Thx,

Smith

---

from: carl@simonyi.com
to: smith@simonyi.com
date: Sat, Sep 5 at 9:45 AM
subject: re: Copyright

I'm SO BAD at this boundaries thing. A workaholic on a Friday is a workaholic on a Saturday and Sunday. And FYI, Monday is Labor Day, so I will be in the Hamptons at a SHAVED cookout.

Okay, I will reach out to them, but remember what I said about the sister? I think that's going to matter as well.

See you Tuesday!

from: smith@simonyi.com
to: carl@simonyi.com
date: Sat, Sep 5 at 9:47 AM
subject: re: Copyright

I'll deal with the sister. Thx.

from: smith@simonyi.com
to: jademassey@yahoo.com
date: Sat, Sep 5 at 11:02 AM
subject: re: no subject

Did you really not read the emails I sent to Iris?

from: jademassey@yahoo.com
to: smith@simonyi.com
date: Sat, Sep 5 at 11:28 AM
subject: re: no subject

Emails, plural? I only saw one. (And I didn't read it.)

from: smith@simonyi.com
to: jademassey@yahoo.com
date: Sat, Sep 5 at 11:31 AM
subject: re: no subject

How are you doing?

---

from: jademassey@yahoo.com
to: smith@simonyi.com
date: Sat, Sep 5 at 11:45 AM
subject: re: no subject

I'm okay. Focused on getting my life back on track. Today I'm sending out résumés and cleaning my apartment. And I'm going to look up the malpractice claim and what all it entails.

How are you?

---

from: smith@simonyi.com
to: jademassey@yahoo.com
date: Sat, Sep 5 at 6:44 PM
subject: re: no subject

That's good.

Me? Oh, at rock bottom. No big deal.

---

from: smith@simonyi.com
to: jademassey@yahoo.com
date: Sat, Sep 5 at 6:45 PM
subject: re: no subject

Joking.

---

from: jademassey@yahoo.com
to: smith@simonyi.com
date: Sat, Sep 5 at 8:20 PM
subject: re: no subject

Um, ha?

from: smith@simonyi.com
to: jademassey@yahoo.com
date: Sat, Sep 5 at 8:27 PM
subject: re: no subject

Things are not great. I messed up with a pretty big client so I'm dealing with that. But it's nothing you want to hear about.

from: jademassey@yahoo.com
to: smith@simonyi.com
date: Sat, Sep 5 at 8:33 PM
subject: re: no subject

Were you in love with her?

from: smith@simonyi.com
to: jademassey@yahoo.com
date: Sat, Sep 5 at 8:38 PM
subject: re: no subject

The client? It's a he. I can't say his name. And no, I wasn't . . .

from: jademassey@yahoo.com
to: smith@simonyi.com
date: Sat, Sep 5 at 8:41 PM
subject: re: no subject

I mean Iris.

---

from: smith@simonyi.com
to: jademassey@yahoo.com
date: Sat, Sep 5 at 8:44 PM
subject: re: no subject

What makes you think that?

---

from: jademassey@yahoo.com
to: smith@simonyi.com
date: Sat, Sep 5 at 8:48 PM
subject: re: no subject

You wrote it. In the email you sent to her.
   (I did read it. Sorry.)

---

from: smith@simonyi.com
to: jademassey@yahoo.com
date: Sat, Sep 5 at 8:50 PM
subject: re: no subject

I wrote that?

---

from: jademassey@yahoo.com
to: smith@simonyi.com
date: Sat, Sep 5 at 8:53 PM
subject: re: no subject

It was heavily implied. You talked about how much you miss her.

from:	smith@simonyi.com
to:	jademassey@yahoo.com
date:	Sat, Sep 5 at 9:04 PM
subject:	re: no subject

I don't think I was in love with her. I do miss her a lot.

from:	jademassey@yahoo.com
to:	smith@simonyi.com
date:	Sat, Sep 5 at 9:42 PM
subject:	re: no subject

You know those cartoons where a giant boulder falls out of the sky and flattens the coyote or bunny or guy with the beard? That's how it feels to me. Like I don't even have the choice to care about anything, because I've been flattened. Just eyeballs staring up into nothing.

Sometimes I cry as hard as I can for as long as I can, as if eventually I'll be finished. Like grief is a marathon and I just have to log enough miles. I wake up looking like I was in a boxing match in the night. People talk undereye bags, but do you know how much your eye*lids* can swell from crying?

I tell myself to get out of bed, but then I think, why bother? Doing anything. We are alive then we aren't. The world is indifferent to whether we're here. What's there to be other than indifferent back?

---

from: smith@simonyi.com
to: jademassey@yahoo.com
date: Sat, Sep 5 at 9:50 PM
subject: re: no subject

I think you should give yourself credit for feeling that way and still getting shit done. You feel like *that*, and yet you're looking for a job and flying back and forth to Virginia to care for your mom? That's impressive as hell.

---

from: jademassey@yahoo.com
to: smith@simonyi.com
date: Sat, Sep 5 at 9:54 PM
subject: re: no subject

Well. Thank you, I guess. I've also started writing poetry, which is weird. I wrote that to you a moment ago and deleted it because it sounds stupid. But since nothing matters, neither does that.

Speaking of moms, how's yours?

---

from: smith@simonyi.com
to: jademassey@yahoo.com
date: Sat, Sep 5 at 9:56 PM
subject: re: no subject

My mom? Why do you ask?

from: jademassey@yahoo.com
to: smith@simonyi.com
date: Sat, Sep 5 at 10:04 PM
subject: re: no subject

You told me she wasn't doing well. That's why you left the funeral.

from: smith@simonyi.com
to: jademassey@yahoo.com
date: Sat, Sep 5 at 10:38 PM
subject: re: no subject

Right. She's okay. I mean, she's still paralyzed. Ha.
    Can I read your poetry?

from: jademassey@yahoo.com
to: smith@simonyi.com
date: Sat, Sep 5 at 10:47 PM
subject: re: no subject

Glad to hear it. Well, I'm falling asleep. Good night.

from: smith@simonyi.com
to: jademassey@yahoo.com
date: Sat, Sep 5 at 11:00 PM
subject: re: no subject

Good night.

I have been thinking about when I started baking, and it was right after the fire. The fire that I probably started.

I was twenty-seven and still at Nose, the perfume shop where I worked for two years between my consulting job and my current job. I was happier at Nose than I had been at Propel, but that's not saying much. It was retail, after all.

I'd also started dating Daniel, which both excited me and made me anxious all the time. My feelings for him kept me alert, on my toes, a constant buzz that fed my nicotine addiction. My smoking had escalated. Before Daniel, I'd gotten it down to one cigarette a night, but it had climbed to three, then eleven or twelve. I was going through three or four packs a week.

That night, we all stood outside the building, those of us who lived in it, and watched the smoke pour out of Mrs. Freder's on the first floor. I had just had a cigarette in my bedroom window an hour earlier. I was pretty sure I had fully extinguished it before dropping the butt down the fire escape, where it would have bounced like a Plinko game onto the littered alley below. (I had no qualms littering back then, though I should've, given my Smokey the Bear exposure as a child.) Of course I had extinguished it. I had squashed it on the ledge and then dropped it below like a million times before. But maybe I'd been too careless, too hungry to light my next. Maybe I'd neglected to notice the trace of a glow at the tip.

Mrs. Freder was crying and meth-head Ernie from upstairs had his arm around her.

When the smoke thinned and we were allowed back inside, we passed through the remains of her ground-level one-bedroom. It was soggy and black, like drenched burned toast, minus a few objects that had survived the rapture. A toaster. The porcelain base of a lamp styled as the figure of a Victorian lady. A red rubber plunger.

I listened as a bulky fireman asked Mrs. Freder if she had left her stove on, perhaps. The stove sat by the window, now open, below my own. Could it have been open before? It was late April and possible.

Tom the landlord, who was always way too nice to be a New York landlord, let her stay in the empty unit across the hall while her unit was being cleaned up. Ernie brought her a small TV with an antenna, and I brought other things: towels, plates and pans, cups and napkins, a lamp, the quilt Daniel's grandmother made for him that he'd brought over after my radiator temporarily broke. When her daughter and son came from Chicago and Miami, she invited me down to meet them. They thanked me for all the dinners I'd delivered to her since the fire.

I couldn't smoke in my window again after that. And since

public smoking never appealed to me, I was left with little choice but to quit.

I started baking because I was restless without cigarettes. I noticed a recipe book with a cheesecake on it in the window display of a bookstore and decided to make that cheesecake. It took me three hours because I fucked it up with too much sugar, nine if you count the cooling period, and by the time that was over, I realized I hadn't craved a smoke.

I learned how to make raspberry tarts and lavender sea salt ice cream, blueberry crème brûlée with lemon glaze, and honey pistachio biscotti. I shared it all with Mrs. Freder and Ernie and then everyone else. I decided I wanted to bake for people and that, if I saved enough money, I would open a bakery. It was the first career idea I ever got really excited about.

All of this is to say, I have mixed feelings about what I did. I'm sorry that I might have burned your apartment up, Mrs. Freder. But I'm also glad it led me to start making people things.

COMMENTS (1):

ChristmasWasMyFavorite: Lavender in ice cream? I'd rather eat pine straw! Or hay! Lol

SUNDAY, SEPTEMBER 6

---

from: jademassey@yahoo.com
to: smith@simonyi.com
date: Sun, Sep 6 at 8:13 AM
subject: no subject

Why don't you think she told me? About the bakery?

---

from: smith@simonyi.com
to: jademassey@yahoo.com
date: Sun, Sep 6 at 11:55 AM
subject: re: no subject

Maybe she thought it was your territory. You're the chef.

---

from: jademassey@yahoo.com
to: smith@simonyi.com
date: Sun, Sep 6 at 12:29 PM
subject: re: no subject

But I don't even like sweets. She knows that. I hate pastries. With
a passion. Actually that's not entirely accurate. What I hate are
desserts. You've just had this beautiful meal, the arc of it has left

you perfectly satiated and grateful and complete, and then out comes a dish that invariably contains something red or pink, and quivering—you're going to close this culinary experience with a *sugar bomb*. It's repulsive. A sloppy, sentimental epilogue to a book that had a suitable ending.

---

from: jademassey@yahoo.com
to: smith@simonyi.com
date: Sun, Sep 6 at 12:32 PM
subject: re: no subject

Hmm. Actually, maybe she thought I would judge her.

---

from: smith@simonyi.com
to: jademassey@yahoo.com
date: Sun, Sep 6 at 1:30 PM
subject: re: no subject

What you're doing right now? That's the worst part, for me, about losing someone. They are no longer around for you to know what they think, or thought. You don't get to assume you know what they'll say and then be surprised when you're wrong. There's no tension. All conversation is imaginary, confined to the echo chamber of your own mind.

I always hated hearing people talk about the dead as if, suddenly after death, their desires became transparent. "She would have wanted you to do this." "He would have wanted that." Who knows what they would want if they were still alive? Isn't that the terrible thing? You have no idea, and you can't ask. You can't rehash the past, or say you're sorry. You can't even tell them you're mad.

My ex-wife used to imply she knew what my dad would want or do even though she never met him. She felt permission to say things like, "What would your dad think?" in this tone like she knew the answer.

---

from: jademassey@yahoo.com
to: smith@simonyi.com
date: Sun, Sep 6 at 2:15 PM
subject: re: no subject

That's not the worst part for me. (Isn't THIS a fun conversation!) The worst part for me is thinking about how now she's just a bunch of memories. What happens when they go?

My mother has always been fond of beautiful things. Fashion and makeup are her food and water. After my father died when I was seven and Iris was three, she started working for Winsome Beauty Brands, a pyramid-style marketing enterprise that she diligently rose to the heights of in the late 1980s. By the time I was twelve, she'd been promoted to national director status. As a national director, she was charged with traveling all over the country leading seminars, and of course we were dragged along. For the next six years (ten for Iris) we lived in Ramada Inns. Always Ramada.

Last night I remembered how in the early Ramada Inn days, Iris and I would camp out in ladies' bathrooms at the hotels, or nearby shopping malls—anywhere with public restrooms—and peek over the stalls to watch grown ladies pee. At twelve, I was too old for it and knew it was dumb, but I liked seeing how happy it made Iris to misbehave in this harmless way, how much delight she got out of being naughty.

Once her foot slipped into the toilet, soaking her sneaker and sock. Our mother's temper was our greatest fear. Terrified, we hurried back to our room and tried to blow-dry her sock and shoe. Our mom was freakishly observant, and I was sure she'd notice. At minimum she'd detect the guilt on our faces. But when she jangled in from work, a cloud of perfume as always, she didn't make a single comment or interrogate either of us. We'd gotten away with it. And that night, we were so proud of ourselves. I remember thinking, Iris and I could get by if we ever needed to run away. We could make it as a team.

What happens when I can't remember our shared life anymore? What becomes of it?

---

from: smith@simonyi.com
to: jademassey@yahoo.com
date: Sun, Sep 6 at 2:28 PM
subject: re: no subject

Would it really be so terrible if you forgot the memory where, as a child, you thought you might have to run away?

---

from: jademassey@yahoo.com
to: smith@simonyi.com
date: Sun, Sep 6 at 2:35 PM
subject: re: no subject

You left out the important part—knowing we could survive together.

from:	smith@simonyi.com
to:	jademassey@yahoo.com
date:	Sun, Sep 6 at 2:41 PM
subject:	re: no subject

You could write them down like she did. I understand what you mean though. I think it's why I kept her stuff in here for months. I didn't want to move it, because once I did, it felt like erasing her from this place.

from:	jademassey@yahoo.com
to:	smith@simonyi.com
date:	Sun, Sep 6 at 2:44 PM
subject:	re: no subject

"Here"? At work on a Sunday, huh?

from:	smith@simonyi.com
to:	jademassey@yahoo.com
date:	Sun, Sep 6 at 3:01 PM
subject:	re: no subject

Yeah.

I mean, you've been through this before, right? With your dad?

---

from: jademassey@yahoo.com
to: smith@simonyi.com
date: Sun, Sep 6 at 3:19 PM
subject: re: no subject

Our dad's death was different. Iris doesn't even remember him. I remember him well from when he was alive, but his death I remember mostly in images of my mother grieving. And as the origin of my, shall we say, preoccupation with health concerns (fine, I'll say it: hypochondria).

---

from: smith@simonyi.com
to: jademassey@yahoo.com
date: Sun, Sep 6 at 3:38 PM
subject: re: no subject

I don't know if this happens with your memories of your dad— but I won't have thought about something for years, then out of nowhere it will percolate. I'll find myself smack in the middle of it again.

When I was a kid, my dad warned me that if I forgot to say grace before bed, I'd turn into a cow in my sleep.

"Do you want to wake up a cow?" he'd say, and I'd press my hands together and close my eyes.

My whole childhood I believed that if I didn't pray before I went to sleep, I'd wake up a farm animal. I'd completely forgotten this until last year, when I saw a cow on a billboard in Midtown. I saw that cow, and it returned to me vividly, including the prayer: *Bless my mom. Bless my pop. Grant us mercy until we plop.*

from:	jademassey@yahoo.com
to:	smith@simonyi.com
date:	Sun, Sep 6 at 3:43 PM
subject:	re: no subject

Until we *plop*?

You called him Pop? Were you close?

from:	smith@simonyi.com
to:	jademassey@yahoo.com
date:	Sun, Sep 6 at 3:51 PM
subject:	re: no subject

No, I called him Dad.

Yeah, it's ridiculous. He wrote it. And was probably drunk when he did.

Were we close? I mean, he was my dad, so sure. But he drove, so he was gone a lot.

from:	jademassey@yahoo.com
to:	smith@simonyi.com
date:	Sun, Sep 6 at 3:54 PM
subject:	re: no subject

Drove? Like as a trucker?

from:	smith@simonyi.com
to:	jademassey@yahoo.com
date:	Sun, Sep 6 at 3:55 PM
subject:	re: no subject

Yes.

---

from: jademassey@yahoo.com
to: smith@simonyi.com
date: Sun, Sep 6 at 3:58 PM
subject: re: no subject

Oh, gotta run. I have a call about a possible job. I lost track of time!

Thanks for talking.

---

from: smith@simonyi.com
to: jademassey@yahoo.com
date: Sun, Sep 6 at 3:59
subject: re: no subject

Good luck!

January 18 | 6:45 AM

Well, I told my mother I have cancer. My sister made me. She arrives Tuesday.

It has left me thinking about family.

I discovered thrift shops in Somerville, Massachusetts, during my freshman year of college. They were miraculous. I had no idea how I had lived eighteen years without being inside one. I had heard of them, of course. I'd just never been to one, and it was astonishing: you could get barely used, gorgeous items for single digits!

I would cash my paycheck from restocking books at the campus library and go straight to Summer Street Seconds. I bought what I felt like wearing, the things I wasn't allowed to buy as a kid and teenager, things my mother would have vetoed with disgust. I mixed black and brown. I wore hot pink tights. White after Labor Day! Open-toed sandals with "stockings"—lacy ones, no less!

My favorite shoes ever were a pair of violet kitten-heel boo-
ties that I wore on my first college date. He was my Philosophy
101 TA, a senior. He had eyelashes so long that one girl changed
sections because she claimed she got dizzy whenever she
looked at him. He called me quirky, and said he had assumed
from my style that I was gay. He smoked Black & Milds and
didn't believe in a distinction between art and life. He explained
postmodernism to me like this: *The Simpsons.* I pretended to understand. Our mom had not allowed us to watch *The Simpsons*,
as she felt it "glorified mediocrity." Also, that Bart disrespected
his parents—"Honor thy father and mother" was one of her favorite lines of scripture.

Those heels stayed with me for eight years. I wore them
studying abroad in Paris, walking through the Latin Quarter,
pretending to be French. As a consultant, I wore them to bars
and clubs and rooftop parties in Manhattan and Brooklyn. When
I was twenty-six, they finally wore out. The heel snapped, and
the cobbler on Flatbush Avenue near my apartment scoffed at
my plea to save them.

"These shoes were not made to last this long," he said in a
thick Italian accent. "You have done more in them than they were
meant for already."

But my love of thrift shops did not subside. One afternoon
a few years ago, I wandered into a Goodwill to browse. In the
corner, I found a pile of camouflage bags, stuffed full and worn.
The bags, a troubled Goodwill employee told me softly, were the
unclaimed belongings of soldiers who had died while deployed.
They were unclaimed because there was no one to take their
stuff after they were gone. Their last names, as always, were
stitched onto the bags in block lettering. She told me this as if

she needed to get it off her chest. She wasn't comfortable with the bags being up for grabs like that.

I read through the names, feeling for each one, but the bag I'll never forget, the bag that still haunts me, was the one belonging to W. Shone.

SHONE, W.

Once, he had shone. Now, here he was. The poetry of it broke my heart.

I have a mom. A mom who may hate my sense of fashion, but who is coming on Tuesday nonetheless. I will do my best to remember that there is a kind of blessing in that.

COMMENTS (1):

ChristmasWasMyFavorite: Isn't the past tense of shine SHINED?

MONDAY, SEPTEMBER 7

from: carl@simonyi.com
to: smith@simonyi.com
date: Mon, Sep 7 at 9:18 AM
subject: Hi! Please Do NOT Take Personally

Happy Labor Day from Montauk!

I forgot that sand makes me anxious, so I've retreated to a café to familiarize myself with our client list. Question: is this a *normal* number of clients who aren't making us any money? I am confused about how this industry works. It seems like we have a lot of clients who are dormant, and very few who are actually worth our time.

I am very excited about our new client Zahara Ferringbottom, however. How does this look for bio copy on our site:

> *In the lineage of Serbian performance artist Marina Abramović, Zahara Ferringbottom, author of the forthcoming memoir <u>Art Precedes Life</u> and internationally renowned performance artist, relentlessly pursues walls while clad in shapewear. Her work invites the audience to consider how we limit our souls in service*

of our bodies. In other words, she wears a leotard and runs at walls . . . and you can't look away.

See you tomorrow!
CVS

---

from: smith@simonyi.com
to: carl@simonyi.com
date: Mon, Sep 7 at 9:24 AM
subject: re: Hi! Please Do NOT Take Personally

Doesn't she run UP walls?

I don't know what list or other records you took with you to Montauk, but a reminder (again) not to take documents from the office, please?

To your question, we're definitely in a bit of a slump, yes.

---

from: carl@simonyi.com
to: smith@simonyi.com
date: Mon, Sep 7 at 9:30 AM
subject: re: Hi! Please Do NOT Take Personally

Her publicist wrote "up" walls, but I figured that was a typo because of gravity.

As for the slump, perhaps it would be useful to revisit this idea of renaming.

What about: RAISIN' BRAND

---

from: smith@simonyi.com
to: carl@simonyi.com
date: Mon, Sep 7 at 9:31 AM
subject: re: Hi! Please Do NOT Take Personally

No puns, remember?

    It's a good idea to check on the ZF question later this week.

---

from: contact@lassimariset.com
to: smith@simonyi.com
date: Mon, Sep 7 at 10:19 AM
subject: re: Congratulations!

---

can u get me on tv or . . .

---

from: jademassey@yahoo.com
to: smith@simonyi.com
date: Mon, Sep 7 at 10:20 AM
subject: no subject

Do you think it's stupid that I quit my job?

---

from: smith@simonyi.com
to: jademassey@yahoo.com
date: Mon, Sep 7 at 10:55 AM
subject: re: no subject

I'm not sure I know enough about the situation to weigh in.

from: jademassey@yahoo.com
to: smith@simonyi.com
date: Mon, Sep 7 at 11:18 AM
subject: re: no subject

You know that I was a chef at a Michelin restaurant. Two star. Which I left without another job to replace it. To spend some time with my mom, who isn't like yours. My mom can walk, and feed herself, and even drive. She'd manage without me.

I mean, she'd struggle.

You deal with careers, right? Do you think it was stupid?

from: smith@simonyi.com
to: jademassey@yahoo.com
date: Mon, Sep 7 at 11:40 AM
subject: re: no subject

It was bold. Rash, perhaps. But you're obviously talented. You'll land on your feet.

from: jademassey@yahoo.com
to: smith@simonyi.com
date: Mon, Sep 7 at 11:44 AM
subject: re: no subject

My mother and I don't even get along.

---

from: smith@simonyi.com
to: jadomassey@yahoo.com
date: Mon, Sep 7 at 12:00 PM
subject: re: no subject

Oh? Why is that?

---

from: jademassey@yahoo.com
to: smith@simonyi.com
date: Mon, Sep 7 at 12:05 PM
subject: re: no subject

Did Iris talk about her?

---

from: smith@simonyi.com
to: jademassey@yahoo.com
date: Mon, Sep 7 at 12:06 PM
subject: re: no subject

Not much. No, really not ever, actually.

---

from: jademassey@yahoo.com
to: smith@simonyi.com
date: Mon, Sep 7 at 12:40 PM
subject: re: no subject

Let me think of an example.

Okay, the reason we lived in Ramada Inns specifically is because my mom's boyfriend—the one she had after our father died—owned a slew of them, and so we lived there for free. His name was Donovan, he was married, and she would fly out to LA once a month for a weekend to visit him. Sometimes he would come visit us in one of the towns where we were living, but he wouldn't stay at the Ramada. Mom would leave us there and go meet him at a Hilton or a Hyatt or a W, or some hotel we didn't know the name of. We just knew it was fancier.

Those weekends, Iris and I would dress up in her clothes and put her makeup on each other. This wasn't out of admiration. It was a game: who could make the other one look the most like her, strike the closest balance of gaudy and clownish, apply the bright fuchsia lipstick outside the lines of the lips in the precise way that she did to "enhance" the shape of "the lip," mimic the orange streaks of blush on the cheeks just under the bones (early contouring—if you know what that is—though not called that then, and definitely the wrong shade for it). After you finished applying makeup on your subject, you spun her around to face the mirror, and she would give you a ranking from one to ten. Ten meant you looked just like our mom. One would mean you looked nothing like her, but we never gave ones, or anything lower than a six for that matter.

Then we'd pretend to be her, prancing around the room casting about insults, complaining about the quality of the food and the watered-down iced tea. ("This watery tea is inexcusable!" she'd exclaim at the counter of a Wendy's, as if it were the Rainbow Room.) We'd laugh our faces off and then try to find free Pay-Per-View on TV. (Occasionally, the Ramada rooms in those days had cable that had been misconfigured such that the porn channels would come through in patches here and there.)

Then we'd take off the makeup and dresses and pantyhose, and return everything to its proper place, double- and triple-checking to make sure we'd put everything back in its exact spot, carefully removing any of our strands of hair from her brush, all within at least an hour before she was due to come home (though she never did, not those nights), just in case, for once, she kept her promise and returned. We would close the door behind us quietly and retire in one of our rooms, usually mine, where we'd find a movie on TBS or a talk show and leave the TV blaring until we fell asleep in the same double bed. In every hotel in those years, even when we got our own rooms, we only ever slept in one room, in one bed.

One time, she came home early. Way early. By her smeared mascara, I gathered that she and Donovan had had a fight. When she walked in, Iris had one leg in her pantyhose, one leg out, and I was zipping up a pencil skirt. She beat us with her hairbrush.

She's not as bad now. Not nearly. She hasn't been for years, since Iris and I both moved away. But of course I have resentment from childhood, yada yada.

---

from: smith@simonyi.com
to: jademassey@yahoo.com
date: Mon, Sep 7 at 12:54 PM
subject: re: no subject

I understand. I also grew up in an abusive household.

---

from: jademassey@yahoo.com
to: smith@simonyi.com
date: Mon, Sep 7 at 1:20 PM
subject: re: no subject

Whoa, there. I don't know if I'd call it abuse (or a household, for that matter). The hairbrush thing was . . . it was what it was. She wasn't typically physical. So at least, not in that sense.

Emotionally, maybe. Our mom thought it was "creepy" that we always shared a bed.

"Girls, that's creepy," she'd say over a Styrofoam cup of hotel-lobby coffee as we followed her out to the car, our book bags dangling from our right shoulders. (Carrying a book bag on one shoulder, as opposed to on both, was in style in those days in most towns, though not all of them; you couldn't be sure if the one-shoulder hang was going to be in or out, so you had to study the crowd from a distance on your first day and switch it up if you'd bet wrong.) "You're both teenagers. Sleep in your own beds."

But Iris wasn't a teenager, yet. I would wonder if my mom just forgot. Once, I dared to remind her: Iris was twelve.

"I'm rounding," she said. From then on, she rounded Iris's age up, I guess to prove herself right.

So yeah, maybe.

The weird thing is—since Iris died, she's been completely different in a way that is alarming. I mean, I don't want her to be *mean*. But she's not herself, and not just in the sense that she's suddenly scribbling notes in the margins of her Bible. She's this ghost of a person who just moves about with no opinions on anything. She lets me make all the decisions. She checks out. I have to repeat myself several times to get a response from her. Last week, the cat ate half of her plate of spaghetti while she was sitting there, and she didn't notice until he started puking it up on the table. I came out of my room to find Mistoffelees hacking up a hairball covered in tomato sauce while my mom wondered aloud why the hairball was red. I actually find myself missing the old her.

from: jademassey@yahoo.com
to: smith@simonyi.com
date: Mon, Sep 7 at 1:30 PM
subject: re: no subject

God, I just realized I must sound terrible. Your mom is paralyzed and I'm complaining about how mine gets easily distracted and is much nicer than she used to be.

from: smith@simonyi.com
to: jademassey@yahoo.com
date: Mon, Sep 7 at 1:35 PM
subject: re: no subject

Apples and oranges. I'm not offended.

from: jademassey@yahoo.com
to: smith@simonyi.com
date: Mon, Sep 7 at 1:46 PM
subject: re: no subject

So you *don't* think I'm stupid for quitting necessarily? As a data point, I also didn't get along very well with the head chef.

from: smith@simonyi.com
to: jademassey@yahoo.com
date: Mon, Sep 7 at 1:52 PM
subject: re: no subject

I suppose my first question is, can you afford to be unemployed? I'm assuming the answer is yes.

---

from: jademassey@yahoo.com
to: smith@simonyi.com
date: Mon, Sep 7 at 2:04 PM
subject: re: no subject

For now. I have savings. And Iris left me hers, not that I would dip into that unless it was for something really important.

---

from: smith@simonyi.com
to: jademassey@yahoo.com
date: Mon, Sep 7 at 2:18 PM
subject: re: no subject

Honestly? I think it's nice you are devoted to your mom despite the fact that it isn't easy. So devoted that you quit your job. I admire it.

---

from: jademassey@yahoo.com
to: smith@simonyi.com
date: Mon, Sep 7 at 2:37 PM
subject: re: no subject

If I didn't, I'm afraid I'd regret it.

---

from: smith@simonyi.com
to: jademassey@yahoo.com
date: Mon, Sep 7 at 2:56 PM
subject: re: no subject

I'm not sure I believe in regret. Everyone has regret, but that doesn't mean the choices we made were mistakes, or that we even could have acted differently. It just means we look back and *feel* like we could have.

I think regretting is a way to believe (incorrectly) that we have control over life. We get to feel like if we had done something differently, things might have turned out better. But that's just as easily not the case. Maybe if we'd done something different, things would be even worse.

---

from: jademassey@yahoo.com
to: smith@simonyi.com
date: Mon, Sep 7 at 2:59 PM
subject: re: no subject

Okay, fine. But you also care for your mom.

---

from: smith@simonyi.com
to: jademassey@yahoo.com
date: Mon, Sep 7 at 3:19 PM
subject: re: no subject

I haven't seen her in four years.

---

from: jademassey@yahoo.com
to: smith@simonyi.com
date: Mon, Sep 7 at 3:20 PM
subject: re: no subject

Wait, really?

---

from: smith@simonyi.com
to: jademassey@yahoo.com
date: Mon, Sep 7 at 3:22 PM
subject: re: no subject

Yeah.

from:	jademassey@yahoo.com
to:	smith@simonyi.com
date:	Mon, Sep 7 at 3:30 PM
subject:	re: no subject

What's the deal? You don't get along?

from:	smith@simonyi.com
to:	jademassey@yahoo.com
date:	Mon, Sep 7 at 3:48 PM
subject:	re: no subject

Not that. She was a good mom. The kind who made me pancakes in the shape of snowmen for no reason. When I turned sixteen, despite the fact that I'd hardly ever talked to a girl for longer than ten seconds, she slid a condom into my wallet "just in case." But the accident didn't just break her back. It affected her brain (though the doctors claim it didn't, they are wrong). It made her feistier, I guess is how I'd put it. More irritable. She is quicker to anger. Long story short, we haven't been as close in a while.

from:	jademassey@yahoo.com
to:	smith@simonyi.com
date:	Mon, Sep 7 at 3:50 PM
subject:	re: no subject

Did you say she's paralyzed?

---

from: smith@simonyi.com
to: jademassey@yahoo.com
date: Mon, Sep 7 at 3:52 PM
subject: re: no subject

She is quadriplegic.

---

from: jademassey@yahoo.com
to: smith@simonyi.com
date: Mon, Sep 7 at 3:54 PM
subject: re: no subject

God, that's sad. I'd be angry, too.

That must be so depressing for you to watch. Is that why you don't go see her?

Gotta run—have a consultation with a med mal lawyer about Iris. Talk later!

---

from: smith@simonyi.com
to: jademassey@yahoo.com
date: Mon, Sep 7 at 3:55 PM
subject: re: no subject

And I should probably get some work done today now that we've spent the majority of it rehashing our childhoods.

from:	jademassey@yahoo.com
to:	smith@simonyi.com
date:	Mon, Sep 7 at 3:56 PM
subject:	re: no subject

Working on Saturday *and* on Labor Day? Lawyers are one thing, but I didn't know the world of branding was so intense . . .

from:	smith@simonyi.com
to:	jademassey@yahoo.com
date:	Mon, Sep 7 at 4:08 PM
subject:	re: no subject

Ha. Well, I have nothing else to do.

Hey—do you want to have dinner tomorrow? No pressure. I know you're not into publishing your sister's blog, but maybe we could talk about ways we could honor her memory in some other way. (To be clear so that it's not awkward, not as a date.)

from:	jademassey@yahoo.com
to:	smith@simonyi.com
date:	Mon, Sep 7 at 4:27 PM
subject:	re: no subject

Sure. I don't know what that would be. It's not like we're going to erect a statue or something. (Thanks for not pushing me more on the blog, by the way. I'm relieved that's off the table.)

I'm also fine just talking about Iris with someone else who misses her. That sounds kind of nice.

But I can't do dinner. I don't eat at restaurants. Unless it's dim sum. Sorry. I'll be too distracted assessing the food to be a good dinner partner.

Maybe we could just go on a walk on the High Line or something? I'm trying to get out into nature more. (High Line = New York version of nature.)

---

from: smith@simonyi.com
to: jademassey@yahoo.com
date: Mon, Sep 7 at 4:33 PM
subject: re: no subject

A walk it is.

Richie and I decided to go upstate this weekend, and as a life-time New Yorker who grew up jumping turnstiles in the Bronx, he doesn't drive—never even got his license. So today I had to renew mine, which I'd let expire because I also don't drive in New York. (The irony of needing to renew my license right now I won't even bother to point out.)

I was in line at the DMV and cranky like everyone else. It didn't help that the guy in front of me was getting a vanity plate, and couldn't understand the process for doing so.

The DMV employee was telling him he had to submit up to three choices, and this confused him. He didn't understand if that meant he could submit only one, or if he *had* to submit three.

"So I can submit one?"

"No, three."

"You said up to three."

"You can submit one, but you may not get it. Write down your choices here." She slid a piece of paper to him through the window. The woman behind me cursed under her breath, and I consciously fought turning around to commiserate. I took a deep breath as the man wrote on the paper and then slid it back under the window.

"Sir, I said eight characters."

"Oh, come on!" another man hollered from several feet back. But then he started to count his letters, saying them out loud.

"F."

"O."

"R."

"G."

"I."

"V."

"E."

"M."

"E . . . oh. That's nine."

Then he said, how about the number 4? 4-give-me. She typed for a second, consulted the screen, and told him it was taken. So was 4giveMe with no spaces. She offered 4giveYou, 4giveUs, or 4giveme with 3s for the E's. She wrote it down for him.

"That doesn't look right to me," he said, and the guy behind me yelled "Come on!" again. The man interested in forgiveness finally seemed to understand that the people behind him had grown impatient.

"How about 4giveRJ?" he said. It was available.

COMMENTS (1):

BigJessBarbs: Fun Fact: If you write "I am a horrible person with no interpersonal skills" on the DMV application, you automatically get the job!

TUESDAY, SEPTEMBER 8

from: Chad Wotherspoon
to: carl@simonyi.com; smith@simonyi.com
cc: Todd Kohlstedt
date: Tue, Sep 8 at 9:03 AM
subject: re: Copyright Inquiry re: blogs on site

Dear Carl et al,

AMAZING that we're hearing from you on this. Amazing.

No, she didn't sign anything; we ask our contributors solely for license to publish their content on our site. However, her blog was actually just pulled by our new marketing gal Margaux as a potential part of an upcoming promo campaign, so it's serendipitous you reached out! We couldn't find a contact for her, which was a real downer because we need to make sure *we* have the copyright to reproduce it as an e-book for download! Ironies.

Might you be able to put us in touch with next of kin? Was she married? Kids?

Cheers,

Chad

---

from: carl@simonyi.com
to: Chad Wotherspoon
cc: Todd Kohlstedt; smith@simonyi.com
date: Tue, Sep 8 at 9:14 AM
subject: re: Copyright Inquiry re: blogs on site

Hi Chad,

What an utterly exciting and record speed response!

She died without a husband or kids, but we are in touch with her sister, so checking with her should not be a problem. Smith, thoughts?

More soon,

CVS

---

from: smith@simonyi.com
to: carl@simonyi.com
date: Tue, Sep 8 at 9:31 AM
subject: no subject

Carl, I just wanted you to stealthily figure it out, not alert them.

---

from: carl@simonyi.com
to: smith@simonyi.com
date: Tue, Sep 8 at 9:40 AM
subject: re: no subject

Wait, what about this isn't great?

---

from:	smith@simonyi.com
to:	carl@simonyi.com
date:	Tue, Sep 8 at 10:18 AM
subject:	re: no subject

I don't know. It feels different. Icky in some way.

---

from:	Chad Wotherspoon
to:	carl@simonyi.com; smith@simonyi.com
cc:	Todd Kohlstedt
date:	Tue, Sep 8 at 1:21 PM
subject:	re: Copyright Inquiry re: blogs on site

Super! It's a bit late because the others are scheduled to go to press at the end of the month, but we can push it through if we enter it into Habitat soon—can Daryl's team get on that, Todd? We can go ahead and start production. Smith, I'll take you off from here. We'll work on it with Daryl's team—if you could just handle the IP question by EOB on 10/23 at the latest, that'd be fantastic. Does that give you enough time? I can put you in touch with legal to find out exactly what we need from you.

Cheers,

Chad

---

from:	smith@simonyi.com
to:	carl@simonyi.com
date:	Tue, Sep 8 at 1:25 PM
subject:	re: no subject

Carl,

　　I'll handle it from here.

Thx.

---

from: jademassey@yahoo.com
to: donnalionschef@gmail.com
date: Tue, Sep 8 at 1:30 PM
subject: Hello!

Hi Donna!

It's been too long! Hard to believe that it's been twenty years since we were babies just starting school.

How is it going at 85 Cherry? Are you still there?

I left Barn recently and am putting out feelers for what may come next. I'd love to get together for coffee if you have a free moment.

Jade

---

from: Barnes & Noble [bn.com]
to: jademassey@yahoo.com
date: Tue, Sep 8 at 1:51 PM
subject: Your Order Is on Its Way!

Dear Jade,

The following order(s) has shipped and is on its way:

The Year of Magical Thinking (9.99)

H is for Hawk (12.99)

Grief for Dummies (14.99)

Fertility after 40 (15.99)

The Ghost Womb Myth Revisited (4.99)

Subtotal: $58.95

Visit <u>Order Status</u> to track your order. Thanks for shopping at BarnesandNoble.com!

from: HelloCupid
to: jademassey@yahoo.com
date: Tue, Sep 8 at 2:02 PM
subject: SEAFARER1980 is looking at your profile!

JadeJadeJava,

It's been 6 months since you logged in—have you found a match? Let us know! Hearing that we've helped you find love makes our heart go pitter-patter.

And if not, why not come back and visit? People are checking out your profile. Here's a sneak peek at the latest messages you've received:

From SEAFARER1980:

JadeJadeJava,

Nice name. I am, too, a fan of the caffeinated beverage.

A bit about me: I am currently exploring the 112 meditation techniques of Vigyan Bhairav Tantra. Growing my law practice keeps me busy, but I'm always down for exploring ancient spiritual systems.

Speaking of, I like sex—and I don't just mean the act but also the nuances of it, the power exchange that makes people crazy, the quid pro quo.

Shoot me a message if you are intrigued . . .

From DAWGONNIT:

sup

ps write me back if you want a real man and WILLNT USE ME FOR FREE RIDES IT WILLNT WORK

Tuesday, September 8
TherapistAwayNetwork™
Patient Name: Jade Renee Massey
AUTO PROMPT: **What secret question do you hold?**

Tonight I am taking a walk with my sister's former boss, but I need to be certain that it's not a date. He says it's not.

Smith is pleasant enough to talk to. But if I recall correctly, he is short, so it wouldn't work out anyway. Plus I haven't even seen his hands. They could be monstrous.

All of this—and something else. I reached out to Henry today. I know. But I wanted to ask him about whether he thought I have a case against Iris's doctor. He suggested that I drop it and move on, which, if I'd thought about it for five seconds, I could have predicted. He's a doctor, so of course he is going to be on the side of medicine. Like you would be, I imagine, if you were here. Actually, if you were here, you'd say: Why did you *actually* email Henry?

I don't know. Partly what I just wrote. But I guess I also . . . why do I feel like I'm supposed to tell him that I might have a date with someone? It's not a date. Even *Smith* said it's not a date. And I'm not with Henry anymore. There is no reason to think I need to talk to him first. I owe him no heads-up. I don't want to be with Henry anymore . . . do I?

Dear JADE,

Thank you for your submission to TAN™. We will make sure your provider receives this message.

Did you know "secret" is derived from the Latin *secretus*, meaning "separate" or "apart"? When we hold secrets from others, we are keeping them at a distance. Sometimes, by exploring the nature of that distance, we can figure out how it is serving us. Once we understand its purpose, we can ask ourselves—am I still the person I was? Do I really need this secret any longer?

TAN™ is not to be used in case of emergency. If you are in crisis, call 9-1-1.

Sincerely,

Your friends at TAN

---

from: smith@simonyi.com
to: iris@simonyi.com
date: Tue, Sep 8 at 11:59 PM
subject: no subject

Emailing you at your work email since your sister is apparently dipping into your Gmail.

I spent some time with her tonight. Based on her emails, I got the impression that in person she'd be chatty and open, but when she showed up, she was guarded and on edge. (It may have been because she was flustered. I'd suggested we meet at the corner of Twenty-Third and Tenth since she'd be taking the PATH train in from Jersey, but she'd thought I'd said Twenty-Fifth and waited there for fifteen minutes before rechecking her email.)

We met at five. It was a hot day for September, and she kept her arms crossed for the first half hour or so of our walk along the Hudson. But as I spoke about you, she began to relax. Not like it made her happy to discuss you, more like it reminded her that she was sad, and she forgot to be as closed off.

She told me that in the boxes of your things from work she'd found a scarf that belonged to Daniel—evident because his name was stamped on the tag like a child's. She wondered if you'd kept it because you intended to give it back, or because of nostalgia. I told her I'd seen you wear it regularly in the winter, and maybe you simply liked that it was a well-made scarf.

I told her I'd set up you and Richie, and that he was my first roommate in New York. I found myself telling her how he used to sneak into NYU real estate classes to learn how to be a broker until he became one. She looked skeptical, but then when I told her about the coffee sleeves venture and making a killing, she seemed less so. She liked the part about them being environmental.

"He is not who I'd have thought she'd like," she said, "but she seemed to enjoy him." She suggested that sisters never think the men their sisters choose are good enough. (I wasn't sure if she knew about your feelings toward her ex-husband, which of course fall in line with her theory, so I didn't mention them.) I felt a little defensive of Richie. I told her that whatever it was you and Richie had there at the end, you did one over on him. That he spent a full month after you died cocooned on my couch.

"It hasn't been easy for anyone, I guess," she said.

Jade is preoccupied with not forgetting you, worried that she won't remember who you were. In an attempt to reassure her, I said, "Look at how much Iris managed to recall about the past, including the distant past, when she sat down to write. Jade didn't like this."

"Can we not talk about the blog?" she said. "I'm working on feeling better, not worse." She laughed. It seemed forced.

I told her I don't find it sad. I asked if that's why she doesn't want it published.

She said, "We're not ready," meaning, I assume, her and your mom. I dropped it.

She asked more about my business, what I do day to day, and I got the sense that her questioning was more about you than me. She wanted to learn what your daily life had been like.

I didn't plan to spend six hours roaming southern Manhattan with your sister, but neither of us made a move to leave until she started falling asleep on a bench in Union Square Park. The first hour we spent talking about you, but then we turned to other things. Our marriages. Our childhoods.

When I described the night as "shiny," she called me poetic. I've never been called poetic before.

She asked me at some point what my vice is. Maybe because she told me hers is working too hard and drinking red wine, I actually told her the truth. I gamble. (I told her I haven't in a while. I didn't say: a week ago.)

She asked if I do it every day.

I said no, mainly during a crisis. When things are already going badly.

"That makes sense," she said, which surprised me, because it never made sense to me at all. Why on earth would that make sense? "If things are already bad, you blow things up so they can't get worse." A fog had settled around us, which made the West Village streets feel like a stage with no one on it but us.

I like her, Iris. Is it because she reminds me enough of you that it feels familiar? Or could it be more?

At your funeral, the only other time I've ever seen her, I was struck by the way she commanded the room, her generous energy as she hosted people like it was a dinner party. She appeared a person who takes charge.

But I'm seeing another side of her now. She is afraid. She's searching. And she misses you more than she thinks she lets on.

Tuesday, September 8
TherapistAwayNetwork™
Patient Name: Jade Renee Massey

UPDATE to Most Recent Post. *Please enter additional text below. It will appear at the bottom of your post.*

His hands are fine.

THE DANIEL DOTS

At night my dreams take me places I can no longer go in real life. I am with Daniel again. He is lying next to me, spindly and warm. In last night's dream, I used to be sick but now am not, and we are relieved, and we are in love again. Even in the dream, I scold myself: *Things will shift. It is never too good for too long.* But my reservation scatters and fades while the thing that sticks, that weighs me down upon waking, sweaty against my pillow, is the loss.

In the morning light the ache lingers. The cruelty isn't that it's fantasy, but that it's over. I am hungover from a recollection.

Does time forget to put a check on our dreaming? I haven't been with Daniel in three years, can safely say I haven't loved him in nearly two, but last night, I did, and so this morning, I feel the sting of loss again.

Sometimes I wonder how much of this is my cancer mind, my neurons scrambling to make sense of what is happening as malignancy ravages me from the inside out and the drugs ravage me from the outside in.

When I was younger and stupider and loved him despite the signs I shouldn't . . . well, I have done a fine job of writing off that gal as a fool, and in turn, how I felt about him. He didn't deserve my love. Once I figured that out, I scrubbed it clean from my heart. It took time, of course. But sometimes, after I've closed my eyes, the love comes back in full. I awake with the heart of that girl, swollen with hope and belief in a soul she fears will never belong to her completely, which only makes her want it more.

It didn't go as planned.

Daniel was at the foot of our bed wearing my one-piece, palm trees stretched over his rippled chest, distorted.

"What do you think?" he asked. We were packing for a trip to the beach with my friend Sabine and her husband, and my antidepressant had assembled twenty pounds onto my butt, thighs, and stomach, hence the purchase of the conservative, ruffled one-piece, a hideous tribute to the tropics that I only bought because it was the most flattering among the selection at Macy's, and there was no way I was going to a *second* store to stare at my pale, dimpled skin under fluorescent lighting. Apparently, the swimsuit I selected also fit my boyfriend.

"It looks better on you. Great," I said.

"I guess I'm wearing it, then, and you're wearing mine." He threw his bright green surf shorts at me. I batted them away and pulled the sheet up around my thighs. Then he was on top of me, pushing his shorts onto me over the lacy underwear I still wore in those days before I realized that my thumbs are too opposable to wear lacy underwear without ripping holes in it. He pulled the swim trunks up my legs all the way to my waist as I fought, wriggling and winded and hideously conscious of every roll, every lump of flesh. Finally I gave in, a limp seal. My nightgown was twisted around my breasts, and his shorts tangled up in my legs.

"I'm out of breath from four seconds of exercise," I said, panting.

"You put up a good fight," he said from behind me.

I started to cry.

"What's so funny?" he asked, then realized I wasn't laughing.

"Hey," he said, pinching my ass. "You are beautiful." And I cried more because he was being so sweet, but mostly because I felt fat.

Three years later, I was hunched over a toilet in Café Frida west of Central Park. My crinkly peach wedding dress, vintage from a secondhand store on MacDougal, was all bunched up in Sabine's hands as I vomited mucus. Clutching it, she kept telling me to be careful, like I could control the trajectory of my bile.

I was to marry Daniel in a couple of hours because I loved him enough to get married. Loved him so much, in fact, that I was marrying him despite the arguing.

We hadn't gone a day without a fight that I could remember. We'd been to therapy. We'd been on a couples' retreat where we stared into each other's eyes, not blinking, for long stretches. We'd traded a journal back and forth in which we wrote each other letters in an attempt to cut through our defense mechanisms. We set aside one day a week where we were only allowed to enjoy each other's company: Fridays were for being happy; no arguments allowed. Like addicts, we never once made it through a Friday without spiraling into heated tension.

We could scream for hours, tormenting neighbors I'm sure. We were so adept at pressing each other's buttons, we were like two organists playing each other with all four limbs, blasting furious energy through empty space at a moment's notice. We were wildly in love, and because of it, we made each other miserable. It was my wedding day, and I was as sad as I'd ever been.

Plus—and this I never told a soul—I'd begun having feelings for someone else, someone who didn't drain me. It was new, and nothing, but enough of a contrast that I wondered: maybe there's a better way.

Sabine helped me up, and we backed out of the stall. She checked for spots and pronounced me clean. I washed my hands. We made eye contact in the mirror. She asked my mirror self if I was okay. My mirror self nodded, yes.

She gave my mirror self a weird look.

"What are you doing?" I asked.

"I'm sending you a message with my eyes," she said.

"It's not translating," I said.

"You can back out. It's not too late."

She laid out how it would happen. I would tell Daniel that I wasn't ready, that I needed to postpone. She was careful not to use the words "cancel" or "break up." She would tell the guests that I wasn't feeling well enough for the ceremony. I didn't have to face anyone but him. It didn't have to be a humiliating nightmare.

Hearing it spelled out like that, I could picture it, and it wasn't insurmountable. Perhaps if I'd had to face our friends and family members (only twenty or so of them, but still), I'd have been too afraid. But Sabine's offer to handle the logistics, via a watered-down version of the truth that I could wrap my mind around, allowed my gut to prevail. And so I did it. I fucking backed out of my wedding on my wedding day. Like some goddamn Lifetime movie.

It was strangely seamless. Sabine told the guests to go home. Later I slept in her bed, in her pajamas. I had spread my dress neatly across her love seat, as if I might wear it again one day.

Emotionally, however, it was worse than I could have imagined. Later that week, sharing the last meal I'd ever have with Daniel, I wondered, as I would again and again, how I'd ever feel anything but sorrow over choosing not to be with the person I loved most in the world.

It wasn't ever cracked

I had to pull it apart

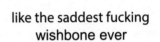

like the saddest fucking
wishbone ever

COMMENTS (3):

BonnieD: :(

ChristmasWasMyFavorite: You should write a romance novel!

BigJessBarbs: News Alert!!! Men you didn't marry don't matter at
the end of your life, sweetheart!

WEDNESDAY, SEPTEMBER 9

from: winsomebeautydorothy@hotmail.com
to: Junior League Singers Full List
date: Wed, Sep 9 at 5:17 AM
subject: "Hands that Work, Hearts Full of Joy" Concert Follow-up +
          Some News

Dearest Fellow Singers,

Congratulations on a truly spectacular performance at the Evergreen Community's Labor Day "Hands that Work, Hearts Full of Joy" on Monday. Judith, our contact at Evergreen, called me this morning to let me know that the residents are still talking about how much they enjoyed hearing the love songs of their youth, which they seldom get to experience in their golden years. Bernice's solo in "I Could Write a Book" was of particular charm to several of the more senior gentlemen. I understand that Judith has received a handful of requests for Bernice to be invited back soon! Just wait until they hear your sheep solo in "Christmas Barnyard Sampler" come the holidays!

And now this email takes a turn, for I have a favor I must ask as director of the Gray Lady Chorus. My eldest daughter (the former chef) is arriving back into town today. I would appreciate your patience at choir practice tomorrow evening, as she does seem to enjoy attending our rehearsals when she is visiting. I understand that some of us, particularly Loretta and Eunice, are not crazy about having an audience when we are in the "learning" stage of our music, but my daughter is single (at thirty-seven), unemployed, suffering from a jaundiced complexion, and in need of positive female role models such as yourselves. I do not imagine it will be forever, but for the immediate future I just need to remind myself that she is trying to feel useful, and allow her to be a "help." Your cooperation is greatly appreciated!

In other news, KellyAnne Smithies has volunteered to host this year's fall cookie baking party. Thank you, KellyAnne!

Sincerely,

Dorothy

---

from: gamblersanon.com
to: smithsimonyi@gmail.com
date: Wed, Sep 9 at 7:03 AM
subject: You're on a streak

Dear Smith,

You have attended Online GA Meetings 7 days in a row.

That's a winning streak. Keep up the good work, and reap benefits you didn't know were possible.

On your team every step of the way,

Gamblers Anonymous

from: smith@simonyi.com
to: Airbnb GUEST EMAIL
date: Wed, Sep 9 at 7:30 AM
subject: re: BOOKING EXTENSION INQUIRY for Thurs, Sept 10—Mon, Sep 14

Hi Travel Man2,

I'm glad to hear that you're enjoying New York enough that you want to extend your stay! You're welcome to stay in my apartment through Monday. One favor—if anyone asks, please just tell them you're my cousin. Just gets a little messy with the co-op board sometimes.

Best,

Smith Simonyi

from: carl@simonyi.com
to: zaharaferringbottom@zaharaferringbottom.com
date: Wed, Sep 9 at 9:05 AM
subject: Clarification

Dear Zahara,

My name is Carl and I'm assistant to Smith. I am writing to clarify a preposition for your biography, which I'd like to post on the Clients page of our site.

Do you run UP walls or AT walls? I'm having difficulty tracking down this information, since your performances are undocumented and no one at MoMA PS1 will get back to me. It *does* seem like an important distinction.

Thanks in advance,

CVS

---

from: jademassey@yahoo.com
to: smith@simonyi.com
date: Wed, Sep 9 at 9:42 AM
subject: ☺

Good morning.

---

from: smith@simonyi.com
to: jademassey@yahoo.com
date: Wed, Sep 9 at 9:50 AM
subject: re: ☺

Good morning.

---

from: jademassey@yahoo.com
to: smith@simonyi.com
date: Wed, Sep 9 at 9:51 AM
subject: re: ☺

Best memory. Go!

---

from: jademassey@yahoo.com
to: smith@simonyi.com
date: Wed, Sep 9 at 11:02 AM
subject: re: ☺

Don't think so hard. Some of us don't* have all day.

*Do, but who's checking?

---

from: smith@simonyi.com
to: jademassey@yahoo.com
date: Wed, Sep 9 at 11:04 AM
subject: re: ☺

My best one is tied up with a bad one is the problem.

---

from: jademassey@yahoo.com
to: smith@simonyi.com
date: Wed, Sep 9 at 11:05 AM
subject: re: ☺

Of course it is.

---

from: smith@simonyi.com
to: jademassey@yahoo.com
date: Wed, Sep 9 at 11:11 AM
subject: re: ☺

What does that mean?

---

from: jademassey@yahoo.com
to: smith@simonyi.com
date: Wed, Sep 9 at 11:12 AM
subject: re: ☺

You're a bit of a pessimist is all. Best/worst memory, go!

from:	smith@simonyi.com
to:	jademassey@yahoo.com
date:	Wed, Sep 9 at 12:29 PM
subject:	re: ☺

All right, here goes. For a while, my dad drove for a company called FasTrans. But the summer before I started second grade, Oscar Mayer, which was based in Madison, expanded its Wienermobile fleet, and my dad became one of a hundred hotdoggers hired to drive the wieners around the Midwest. As a kid I thought it was the coolest thing, of course. For the last three weeks before the start of the school year, he and I handed out wiener whistles (plastic whistles that, you guessed it, were shaped like wieners) at diners, Wal-Marts, 7-Elevens. I was living with my dad in a wiener with a RELSHME plate! I missed my mom, of course, but it was all so new and adventurous that I didn't think of her much. We were just two guys having a blast, living in a hot dog. I'd never been happier.

Then one day I woke up to a man angrily knocking on the window. We weren't supposed to be living in the wiener. My dad told me to clean up the inside, then climbed out and shut the door. While I gathered up scratch-offs and napkins and rock-hard stray French fries in the grocery bag we used for trash, the man yelled at him. My dad stood next to the car in the parking lot of the rest stop, taking it, while I walked the bag of trash across the lot to a dumpster. I understood that what we'd done was shameful because we'd done it to save money.

I found a spot on the curb on the other side of the lot, and as I shimmied the change I'd collected from the wiener in the belly of my T-shirt, I dreamed of hurling it in the man's face. He'd ruined our trip, when all we'd done wrong was sleep.

Driving home, I could tell my dad was embarrassed in front of me. That killed me.

from: jademassey@yahoo.com
to: smith@simonyi.com
date: Wed, Sep 9 at 1:27 PM
subject: re: ☺

Well, I'm glad you have the good part at least? (Not being sarcastic.)

Here's mine. It was a New Year's, and Henry (husband at the time) had insisted we do the "polar plunge": a January 1st collective dip into the Atlantic Ocean at the Jersey Shore with a bunch of other wack jobs who thought this was a good idea.

We'd just run in and run right back out, he said, promising that it would be thrilling and a hearty shock to the circulatory system.

So we drove to the shore wearing our swimsuits under our layers of winter clothes. It was icy even in the car, in the dry heat. For the full hour-long drive I dreaded the "plunge" part, but once we arrived, the energy of the crowd gathered on the beach was infectious.

"One, two, three, go!" a thick, beer-gutted man hollered, and over a hundred of us, middle-aged adults mostly, ripped off our coats and pants and sweaters and socks. In a mad dash we rushed into the surf. Some, including Henry, immediately ducked their heads under, but I hurried in only up to my waist and splashed water onto my chest and arms before darting back onto the sand to fetch my towel.

It was enough. Henry was right—the shock was electric. I ate a hot dog, a delicious hot dog, feeling powerfully, unflappably alive.

It was a great day.

from: smith@simonyi.com
to: jademassey@yahoo.com
date: Wed, Sep 9 at 1:39 PM
subject: re: ☺

You eat hot dogs?

from: jademassey@yahoo.com
to: smith@simonyi.com
date: Wed, Sep 9 at 1:42 PM
subject: re: ☺

Right? I did that day.

from: smith@simonyi.com
to: jademassey@yahoo.com
date: Wed, Sep 9 at 1:46 PM
subject: re: ☺

The reason I told you last night wasn't a date is because in the spring your sister told me you were dating your ex-husband again. I wondered if you still were.

from: jademassey@yahoo.com
to: smith@simonyi.com
date: Wed, Sep 9 at 1:59 PM
subject: re: ☺

That was out of nowhere.

Yes, we were. And Iris would have loved to know it ended. Again. Ended again. She was not a fan, as you probably are aware, since you apparently have heard about him.

---

from: smith@simonyi.com
to: jademassey@yahoo.com
date: Wed, Sep 9 at 2:04 PM
subject: re: ☺

She may have mentioned that she wasn't crazy about Henry 4, as she called him.

---

from: jademassey@yahoo.com
to: smith@simonyi.com
date: Wed, Sep 9 at 2:18 P
subject: re: ☺

Technically he was Henry 3. He was my third Henry to date. But then we broke up for a short time when he felt like he might prefer to date a nurse he worked with, and then changed his mind so we dated again, upon which he became Henry 4. (If you're thinking that I should have seen the pattern, I agree.)

Then we got married, then divorced two years ago. And then, last spring, we briefly dated again. Which I guess would make him also Henry . . . 5?

Let's just say it took me a while to realize it wasn't going to work.

Get this—now he's angling to get together again. Sometimes he does this when he's bored.

I'm surprised to hear that she called him Henry 4. I thought her nickname for him was Only Henry, based on the time he got frustrated at being referred to by her as "Henry 3" and lost his temper.

"There is one Henry now! I am Only Henry!" Iris found the tantrum hilarious.

from: smith@simonyi.com
to: jademassey@yahoo.com
date: Wed, Sep 9 at 2:24 PM
subject: re: ☺

Ah. That explains our favorite drink: the Only Henry, made to perfection by the bartender at Doyle's Bar and Grill on the corner: 1 part whiskey, 2 parts ginger beer, and a squeeze of lime juice. Iris told us she'd invented it but didn't explain the origin of the name.

from: jademassey@yahoo.com
to: smith@simonyi.co
date: Wed, Sep 9 at 2:28 PM
subject: re: ☺

Wow, thanks, sis.

from: smith@simonyi.com
to: jademassey@yahoo.com
date: Wed, Sep 9 at 2:30 PM
subject: re: ☺

Why did you get back together with him so many times?

from: jademassey@yahoo.com
to: smith@simonyi.com
date: Wed, Sep 9 at 2:37 PM
subject: re: ☺

I suppose because I had regrets (even though you don't believe in them ;)). And the regrets made me think I'd made a mistake.

---

from: smith@simonyi.com
to: jademassey@yahoo.com
date: Wed, Sep 9 at 2:39 PM
subject: re: ☺

Is that not what regrets mean? (I do believe they *exist*, I just don't know if we should make decisions in an attempt to avoid future ones.)

---

from: jademassey@yahoo.com
to: smith@simonyi.com
date: Wed, Sep 9 at 3:00 PM
subject: re: ☺

Maybe there's a distinction between regret and nostalgia that I now understand. I miss him sometimes. But that's different from regret. I'm nostalgic for my twenty-three-year-old metabolism, too. Do I wish I was twenty-three again? Lord, no.

Anyway, now that my ex-husband is also my ex-boyfriend, I get to say "How many times does it take a prefix to stick?" That's my new joke.

---

from: smith@simonyi.com
to: jademassey@yahoo.com
date: Wed, Sep 9 at 3:03 PM
subject: re: ☺

Have you considered stand-up?

from:	jademassey@yahoo.com
to:	smith@simonyi.com
date:	Wed, Sep 9 at 3:09 PM
subject:	re: ☺

Does it pay, and can I start tomorrow?

from:	smith@simonyi.com
to:	jademassey@yahoo.com
date:	Wed, Sep 9 at 3:22 PM
subject:	re: ☺

Haha. How did it end this last time? With Henry 3/4/5/Only?

from:	jademassey@yahoo.com
to:	smith@simonyi.com
date:	Wed, Sep 9 at 3:37 PM
subject:	re: ☺

Oh, man. Let's see. Iris had died a week earlier. It was the middle of the night. I was lying next to Henry. And I had the sensation that I'd been falling into a deep well for a long time with him, and that I had just hit the bottom with a thud. I wish I could say it was a dream, but I was awake. And so I couldn't write it off as my asleep brain. I lay there thinking about how I knew everything about him I could know, understood everything we were capable of being. I saw our future stretched out thirty or fifty years, and it was not my future.

I suppose the clinical way of putting it is that we had different ideas of what we wanted out of our lives.

You know I'm about to ask you about your divorce now, right?

---

from: smith@simonyi.com
to: jademassey@yahoo.com
date: Wed, Sep 9 at 3:42 PM
subject: re: ☺

Mine was entirely run-of-the-mill. Woman leaves man because he isn't emotional enough: a classic, cautionary tale.

---

from: jademassey@yahoo.com
to: smith@simonyi.com
date: Wed, Sep 9 at 3:44 PM
subject: re: ☺

All right, I won't press.

---

from: smith@simonyi.com
to: jademassey@yahoo.com
date: Wed, Sep 9 at 3:47 PM
subject: re: ☺

Funny—you and me, both divorced, with no kids and deceased fathers. Real portraits of the American dream.

    And Iris, too!

---

from: smith@simonyi.com
to: jademassey@yahoo.com
date: Wed, Sep 9 at 3:48 PM
subject: re: ☺

(Kidding. I think that came across ruder than I intended.)

from:	jademassey@yahoo.com
to:	smith@simonyi.com
date:	Wed, Sep 9 at 3:50 PM
subject:	re: ☺

I want children. I just wasn't ready before the last year or so, which was a point of contention with Henry. But I've always wanted them. Do you not?

from:	smith@simonyi.com
to:	jademassey@yahoo.com
date:	Wed, Sep 9 at 3:53 PM
subject:	re: ☺

Depends. Not at the moment, no.

from:	jademassey@yahoo.com
to:	smith@simonyi.com
date:	Wed, Sep 9 at 3:56 PM
subject:	re: ☺

And Iris wasn't divorced, you realize.

from:	smith@simonyi.com
to:	jademassey@yahoo.com
date:	Wed, Sep 9 at 3:59 PM
subject:	re: ☺

She left someone at the altar. That's pretty close.

---

from: jademassey@yahoo.com
to: smith@simonyi.com
date: Wed, Sep 9 at 4:01 PM
subject: re: ☺

Were you there for the non-wedding? I don't remember meeting you.

---

from: smith@simonyi.com
to: jademassey@yahoo.com
date: Wed, Sep 9 at 4:11 PM
subject: re: ☺

No. I was wooing a prospective client in Nashville, a singer-songwriter who'd just won a Golden Globe for his score of that TV miniseries *The Underlings*. I really wanted to sign the guy (which didn't happen). And Iris and I had only been working together a year, so I kinda figured she'd invited me out of obligation. The next morning I texted her congrats, and when she didn't respond, I assumed she was having a great time honeymooning in Madrid. I was in Nashville through Monday.

On Tuesday I showed up, and there was a note on my desk. She wrote that she hadn't gone through with it, and so no Spain, but she still needed the couple of weeks off. She didn't respond to my texts later that week, or the following. Two weeks later she was back, saying she didn't want to discuss it.

I always found it odd she came into the office to leave the note instead of just emailing me.

from: jademassey@yahoo.com
to: smith@simonyi.com
date: Wed, Sep 9 at 4:24 PM
subject: re: ☺

I wasn't there, either. I mean, I was *there*—in the park for the wedding. But I wasn't *there* there. I was distracted by some kitchen drama from earlier that morning at the restaurant, wrapped up in my own world. I didn't think to check on Iris beforehand. Until her friend—Nadine, something, maybe?—came out and announced that there would be no wedding, I had been entirely preoccupied. Who knows what the issue even was, surely something to do with my boss, Marcus.

It doesn't surprise me that she left you that note. Was it handwritten? She was oddly fond of handwritten notes.

from: smith@simonyi.com
to: jademassey@yahoo.com
date: Wed, Sep 9 at 4:30 PM
subject: re: ☺

Yes.

from: jademassey@yahoo.com
to: smith@simonyi.com
date: Wed, Sep 9 at 4:53 PM
subject: re: ☺

When she was in sixth grade, we moved midyear (not uncommon for us). We started at a new school just in time for the science fair. The winner got a year of free admission to the science museum, which was a big deal because there was an exhibit where you could make your own candy. Or was it your own soda?

Anyway, Iris really wanted to win, but she was insecure about coming up with a project. She was convinced she'd make a fool of herself. (When you move mid school year as a kid, especially multiple times, there are whole units of knowledge that you miss. In one state, US history is covered in fourth grade, but in another, it's third, and so all the kids already know it—I made it to adulthood thinking the Boston Tea Party was an actual tea party.) It never bothered me that much to be behind in some subjects. We were ahead in others. But Iris got so embarrassed when gaps in her education were exposed—she was always bringing up that she never learned the US presidents, state capitals, or animal classifications, for instance. And this was pre-Internet, so it wasn't like we could just look stuff up. Point is, she wanted me to come up with a science project for her. We made clouds.

And she won!

Which I learned . . . in a handwritten note.

That was the point of this long story.

---

from: smith@simonyi.com
to: jademassey@yahoo.com
date: Wed, Sep 9 at 4:57 PM
subject: re: ☺

What are animal classifications? You *made clouds*?

---

from: jademassey@yahoo.com
to: smith@simonyi.com
date: Wed, Sep 9 at 5:00 PM
subject: re: ☺

You know, like animal kingdoms. Genus. Order.

Making clouds is less complicated than it sounds. It involves an empty glass bottle (my mother's Perrier), steam, and an ice cube.

---

from: smith@simonyi.com
to: jademassey@yahoo.com
date: Wed, Sep 9 at 5:02 PM
subject: re: ☺

I am 100% sure I never learned the animal kingdoms either.

"Making clouds" is kind of beautiful. When do I get to read some of your poetry?

---

from: jademassey@yahoo.com
to: smith@simonyi.com
date: Wed, Sep 9 at 5:06 PM
subject: re: ☺

Ha.

---

from: smith@simonyi.com
to: jademassey@yahoo.com
date: Wed, Sep 9 at 5:10 PM
subject: re: ☺

"Ha" is progress! Last time I asked, you just ignored me.

---

from: jademassey@yahoo.com
to: smith@simonyi.com
date: Wed, Sep 9 at 5:12 PM
subject: re: ☺

[You never hear from me again.]

---

from: smith@simonyi.com
to: jademassey@yahoo.com
date: Wed, Sep 9 at 5:13 PM
subject: re: ☺

☺

---

from: smith@simonyi.com
to: jademassey@yahoo.com
date: Wed, Sep 9 at 9:43 PM
subject: re: ☺

Did I say something?

---

from: jademassey@yahoo.com
to: smith@simonyi.com
date: Wed, Sep 9 at 10:59 PM
subject: re: ☺

Sorry, I was on a flight.

---

from: smith@simonyi.com
to: jademassey@yahoo.com
date: Wed, Sep 9 at 11:02 PM
subject: re: ☺

Where to?

from: jademassey@yahoo.com
to: smith@simonyi.com
date: Wed, Sep 9 at 11:09 PM
subject: re: ☺

Back to Virginia. Just for two days.

I wonder what would have happened between her and Richie.

from: smith@simonyi.com
to: jademassey@yahoo.com
date: Wed, Sep 9 at 11:17 PM
subject: re: ☺

Me too.

from: jademassey@yahoo.com
to: smith@simonyi.com
date: Wed, Sep 9 at 11:19 PM
subject: re: ☺

How is he doing?

from: smith@simonyi.com
to: jademassey@yahoo.com
date: Wed, Sep 9 at 11:25 PM
subject: re: ☺

He still isn't really getting back to me, so I don't know.

from:	jademassey@yahoo.com
to:	smith@simonyi.com
date:	Wed, Sep 9 at 11:27 PM
subject:	re: ☺

Is that normal?

from:	smith@simonyi.com
to:	jademassey@yahoo.com
date:	Wed, Sep 9 at 11:30 PM
subject:	re: ☺

Not really. Anyway, you've had a lot of change these last few months. Sister. Job. Re-re-break up.

from:	jademassey@yahoo.com
to:	smith@simonyi.com
date:	Wed, Sep 9 at 11:34 PM
subject:	re: ☺

And I dyed my hair this morning. I'm a redhead now. It's possible I look like a Disney witch, given that a few minutes ago, my mother described it as "purple."

from:	smith@simonyi.com
to:	jademassey@yahoo.com
date:	Wed, Sep 9 at 11:43 PM
subject:	re: ☺

I liked your hair color before. But I'm sure it looks lovely now, too.

from:	jademassey@yahoo.com
to:	smith@simonyi.com
date:	Wed, Sep 9 at 11:49 PM
subject:	re: ☺

Thanks. That's nice of you to say. Time for bed. G'night.

from:	smith@simonyi.com
to:	jademassey@yahoo.com
date:	Wed, Sep 9 at 11:54 PM
subject:	re: ☺

Good night, Disney witch.

I'm in love. It hit me this weekend. I didn't see it coming. For, well, a number of reasons. First of all, he's beefy. Hugging him is like holding four people crammed into the skin of one human. He gels his hair, reads Nicholas Sparks novels, and believes in *The Secret.* And yet every day, he surprises me. He's a power-lifter passionate about global warming. He's thoughtful in small ways, like noticing I've stopped putting lemon slices in my water (because of mouth sores, a fun chemo side effect). He smells like a combination of mint and that body spray teenage boys wear—but I actually *like* it.

It feels like it did when I was fourteen: I miss him after forty-five minutes; I read and reread his texts. His arrival is an event I prepare for, my preparation a ceremony. For once, lately, it's not a ceremony of death, but a ceremony of life.

And even though I have the mouth sores, and I'm self-conscious my hair has finally started falling out, and I have no idea why he's attracted to me at the moment, we're happy.

This past weekend we went upstate. For years I've slept with my suitcase by the wall next to my bed, rather than stowed. The reason in my consulting days was that I always figured that I'd soon be packing it again, so why bother? But the habit stuck even after the traveling stopped, and for years now it's sat collecting dust. Last weekend, however, it finally got some use. I lugged it down my building's four flights even though we were only going for three nights. My few outfits and bag of toiletries/meds slid around inside.

I returned from our trip upstate with four dresses, two skirts, a faux fur shrug, and a pair of sequined stilettos. It's possible that I will never wear much, or any, of this outside my apartment. These days I don't have much energy to get out, apart from work. (If Jade had her way I wouldn't still be going to work at all—I've tried explaining to her that I actually like it, and besides, I'm only part-time since chemo started.) I won't be showing up to either of those in glamour wear. But when Richie and I found ourselves wandering into a thrift store in Saugerties, New York, and I started ogling garments, he convinced me that only-inside-my-apartment is good enough. Later that night, we said the L word. And who knows, maybe I have a whole lifetime of parties ahead of me. I haven't given up yet. So, $113 poorer, here I sit, wearing pink fur and sequins, typing on my couch.

I left for Saugerties with a half-empty suitcase and a fling, and came back with one full of shiny things and a boyfriend. Not bad for a weekend, I think.

COMMENTS (2):

DyingToBlogTeam: Happy Groundhog Day!

AnikaMommyof3: Iris, we've been calling you. No need to hide, we know about the cancer. Clara ran into Jade at Whole Foods, and then someone in Morgan's Facebook mommy group posted a link to your blog as the Friday Morning Gratitude Read. Imagine Morgan's surprise when she saw it was by you, and it was about having cancer, not mono. Point being, we are here for you and praying for you, sweetie. And can't wait to meet the new beau! Xo

THURSDAY, SEPTEMBER 10

from: harvwashburn55@hotmail.com
to: smith@simonyi.com
date: Thu, Sep 10 at 10:12 AM
subject: A "Hairball" Idea: Grooming Salon for Pets and Their Humans

Dear Sir or Madam,

I am writing with an idea that I am 100% confident will revolutionize the grooming industry. This is your one and only opportunity to be a part of it, should you so choose.

Picture: A salon . . . for both pets, and the humans they call parents.

How often is it that you want to get a haircut but you also need to get your dog groomed, and you feel you must choose? No longer.

At *The Groom Room* we will do both, simulcraneously.

I have some investment already. Sure, I need more. I've applied to be on *Shark Tank*, and that will prove helpful once I'm cast.

Please respond at your earliest convenience, as this is not the kind of idea one should "sit" on. I must establish a brand and identity.

Harvey Washburn

Bloomington, Indiana

---

from: carl@simonyi.com
to: smith@simonyi.com
date: Thu, Sep 10 at 10:15 AM
subject: Fwd: A "Hairball" Idea: Grooming Salon for Pets and Their
            Humans

Morning, Boss!

What do you think? "Hairball" indeed, but not all hairball schemes are bad . . . I once shoved a futon out of a second-story window to spare my father from having to haul it down the excessively narrow stairwell of my dorm. Given that he was later diagnosed with a triple hernia after merely transferring some urns of sweet potato vine from our east veranda to our west, it was clearly the right choice.

CVS

---

from: smith@simonyi.com
to: carl@simonyi.com
date: Thu, Sep 10 at 10:20 AM
subject: re: Fwd: A "Hairball" Idea: Grooming Salon for Pets and Their
            Humans

Absolutely not. Don't respond.

from:	carl@simonyi.com
to:	smith@simonyi.com
date:	Thu, Sep 10 at 10:25 AM
subject:	re: Fwd: A "Hairball" Idea: Grooming Salon for Pets and Their Humans

Now that I think about it, the fact that the futon didn't break is sort of a miracle. But truthfully—can we really afford to be turning down work right now?

from:	jademassey@yahoo.com
to:	smith@simonyi.com
date:	Thu, Sep 10 at 12:11 PM
subject:	Divorce

I take it back. I *am* going to press you on it. I'm too curious.

from:	smith@simonyi.com
to:	jademassey@yahoo.com
date:	Thu, Sep 10 at 12:14 PM
subject:	re: Divorce

About?

from:	jademassey@yahoo.com
to:	smith@simonyi.com
date:	Thu, Sep 10 at 12:17 PM
subject:	re: Divorce

What was your relationship with your ex-wife like?

---

from: smith@simonyi.com
to: jademassey@yahoo.com
date: Thu, Sep 10 at 12:21 PM
subject: re: Divorce

Oh, boy.

---

from: jademassey@yahoo.com
to: smith@simonyi.com
date: Thu, Sep 10 at 12:33 PM
subject: re: Divorce

No rush. I'm here all day. Just driving my mom around . . .

---

from: jademassey@yahoo.com
to: smith@simonyi.com
date: Thu, Sep 10 at 1:40 PM
subject: re: Divorce

Scratch that: I'm bored and refreshing my email incessantly, so anytime now . . .

---

from: smith@simonyi.com
to: jademassey@yahoo.com
date: Thu, Sep 10 at 2:20 PM
subject: re: Divorce

Maybe I should just see if my old therapist will send me her notes, and you can read those. She was always scribbling away. I'm sure they're juicy.

---

from: jademassey@yahoo.com
to: smith@simonyi.com
date: Thu, Sep 10 at 2:24 PM
subject: re: Divorce

You really don't want to talk about it, huh?

---

from: smith@simonyi.com
to: jademassey@yahoo.com
date: Thu, Sep 10 at 2:29 PM
subject: re: Divorce

Just don't tell me what they say.

---

from: jademassey@yahoo.com
to: smith@simonyi.com
date: Thu, Sep 10 at 2:30 PM
subject: re: Divorce

All right, all right. I'll drop it.

---

from: smith@simonyi.com
to: jademassey@yahoo.com
date: Thu, Sep 10 at 2:34 PM
subject: re: Divorce

I'm struggling with how to describe it. Maybe I'll just tell you a story.

from:	jademassey@yahoo.com
to:	smith@simonyi.com
date:	Thu, Sep 10 at 2:36 PM
subject:	re: Divorce

That works.

from:	smith@simonyi.com
to:	jademassey@yahoo.com
date:	Thu, Sep 10 at 3:00 PM
subject:	re: Divorce

The day before Clementine left me, I came home to find her on the balcony clutching a shimmery silver envelope and screaming, "FLY, DAMMIT!" at the ground. Next to her foot was half a butterfly. Or rather, a whole butterfly, folded. It wasn't moving. Inside the envelope, she showed me, were dozens more, also folded. "Hibernating," she explained. The butterflies, according to the company she'd purchased them from, were supposed to awake upon being flung, and fly away.

She has a slight accent from growing up in East Texas, which gets stronger when she gets mad.

"FLY, FUCKER!" she was yelling in her twang, so full of rage at the poor insects that I suspected (correctly) it had something to do with me.

"Maybe they're just hibernating better than they're supposed to," I said. I'd never heard of hibernating butterflies. I pulled out a third and mimicked her technique. It fell. I asked what they were for.

She told me she wanted to release them at a baby shower for her friend who was having her "rainbow babies," a set of twins. I didn't remember anything about such a person, or what rainbow babies meant. This astounded and irritated her.

"The IVF one?" she said. "She's had a bunch of miscarriages, and so these twins are a godsend? We talked about rainbow babies for, like, half an hour the other night."

I still didn't remember. Weary of me, she reached into the pocket of her sweater, and I noticed a box of Marlboros peeking out of it. I had never seen her smoke. I didn't know she did. She lit a cigarette and sat in one of the patio chairs her mother had given us for Christmas. I sat in the other, wondering if I was allowed to ask when she started smoking. But she beat me to the questioning.

"Why did you marry me?" she asked.

I told her because I loved her, obviously. I asked back: why did she marry *me*?

"You weren't a dick. That's rare here," she said, referring to New York City. She said she found it attractive that I'd come from nothing, made myself successful. And that when she'd learned I'd lost my dad and was taking care of my mom, she saw me as a kind of hero.

"But?" I said, because it was clear one was coming.

"But you're more stoic than heroic."

It stung, and I told her so. Then I asked when she started smoking. She looked at me, disgusted, and said that she'd been smoking since I met her.

"You couldn't smell it on my breath?" She seemed to suggest that me not knowing she was a smoker was a metaphor for much more. I wasn't observant enough or something.

The next morning before work, I had an impulse to go to the window and check the ground. The folded-up butterflies were gone.

---

from: jademassey@yahoo.com
to: smith@simonyi.com
date: Thu, Sep 10 at 3:08 PM
subject: re: Divorce

What do you make of this story you chose to tell?

---

from: smith@simonyi.com
to: jademassey@yahoo.com
date: Thu, Sep 10 at 3:12 PM
subject: re: Divorce

I was fantastic at disappointing her, and she was fantastic at making me feel disappointing. And even fucking butterflies couldn't get off the ground in our presence.

---

from: jademassey@yahoo.com
to: smith@simonyi.com
date: Thu, Sep 10 at 3:20 PM
subject: re: Divorce

Did you really not know she was a smoker?

---

from: smith@simonyi.com
to: jademassey@yahoo.com
date: Thu, Sep 10 at 3:21 PM
subject: re: Divorce

I really didn't.

from: jademassey@yahoo.com
to: smith@simonyi.com
date: Thu, Sep 10 at 3:33 PM
subject: re: Divorce

She must not have smoked *that* much then. Did you know Iris was a smoker?

from: smith@simonyi.com
to: jademassey@yahoo.com
date: Thu, Sep 10 at 3:35 PM
subject: re: Divorce

By the time I hired Iris, she had quit. I never knew she smoked till I read her blog. How long, do you know?

from: jademassey@yahoo.com
to: smith@simonyi.com
date: Thu, Sep 10 at 5:10 PM
subject: re: Divorce

The first time I saw Iris smoking, she was thirteen. We were living in Little Rock, and I found her squatting behind a dumpster in the parking lot, her arms wrapped around her bony little knees, puffing on a Camel. She frantically put it out and begged me not to tell our mom, but of course I wouldn't have. It was two against one.

I told her smoking was stupid, but that's all I said. I could have told her to give me the pack.

In my mind, I was already on my way out, counting down the months until I could start culinary school, move to one city and stay there, with my own room that wasn't a hotel room. Iris, though, was a little kid when we became transient. The bulk of her childhood was spent on the move. It's hard to have no friends and live on pizza and Chinese takeout and cold cuts on white bread that you eat on hard, scratchy sofas. Changing schools every few months, in a new town in a new state with people who have known each other for years and have their cliques and norms and inside jokes. Trying to break into that again and again, withstand the awkwardness, the discomfort—no wonder she started smoking. It gave her something to do with her hands, if nothing else. *I* certainly never got used to the conversation:

"What do you mean, you live in a hotel?"

"Have you heard of Winsome Beauty Brands? Our mom is a national director, and so we move around a lot."

"But why do you live in a hotel?"

So I joined her behind stinky dumpsters along highways, and later, once Mom finally settled down in Virginia, behind the toolshed where she stored all of our stuff from childhood that she hadn't thrown away—our drawings and certificates and diplomas all became stiff and blurred in the first winter's snow. I didn't smoke with her, but I sat.

One time I *almost* scolded her. I was twenty-four. She was twenty. We were at this club in Soho, talking to some guys, and I went to the bathroom. When I came back out, they were all gone. I figured she'd stepped outside for a cigarette. But it was February in New York, when "freezing" is an understatement. (These were the days before cell phones were ubiquitous, and though she had a flip phone, I didn't.)

I passed by the bouncer and coat check where our coats were— Iris had the tag—letting him stamp my hand so I could get back in. Shivering in my dress, I scanned the sidewalk and spotted the front tips of her heels poking out from the other side of the building, a poof of smoke rising against the blue Manhattan skyline.

"Dammit, Iris, it's freezing!" I yelled. I hurried over, preparing to tell her once and for all that her smoking had gotten out of hand because she had scared me, and it was fucking cold, but when I reached the corner she was crying.

I asked her what was wrong. She didn't answer. I put my arm around her, holding my breath and trying not to lose my temper as she took drag after drag until all that was left was the butt.

"Do you want to talk about it?" I finally asked, relieved we could go back inside. She shook her head.

As we hobbled back—I could no longer feel my toes—she said "Thanks for not getting mad at me." And I was glad that I hadn't, after all. We both were so conditioned to brace ourselves for anger, stiffening up like abused cats. We tried to give each other understanding.

But if I *hadn't* let it go, if I'd been a bossier big sister—would she have continued? Would she have gotten lung cancer?

I just made this about me. Sorry.

---

from: smith@simonyi.com
to: jademassey@yahoo.com
date: Thu, Sep 10 at 5:24 PM
subject: re: Divorce

Are you kidding? I would much rather talk about you than me.

I don't think you should blame yourself. One conversation, or even two, would not have changed things.

---

from: jademassey@yahoo.com
to: smith@simonyi.com
date: Thu, Sep 10 at 6:10 PM
subject: re: Divorce

If you say so.

---

from: smith@simonyi.com
to: jademassey@yahoo.com
date: Thu, Sep 10 at 6:12 PM
subject: re: Divorce

Let's get back to the lighter stuff. If you lived on cold cuts, how on earth did you end up a chef?

---

from: jademassey@yahoo.com
to: smith@simonyi.com
date: Thu, Sep 10 at 6:22 PM
subject: re: Divorce

I guess because I used to cook with my dad. But that wasn't when I knew I wanted to be a chef.

---

from: smith@simonyi.com
to: jademassey@yahoo.com
date: Thu, Sep 10 at 6:25 PM
subject: re: Divorce

When did you know?

from: jademassey@yahoo.com
to: smith@simonyi.com
date: Thu, Sep 10 at 6:38 PM
subject: re: Divorce

South Carolina. Tina Christine DuPree's house. My one friend during the six months we were there. Her mom taught me how to cook country fried steak by slapping two bloody filets on the counter, guzzling what remained in a bottle of red wine, and handing the empty bottle to me to pound the steak flat. I was eleven, and hooked.

from: smith@simonyi.com
to: jademassey@yahoo.com
date: Thu, Sep 10 at 6:40 PM
subject: re: Divorce

God bless bloody filets and Tina Dupree's mom.

from: jademassey@yahoo.com
to: smith@simonyi.com
date: Thu, Sep 10 at 6:44 PM
subject: re: Divorce

Damn right.
 My mom's choir practice is starting. Talk later.

I love to bake but am not a big cook. Like my mom, I prefer order-ing in to having to construct a meal on the fly. Tonight I decided to pick up sushi on my way home from work, and as I waited for my order at Abi Sushi, my favorite Japanese takeout restaurant in my neighborhood, "Fast Car" by Tracy Chapman came on the restaurant's scratchy speaker.

It took me back to 1999, the summer before my senior year of high school. My mom, sister, and I were driving down a South-ern California highway in the apple-red '99 Camry my mom re-ceived as a job perk earlier that year. We were in the silent part of an argument I don't remember—the pause between accusa-tions and defenses over something petty. Who got what room in the apartment my mom's boyfriend Donovan had rented for us for the summer so we could be closer to him (and his wife and children).

We each raged out a separate window—Jade in the back seat, me in the passenger seat (my perk of being the one who still "lived there"), my mom staring ahead. Jade had a quick vacation from culinary school for the month of August and, upon hearing that my mom and I were now in the beautiful land of SoCal, decided to join us for the month and sublet her room in New York rather than attempt to live on the fumes of her student loans.

And I was still mad at her for leaving me alone with our mom four years earlier. It's not that she had done anything wrong. I would have done the same thing. I think I missed her more than I was willing to acknowledge.

After a few minutes, Jade passed up a CD and asked me to put it in the Toyota's player. It was Tracy Chapman. I had never heard of Tracy Chapman. It took only a minute or so for her voice to mesmerize me, for her low, gravelly tone to disarm me completely.

Later that week, I read up on her at a computer in the complex's business center. She grew up in Ohio, and her parents divorced when she was four. She lived with her mom and older sister in poverty until she escaped, thanks to a need-based scholarship to a fancy private high school in the Northeast. At one point, she told a reporter, "The idea of being famous doesn't appeal to me because I hate parties and it seems like it might be one big party."

My dad died when I was three. But to me, the idea of life being one big party sounded fantastic.

I applied to Tufts, where Tracy Chapman had gone to college, and wrote my admissions essay about my nomadic existence. I'd managed to get all As throughout high school, and to my shock, I was admitted with a full-tuition merit scholarship. I fled to Medford, Massachusetts.

At Tufts, I majored in English because it was the most interesting, and took my career counselor's advice senior year, accepting a job in consulting. Consulting had been pitched to me as "problem solving." I'd wanted a job that would make me feel useful, and problem solving sounded like such a thing. (In fact it was capitalized: Problem Solving.)

Turned out that the other aspects of the job were what defined it. The travel was familiar, but the rest was new to me: business-class everything, carefree spending (all travel being expensed), colleagues who bought $6,000 watches. I had gone to Tufts in search of myself, then gone into consulting in search of a purpose, but at twenty-two I felt less real than ever before. At least growing up in hotels, I could feel the earth beneath me. Now, I lived a life in which all anyone talked about was credit card points: at dinner, we'd order one of everything and battle to get the bill for the points. It turned into a game. Everyone guessed the size of the bill, and whoever was closest won the check. We abandoned the leftovers.

As one year turned into two, and two into four, I became more integrated into the realm of people who fancy themselves immune to the grit of surviving. I'd fled that grit, leaving my mother with it in Arizona. But I found that I preferred it to a life of needs manufactured out of excess. I was haunted by the feeling that my life was inconsequential, perhaps because there were, literally, no consequences. Money, it turned out, was like the hot boyfriend who is appealing until you discover the toll that being with him takes on you as a person. I remember one day wandering into a bookstore in some city where I'd been flown in to Problem Solve, and spying a copy of *The Unbearable Lightness of Being* on a table of Must-Reads. The title alone brought tears to my eyes. My life had become so unbearably light. Was I even there? I was a guest at one big party, and Tracy Chapman was right—it wasn't what I wanted.

The day I spent $1,500 on a trench coat—Burberry, on sale—was the day I knew I had to get out, or whatever incipient me existed somewhere inside, the me I had yet to discover, would die. That purchase was proof that I was starving her. I sold it to the highest bidder on eBay and wrote my letter of resignation.

The job at Nose was my lifeline. Jade thought I'd lost my mind, giving up a prestigious partner-track position to work the counter at a perfume shop in the Village. She interpreted it as some kind of Stockholm syndrome, my return to the beauty industry, the bane of our upbringing.

Who knows? Maybe it was. But the way I saw it, I needed a hands-on job—a *human* job—to pull me back to reality, and the listing that caught my eye at that exact moment happened to be one for which I was qualified thanks to my experience with my mother's company. (I left consulting off my résumé, of course, for fear of being deemed overqualified.)

My first task was to stand on the sidewalk and spray perfume in the air just before people approached. It earned me more looks of disdain, anger, and annoyance than I could track in a given week. It also made me feel like I was reconnecting to the planet. People cursed at me! Shoved me aside! I was alive again.

I stayed at Nose, riding life like a tube down a river, and driving my sister crazy in the process, for two years. Until I discovered baking. When I quit, I used some of my savings to attend the Tufts Entrepreneurship Incubator, where I met Smith, my current boss. And I didn't leave the earth again.

Now, sixteen years later, Tracy Chapman made me nostalgic for that SoCal drive that would come to define my future. I sit here watching towers of snow form in the dark yard behind my fire escape, and yet I'm in that Toyota, basking in the luxury of our rage. The closeness of our bodies, their warmth and infuriating connection. The horizon that, though I was passive toward it, seared its blue-on-blue line onto my memory. The bright hunger I felt as a teen. The sharpness of my mind that loathed its own sharpness.

Even then, I was aware that one day I would be grateful for that moment. And here I am.

COMMENTS (7):

BigJessBarbs: That Tracy Champer sure does have a deep voice for a woman!!

AnikaMommyof3: Thanks for returning my text, Iris. I understand if it's easier right now for you to talk to strangers, but just reminding you that we are here if you need us: Lesley, Clara, Morgan, and me.

ClaraWaters: Yes, me, too!

MorganKip-Hamp: If not for Propel we all wouldn't have met, though! S S

AnikaMommyof3: Not the time or place, Morgan.

ClaraWaters: Morgan can we push playdate tomorrow to 10:15? Saunders is still awake and I swear he's going to be napping by 9.

MorganKip-Hamp: Sure, just text me.

MONDAY, SEPTEMBER 14

from:	smith@simonyi.com
to:	jocelynvoight@greenberrymurder.com
date:	Mon, Sep 14 at 9:06 AM
subject:	Letter from a fan!

Dear Ms. Voight,

I was thrilled to learn recently of your "murder mystery weekend" series from a friend who was a passenger on the Grand Star DEATH LIVE! Cruise. The notion of live, interactive entertainment sustained by a cast in character for over forty-eight hours, including through six gourmet meals, is stunning, and she tells me that you pulled it off with incredible skill. To think that you scripted the entire thing! To be performed on a boat, no less! I had to read the brochure several times to believe it.

If I may, I think you are selling yourself short in your current branding and marketing approach. For instance, "Mingle with murderers" is cute, but it sounds a little bit like you're bringing in a theater group from the local prison. Same with "If you're lucky, you'll come out alive." I'm envisioning being chased around by a gaggle of actors, and frankly, that sounds a little tiring. The reference to the "bloody deck" leading you to "lose your lunch" is quite evocative—of seasickness.

Would you be interested in having a conversation about some ideas for taking your brand to the next level? (Or should I say— deck? ;))

Sincerely,

Smith Simonyi

President

Simonyi Brand Management

---

from: carl@simonyi.com
to: smith@simonyi.com
date: Mon, Sep 14 at 9:45 AM
subject: re: Today's Agenda

Boss,

What do we think of Iris's book as a quiz in a women's magazine? "Live Your Best Life!" kind of thing?

Or even a listicle! "10 Ways to Improve Your Life at Its Conclusion."

CVS

---

from: smith@simonyi.com
to: carl@simonyi.com
date: Mon, Sep 14 at 10:07 AM
subject: re: Today's Agenda

No.

---

from: carl@simonyi.com
to: smith@simonyi.com
date: Mon, Sep 14 at 10:22 AM
subject: re: Today's Agenda

In that case, here's what I've got. My fraternity brother Stephen Ferrano who is now working at Walrus Press (indie house—v. small) is willing to read Iris's manuscript.

He does express concern that it is the length of a novella but no one reads novellas, especially not ones by dead people. Plus, this isn't even fiction. Do you remember the memoir by the guy who BLINKED THE WHOLE THING BECAUSE HE COULDN'T MOVE? That's the only memoir he could think of that's so short. And he had an excuse for it being so short, which is that he was BLINKING IT. AND he was almost dead.

Iris could still type, so one could make the argument that she should have typed more pages.

I'll let you know what he says, but it sure would be exciting if we had multiple publishers interested! We could do the thing, what's it called, when they have to bid for the book? An auction! Carl

---

from: zaharaferringbottom@zaharaferringbottom.com
to: carl@simonyi.com
date: Mon, Sep 14 at 11:24 AM
subject: re: Clarification

In regard to prepositions.

Thank you for your email.

Up or at walls.

As my senior thesis in art school, I chiseled a hole through the wall of the art building. No, it was not legal. No, my adviser didn't know. Night after night, I burrowed with my tools in the dead hours of the morning, destroying the exalted stone bearings of Arthur K. Billingsley Memorial Hall, circa 1892.

Up?

Or at?

I subvert.

---

from: carl@simonyi.com
to: smith@simonyi.com
date: Mon, Sep 14 at 11:31 AM
subject: Fwd: re: Clarification

Boss,

Just forwarding so you are aware that our new client is a batshit lunatic. That's all for now! Off to Kundalini lunch hour.

Tootles.

MESSAGES

Mon., Sept. 14, 11:40 AM

JADE: I've got it! I'm going to open her bakery. What do you think?

SMITH: That you hate desserts.

JADE: True. However: 1. Baked goods are not necessarily desserts. They can (and should) stand alone. THAT I'm fine with.

JADE: 2. I don't have a job right now.

JADE: 3. She left me her savings, with which she was going to open a bakery.

JADE: 4. I know how to cook.

JADE: 5. You can help me brand it (please?).

SMITH: Those are not bad reasons. Of course I will help you.

It's happened—my tumors have shrunk dramatically. The lesions are nearly invisible.

They can't call it "remission" yet, or "NED" (no evidence of disease), because my particular cancer is very responsive to chemo in the short term but does often come back once chemo stops. Dr. Hsu says that for this reason, I shouldn't get too excited. But he also says it's definitely a sign in the right direction, and that, if anything, it means I will probably live beyond the original sell-by date he gave me in December.

I admit I'm surprised. I was hopeful, but not especially optimistic. Everyone but Richie seems surprised, too. Richie says he always knew I would get better. Jade has already started talking about plans for an "Iris Beat Cancer" party. I told her not to jinx it.

But I *do* feel like something is changed. Here—God willing—on what may be oh-my-god-is-it-the-other-side-of-cancer, I feel different.

My whole life I have been focused on how I should change, searching for what I can do to become better in some way. I've devoted thousands of hours to working on my flaws in my head, entertaining a perpetual roster of hypotheses: *What if I meditated—would I be less anxious? What if I cut dairy, wheat, or sugar? If I became a marathoner, or volunteered, or studied Buddhism, or became a blonde, would the dissatisfaction that eats away at me from the inside finally go away?*

I'd try a new diet. Or kind of yoga. Or self-help book. And if it resonated in some way, I'd see myself from a new perspective:

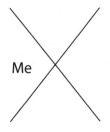

Me

Also me

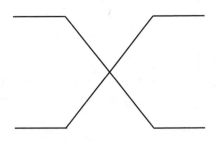

Also me

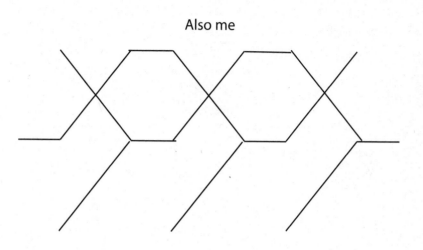

But no matter how far I stepped back or how wide the frame, what I saw wasn't enough. There was always more room to improve, more to be done to uncover that superior, elusive "me" out there, waiting. She was made up of the same pieces, maybe, but in a different pattern:

Me

Better

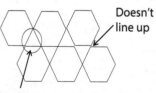

Doesn't line up

Pointless space

Dying has turned out to be the world's fastest-acting perspective check.

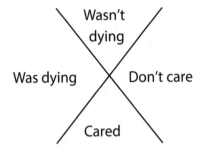

I don't care that I can't meditate. I don't care that I fucking love sugar, and that I have the thighs to show it, even with cancer. I don't care that I curse too much, and don't always vote, and once kissed my friend's boyfriend, and liked *The Fountainhead*, and don't recycle when it's inconvenient, and lied one time to a cop by telling him I was heading to tutor poor kids to get out of a speeding ticket. I don't care that my teeth are crooked because I never had braces, and that the birthmark on my right eyebrow makes my face look sort of lopsided (Christ, I don't even have hair now).

Because I'm here. I'm *still here*.

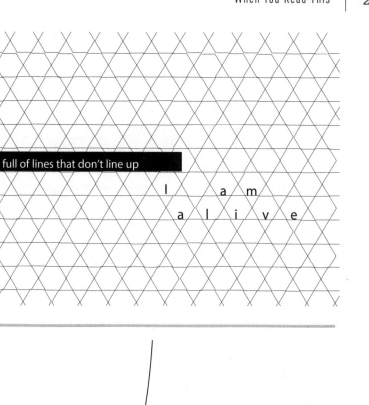

full of lines that don't line up

I   a   m
a   l   i   v   e

I can fall asleep

and wake up.
wake up.
wake up.

COMMENTS (5):

DyingToBlogTeam: May you march forth on March the Fourth!

BonnieD: HOORAYYYYYYYY!!!!

GloriaGlowing: Wow, this is heartening. I didn't think chemo could work so well. Thanks for sharing.

IrisMassey: Gloria: like I said, my particular kind of cancer (small cell) is especially responsive to it at first. But also to be honest it may have been more than just the chemo . . . alternative medicine kind of thing. If you want to hear more give me your email and I'll message you privately. ;)

ArduousArdvark: sell by date lulz

ONE MONTH LATER
MONDAY, OCTOBER 12

from: wally@homilypines.com
to: smith@simonyi.com
date: Mon, Oct 12 at 11:03 AM
subject: Checking in

Hiya Smith,

Hope you're doing well. Your mom asked me to get in touch due to things aren't going so hot with the new roommate Martha Stevenson. I guess she isn't all that new anymore, given it's been over a month they've shared a room. She and Martha can't seem to agree on who chooses what goes on the TV, and since Martha is the one who *can*, well, she ends up commandeering the remote for the most part. Not that your mom lets her be a channel tyrant without a fight. She hollers until Martha changes it back. And then she falls asleep and Martha switches it and the cycle repeats.

I worry the stress isn't good for either of them, and I even tried instituting a rule where every other hour is Martha's, and every other hour is your mom's, but then somebody has a nap and the schedule gets off and the fighting starts up again. Maybe she'd listen to you? It could be a good time to come out, you know, if you want to see the new room and meet Martha and talk to your mom about how cooperating is better for her health and frankly for all of us.

Let me know what ya think,
Wally

---

from: sandra.p.willoughby@thelanding.com
to: smith@simonyi.com
date: Mon, Oct 12 at 11:22 AM
subject: Issue of concern

Dear Smith:

A concern has been raised that there has been a great deal of traffic in and out of your unit recently. While co-op guidelines permit sublets of greater than 30 days subject to board approval, shorter stays as well as guests whom the board has not approved are not permitted.

I trust that you will see to this matter promptly and cease whatever operations seem to be taking place in 12D, as The Landing is neither a hotel nor a hostel but a reputable community that is home to 40 upstanding New York residents such as yourself.

Please let me know if you have any questions.
I am,
Sandra Willoughby
President
The Landing Co-operative

from: hbclark@bellemagazine.com
to: smith@simonyi.com
date: Mon, Oct 12 at 11:31 AM
subject: Your message

Smith,

I got your message. No hard feelings at all about the past. Yes, I was Clementine's friend first, but I still consider you my friend as well. Divorces happen, especially at our age. Clementine is doing great as far as I know, and I hope you are, too. (I haven't kept in super close touch with her over these last few years.) Would it be weird if you had reached out to me to, say, ask me out? Sure. I'd obviously have to say no. But solely in a professional capacity? Of course I'm up for discussing your new client.

A chef! I'd love to hear more about her decision to leave a restaurant as prestigious as Barn to embark on an unknown future, particularly in something as quaint as baking.

I'd be interested to see a draft of an essay on her decision to start her sister's bakery. <800 words, first person, not too heavy on the death stuff? Can I get a draft end of week?

xo

Hadley

from: jademassey@yahoo.com
to: smith@simonyi.com
date: Mon, Oct 12 at 11:32 AM
subject: Thank you . . . again

Hey Smith,

Thank you for coming with me (again) to check out the space in Chelsea (both times), but I've decided to keep looking. It just didn't give me a good vibe. It was the same problem with the Battery Park one, but different. Like something bad had happened in there or something. Maybe someone was killed there, I don't know.

Does it feel like we're moving fast on this? It feels extremely fast to me. Are we still on for dim sum later?
Jade

---

from: smith@simonyi.com
to: jademassey@yahoo.com
date: Mon, Oct 12 at 11:34 AM
subject: re: Thank you . . . again

I believe that if someone is murdered in a property that is up for sale, it has to be disclosed.

---

from: jademassey@yahoo.com
to: smith@simonyi.com
date: Mon, Oct 12 at 11:39 AM
subject: re: Thank you . . . again

Butchered nonfatally, then. Stabbed and survived. I understand that no one "disclosed" anything, but I get a queasy feeling in there.

What is happening with Richie? Is he going to give the green coffee sleeves to us for free, since it was Iris's dream and he was sleeping with her before she died?

---

from: smith@simonyi.com
to: jademassey@yahoo.com
date: Mon, Oct 12 at 11:46 AM
subject: re: Thank you . . . again

Isn't the priority to find a space, get permits, and then, well, figure out what this bakery *is*?

---

from: jademassey@yahoo.com
to: smith@simonyi.com
date: Mon, Oct 12 at 11:50 AM
subject: re: Thank you . . . again

FYI, I meant "green" as in environmentally friendly, not green like the color. Or are they also *not* green in that sense? I thought you said they were recycled from local trash. That was my interest. Now I can't remember if that's true or not. If they aren't, I'm not interested and we should go back to the drawing board on coffee sleeves.

---

from: smith@simonyi.com
to: jademassey@yahoo.com
date: Mon, Oct 12 at 11:59 AM
subject: re: Thank you . . . again

The sleeves are recycled, yes, though again, I don't think that's our focus right now.

MESSAGES
_____

Mon., Oct. 12, 12:06 PM

JADE: Switching to text bc on my way to Pilates. Are you still gambling
online? What, poker?

SMITH: Where did that question come from? Did you get my email
about the essay in Belle? It would be great press for the bakery.

JADE: Oh, right. Opening email now . . .

JADE: Her name is HADLEY? Is she a grown-up, or six?

JADE: Wait, she's hitting on you! Your ex-wife's friend is begging you
to ask her out.

SMITH: She explicitly says that if I asked her out, she would say no.
How is that begging me to ask her out?

JADE: Telling you not to ask her out is her way of screaming ASK ME
OUT.

SMITH: This essay opportunity is a really easy way to get the word
out about the bakery. Two words: free publicity. Plus I think it
pays. By the end of the week can you have something?

JADE: I don't know if I have time to write an essay. I don't know what
I would write. I'm not a writer. I'm not even a baker, yet. I still
have that to figure out. And I have to go back down to Virginia
Thursday because my mom decided to host her entire church
congregation at her house this weekend and somehow thinks
this is something she can manage on her own.

SMITH: Oh come on.

JADE: "Come on" re: her wanting to date you, or the essay?

SMITH: Both!

JADE: Okay, I'll try to put together something.

SMITH: Jade, I wouldn't ask someone out right now, when you and I
are kind of . . . you know. Dim sum sounds good, let me put it
that way.

JADE: Why did you say my name like that? And why wouldn't you ask
someone out right now?

SMITH: Is this a trick question? Are you trying to get me to say that
we're dating? Fine, we're dating.

JADE: We're not dating. We can't be dating.

JADE: ARE we? We only kissed once.

SMITH: Twice. So glad they were memorable.

JADE: You don't want kids. That won't work for me.

SMITH: Can we talk about this later?

JADE: So it's true! You don't want kids!

SMITH: I never said that! I said it depends!

JADE: On?

SMITH: The person! The future! I don't know. You won't even say we're
dating!

JADE: Pilates is starting. I have to go.

JADE: I'm just saying there's no point in us dating if you don't want
kids, so we can save ourselves the trouble.

1:32 PM

JADE: I can't believe you didn't write me back during all of Pilates.

JADE: I can have something to you by the end of this week, fine.

SMITH: Thank you.

JADE: And yes to dim sum. See you at 6.

from:	smith@simonyi.com
to:	iris@simonyi.com
date:	Mon, Oct 12 at 4:19 PM
subject:	no subject

Richie is still avoiding me. Does he suspect the gambling? I don't gamble money I borrow from him. I've barely logged on in the last few weeks.

I know money is money, and the reason I need to borrow is because I keep losing what I have, but I didn't borrow *in order* to gamble is the point I think I need to make clear to you.

To me. The point I need to make clear to myself.

God, I'm so full of shit.

On a Saturday morning six weeks after my wedding day that wasn't, I still hadn't returned a single gift. They sat piled in a corner of my studio, mostly wrapped. I was wandering home in my clothes from the night before. Unable to be with either of the men I cared about, I'd gotten smashed and slept with the bartender. At the corner of Ninth and Court Streets, a block from my place, a little boy manned a lemonade stand. He held out a paper cup to me, but all I had on me was a credit card. I said sorry. He told me I could have it, anyway. The gesture gutted me. I took it from him, but when I got to the end of the block, I dropped it into the trash can, full, because I couldn't bear it.

I wish I could go back and talk to that girl. I wish I could grab her and say, "You're not a bad person. You're not a failure. Now, drink the fucking lemonade because that kid can still see you."

COMMENTS (1):

SP2004: you are not a bad person just for cursing but cursing IT-SELF is bad because it is toxic and spreads to babies

FRIDAY, OCTOBER 16

---

from: smith@simonyi.com
to: jademassey@yahoo.com
date: Fri, Oct 16 at 8:56 AM
subject: hi

Good morning. How's it going in Virginia? How was your trip down yesterday?

---

from: jademassey@yahoo.com
to: smith@simonyi.com
date: Fri, Oct 16 at 9:17 AM
subject: re: hi

Okay. I made my mother the best omelet of my life this morning (I sampled it) (ate half). In my industry, we say that there are two options for an omelet: transcendent, and tastes like eggs. Today's was the former. That is more difficult than it sounds. I mean, there are entire books written on eggs. Not cookbooks. Philosophical *treatises*. To me, the perfect omelet is made with nothing but a fork. But there are people who would argue that a spatula is acceptable. Others would say it's too violent, on par with tongs. You don't know violence until you've watched delicate greens quiver under giant metal teeth.

---

from: smith@simonyi.com
to: jademassey@yahoo.com
date: Fri, Oct 16 at 9:29 AM
subject: re: hi

You were going to get me the draft by today?

---

from: jademassey@yahoo.com
to: smith@simonyi.com
date: Fri, Oct 16 at 9:36 AM
subject: re: hi

Shit.

---

from: jademassey@yahoo.com
to: smith@simonyi.com
date: Fri, Oct 16 at 9:38 AM
subject: re: hi

I can have something to you by this afternoon.

---

from: smith@simonyi.com
to: jademassey@yahoo.com
date: Fri, Oct 16 at 9:55AM
subject: re: hi

Jade, you haven't even started? What did you do Wednesday night when you left the bar to write?

---

from: jademassey@yahoo.com
to: smith@simonyi.com
date: Fri, Oct 16 at 10:01 AM
subject: re: hi

Packed! I said I was leaving to write *and* pack.

I also binge-watched this web series called *The Uncertain Detective*. This woman is concerned because her dog doesn't recognize her, so she thinks her dog is a clone. But it turns out the reason her dog doesn't recognize her is that *she* is the clone. You should check it out.

I'll have something to you by this afternoon. I'm writing RIGHT NOW.

---

from: ronaldglass@apexunitedcitizens.com
to: smith@simonyi.com
date: Fri, Oct 16 at 10:20 AM
subject: Re-branding

Dear Mr. Simons,

My name is Ronald Glass. I am the founder of Apex United Citizens. You may have heard about Apex in the media as of late, but I ASSURE YOU THAT THESE RUMORS ARE FALSIFIED.

Apex is a community of individuals seeking to expand their minds and hearts through the Apex curriculum, which I have recently revamped in light of rumors THAT ARE WHOLLY AND FULLY UNTRUE.

I am seeking assistance in re-branding Apex, and would welcome a meeting with you per this matter.

As a token of my appreciation, I am providing below a "glimpse" of what is in store for anyone (you?) who chooses to join Apex. It is a pearl of wisdom that, this time, is for free! There is more where it came from.

Sincerely,

Ronald P. Glass

The Meaning of Life in Less Than 300 Words
BY RONALD P. GLASS

So I hear you wish you had a different breakfast cereal in the cabinet. I hear you wish you had a different couch, such as the one possessed by your neighbor, with the reclining option and the flap that folds up to expose a convenient and reliable cup holder for containers of all sizes. You are tired because you are sick, born with an illness you have no control over. It is called being a *Homo sapiens.*

But I will tell you a secret. Here are three ways to make your own nature work for you not against you, such as in the style of "judo."

1. If you had those other things or if you were as healthy as a robot-human, you would still wish you had something different. It is the human condition to wish for "the Different." Pretend you are someone else wishing they were you, and you will begin to see "the Positive" aka "the bright side" because you have taken on a new perspective of another envious, unsatisfied human except that human is looking at you!!!!!!
2. Or you can just try to focus on the good things.
3. **Best Way** In the style of "smile and you will be happier" and also "the power of positive thinking," think of yourself as happy and you will be. <u>This is my favorite of the methods</u>.
   a. We create reality with our beliefs.

b. If you visualize yourself as happy you become it.

c. The same applies to eternity.

d. If you believe in eternity, it exists. If you don't, it doesn't.

e. So visualize happiness and eternity and you'll be happy for eternity! Or don't, and you won't. But whatever you do, don't visualize unhappiness and eternity!

---

from: carl@simonyi.com
to: smith@simonyi.com
date: Fri, Oct 16 at 10:28 AM
subject: Fwd: Re-branding

Boss,

I just googled Apex. Let me put it this way:

"Oxygen restriction," and "twelve missing people."

I feel this is truly an ethical conundrum for us. On one hand, this man seems truly terrible. On the other, we need the business.

Thoughts?

---

from: smith@simonyi.com
to: carl@simonyi.com
date: Fri, Oct 16 at 10:43 AM
subject: re: Fwd: Re-branding

Absolutely not. Don't respond.

And while we're on the subject, because this seems to keep coming up, please remember what I said about communicating with clients without my approval. This includes both prospective and former clients as well.

from:	carl@simonyi.com
to:	smith@simonyi.com
date:	Fri, Oct 16 at 10:50 AM
subject:	re: Fwd: Re-branding

Got it. Quick question: Does "former clients" include Phil?

from:	smith@simonyi.com
to:	carl@simonyi.com
date:	Fri, Oct 16 at 10:53 AM
subject:	re: Fwd: Re-branding

Yes. It includes Phil.

from:	carl@simonyi.com
to:	smith@simonyi.com
date:	Fri, Oct 16 at 11:58 AM
subject:	re: Fwd: Re-branding

I understand. But there is going to be a wee problem with that policy, given that Phil has just hired me. We've sort of been in touch. But don't worry, I will only do my work for him during lunch hours and weekends, and I am sure we will get him back to SBM in no time.

I remain your loyal intern M-F, 9–5. Despite what others are saying, I'm sure you had a good reason for doing whatever you did.

Please don't fire me. I need this internship and a subsequent LOR.

Carl

from: smith@simonyi.com
to: carl@simonyi.com
date: Fri, Oct 16 at 12:08 PM
subject: re: Fwd: Re-branding

Seriously, Carl??

from: carl@simonyi.com
to: smith@simonyi.com
date: Fri, Oct 16 at 12:17 PM
subject: re: Fwd: Re-branding

I suggest we focus on the silver lining: so far I have picked up on no plans of his to sue you. Yay?

from: jademassey@yahoo.com
to: smith@simonyi.com
date: Fri, Oct 16 at 6:31 PM
subject: My Essay

BELLE COLUMN: *CAREER CHANGERS*

"GARNISH WITH SALT"

by Jade Massey, Owner of _____[Name of Bakery TBD]

I don't actually like pastries, which you would think would be an issue when opening a bakery. But listen to my story, and you might understand where I am coming from.

Not long ago I was working 15-hour shifts seven days a

week at one of New York City's most demanding restaurants. I loved cooking, but I was tired.

Last winter my younger sister by four years was diagnosed with terminal cancer and died in May at age 33.

Several months later, I stumbled on a dream of hers about which I hadn't known. She had been an administrative assistant by day, but a baker by night. She had dreamt of opening a bakery. And she'd never told me.

First, the obsessing commenced: *Why* hadn't she told me about her dream? Images of my flawed sister-ing took over my brain as I recalled the incidents that might have inspired her to withhold her aspiration from me. Was I too bossy? Too opinionated? Did I make her feel, in some way, like she couldn't achieve her goal?

Then came the curious thought, a natural one given my circumstances and my sister's—should I try to fulfill her dream, the one she didn't have time to complete? She was gone. And, of course, I am a chef. It almost made too *much* sense.

But there was a problem. I loathe pastries. I don't like sweets, in general, particularly when they are baked and involve flour. Since I was a small child I've preferred salt to sugar. Bitter cocoa I can stomach; milk chocolate just tastes cloying. Flaky crust, to me, was never a delicacy; it was decay. I saw the feathering not as light and airy but as the peeling off of layers of skin. It didn't help to learn the extent to which refined sugars and flours (paired with trans fats, no less) destroy our insides.

My sister could see the beauty in them nonetheless, and while I admired that in her, I didn't share it. Until I realized that perhaps I could by sheer will.

Just over a month ago I began pursuing my sister's dream. I am using this opportunity to explore what I think of as the

"anti-pastry"—it satisfies many of the same desires as the traditional pastry, but is different, as well. It contains less sugar
than the traditional pastry. It is safe for those with common
food allergies—all of my pastries are gluten-free, and some
are dairy and nut free. And every (okay, maybe not every, but
most) pastry is garnished with my personal favorite ingredient
of all time: salt.

Jade's Light-as-Air Brazilian Cheese Popovers

Despite the fact that these require you to bake with tapioca flour,
which is the glitter of the kitchen in that it gets absolutely everywhere, I think you'll find that they're worth the mess.

INGREDIENTS

    1 cup almond milk (or substitute coconut)

    2 tablespoons olive oil

    $1^{1}/_{2}$ cups tapioca flour

    2 egg whites

    $^{1}/_{4}$ cup shredded Parmesan

    $^{1}/_{4}$ cup shredded cheddar

    2 teaspoons salt

Yield: 6 popovers

Preparation time: 30 minutes

Preheat oven to 400 degrees. The rack should be on the middle
setting. Generously grease a bouchon pan with butter or canola oil.

In a saucepan, mix the milk and olive oil. Bring to a boil.

Combine the mixture in a bowl with the tapioca flour. Mix,

either with a hand mixer or a spoon—beware, the mixture is hot! Add the egg whites, cheeses, and salt. Mix until the dough contains only small lumps. It will be sticky and a bit runny.

Place the pan in the oven for two minutes to heat it up.

Spoon the dough into six cups of the pan so that each cup is full.

Cook for 20 minutes, or until the tops are plump and tinged golden. Do not check on the popovers by opening the oven until at least 18 minutes have passed. This could cause them to collapse.

Serve warm. They don't save well. If you store them, you'll be disappointed.

Enjoy!

---

from: smith@simonyi.com
to: jademassey@yahoo.com
date: Fri, Oct 16 at 6:48 PM
subject: re: My Essay

What's the name of the bakery? I can't send this over with blank lines where the name of the bakery should be.

And what's a bouchon pan?

---

from: jademassey@yahoo.com
to: smith@simonyi.com
date: Fri, Oct 16 at 7:20 PM
subject: re: My Essay

Can you write TBD?

Same as a mini popover pan.

from: smith@simonyi.com
to: jademassey@yahoo.com
date: Fri, Oct 16 at 7:32 PM
subject: re: My Essay

No, I can't write TBD.

Is that something people own? Can they just use a muffin tin?

from: jademassey@yahoo.com
to: smith@simonyi.com
date: Fri, Oct 16 at 7:34 PM
subject: re: My Essay

No. It needs to be a bouchon/popover pan. The wide bottom of a muffin pan will cause the bottoms to burn before the middle is done, and you'll wind up with gooey blobs.

Fine. The name of the bakery is SALT.

from: smith@simonyi.com
to: jademassey@yahoo.com
date: Fri, Oct 16 at 7:35 PM
subject: re: My Essay

SALT? Really?

from: jademassey@yahoo.com
to: smith@simonyi.com
date: Fri, Oct 16 at 7:37 PM
subject: re: My Essay

You don't like it? It's, like, the anti-bakery name. Salt.

---

from: smith@simonyi.com
to: jademassey@yahoo.com
date: Fri, Oct 16 at 7:41 PM
subject: re: My Essay

Okay. Salt.

Also—not to be too nitpicky, but are these really a pastry you're going to be able to serve at the bakery? If they need to be served warm?

---

from: jademassey@yahoo.com
to: smith@simonyi.com
date: Fri, Oct 16 at 8:09 PM
subject: re: My Essay

I never said *I* was going to serve them. If that was a condition, you should have said so. Fine, here's a more traditional baked good:

Jade's Orange-Kissed Chocolate Chip Cookies

INGREDIENTS

$1\frac{1}{2}$ sticks of butter, melted

1 cup brown sugar, packed

$\frac{1}{2}$ cup granulated sugar

2 large eggs

1 egg yolk

2 teaspoons vanilla extract

1 teaspoon orange extract

$\frac{3}{4}$ cup coconut flour

1 teaspoon baking soda

1 cup chocolate chunks

A bit of orange zest

A bit of salt

Yield: 12 jumbo cookies

Time: 30 minutes

Preheat oven to 325 degrees. Grease two baking sheets or line with parchment paper.

In a large bowl, whisk together melted butter, brown sugar, and granulated sugar. Mix in the eggs and yolk, vanilla, and orange extract.

Add the flour and baking soda.

Add the chocolate chunks and orange zest.

Place up to six golf-ball-size balls of dough far apart on one baking sheet—only six because they will spread.

Bake 20 minutes or so.

Allow to cool fully—if not adequately cooled, they may crumble. Once cooled, however, they will hold. Have faith.

Sprinkle with sea salt.

---

from:	smith@simonyi.com
to:	jademassey@yahoo.com
date:	Fri, Oct 16 at 8:23 PM
subject:	re: My Essay

Does this work with the last part of your essay? About the sugar?

---

from: jademassey@yahoo.com
to: smith@simonyi.com
date: Fri, Oct 16 at 8:29 PM
subject: re: My Essay

Look, baked goods have sugar, okay? Or they suck. You wanted something fast. I can't come up with the perfect recipe in a week. It's not *that* much sugar. It's less sugar than many cookie recipes.

But you're right, it's probably not in the spirit of the bakery. Maybe this essay is a bad idea . . .

---

from: smith@simonyi.com
to: jademassey@yahoo.com
date: Fri, Oct 16 at 8:35 PM
subject: re: My Essay

I don't care if it has sugar. I just didn't know if we should cut the line about the sugar if it's going to be followed by a recipe with sugar. If it's less sugar than normal, that seems fine.

---

from: jademassey@yahoo.com
to: smith@simonyi.com
date: Fri, Oct 16 at 8:39 PM
subject: re: My Essay

Cut the line, I don't care.

---

from: smith@simonyi.com
to: jademassey@yahoo.com
date: Fri, Oct 16 at 8:42 PM
subject: re: My Essay

Nope! Looks great! Sending as is.

I've been thinking about how brief life is, even for those who get to live the longest. Say each year of your life gets a dot. If you survive to age ninety:

•   •   •   •   •   •   •   •   •   •

•   •   •   •   •   •   •   •   •   •

•   •   •   •   •   •   •   •   •   •

•   •   •   •   •   •   •   •   •   •

•   •   •   •   •   •   •   •   •   •

•   •   •   •   •   •   •   •   •   •

•   •   •   •   •   •   •   •   •   •

•   •   •   •   •   •   •   •   •   •

•   •   •   •   •   •   •   •   •   •

That's it. Your ninety years fit easily on an index card.

Before my diagnosis, I had sort of figured that I'd be a fortunate one, that I had around this many left:

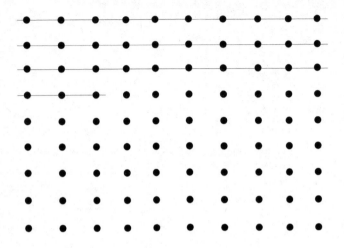

Then I found out I didn't have any left.

Then I found out I *might* have some left.

Who knew dying would be so much like a finicky lightbulb.

A woman I knew once said she feared she was addicted to starting over. That seemed so sad to me at the time. Now it seems less sad than not starting at all. I decided to open a bakery but never made it out of the planning stage. I wanted a family. I always wanted to go on a cruise, of all things, and never went.

If I have more dots left, I will start over. I will open my bakery. I will try to have a kid. I will take the tackiest, most garish cruise I can find.

Please let me have them. Please.

COMMENTS (1):

BigJessBarbs: Do NOT book a cruise on Princess Ocean Adventures, I swear to God I got thrown off that boat during a storm in '88 do NOT get me started.

MONDAY, OCTOBER 19

---

from: smith@simonyi.com
to: jademassey@yahoo.com
date: Mon, Oct 19 at 11:49 AM
subject: Hello?

Did you get my texts?

---

from: jademassey@yahoo.com
to: smith@simonyi.com
date: Mon, Oct 19 at 12:08 PM
subject: re: Hello?

Sorry, swamped. The all-church supper was last night and I had to cook for one million church ladies. Then today I had to clean up after one million church ladies, plus talk with another attorney about the suit against Jade's doctor. He *also* says I don't have a case, but I don't buy it. So many of these guys are only in it for the money. If they don't think they can earn enough to make it worth their time, they'll tell you that you have no case. On top of all this, my mother has decided to start selling Winsome again

254 | *Mary Adkins*

because she is feeling better, which means I'm going to have to start driving her around door to door since there is no way I'm letting her behind a wheel after she knocked over her neighbor's trash can on our way to the grocery store.

What's up? Oh, also, can we plan to go look at this new space I found when I'm back on Friday? It's a newly renovated former vegan sandwich shop in Greenpoint. Apparently a benefit of taking over a lease from a former food service business is that you can inherit permits. That would be a huge load off, given that I already feel lost in the labyrinthine bureaucracy of that nonsense, and I've hardly glanced at it. But even apart from the administrative convenience, I think this spot could be The One. I have an exceptionally good feeling about it. And if it is, we'll need to have everything ready to go—deposit and so forth—so I may have to ask you to run to the bank for me sometime between tomorrow and Thursday. Would you mind?

---

from: smith@simonyi.com
to: jademassey@yahoo.com
date: Mon, Oct 19 at 12:50 PM
subject: re: Hello?

Belle doesn't want the essay. The editor doesn't think it works.

---

from: jademassey@yahoo.com
to: smith@simonyi.com
date: Mon, Oct 19 at 12:54 PM
subject: re: Hello?

What do you mean? What doesn't work about it for Hadley? It was the sugar? I'm such a hypocrite. I took the easy way out.

---

from: smith@simonyi.com
to: jademassey@yahoo.com
date: Mon, Oct 19 at 1:00 PM
subject: re: Hello?

It wasn't the sugar. She feels the essay lacks authenticity.

---

from: jademassey@yahoo.com
to: smith@simonyi.com
date: Mon, Oct 19 at 1:14 PM
subject: re: Hello?

Um, excuse me—this is coming from a *women's* magazine?

---

from: smith@simonyi.com
to: jademassey@yahoo.com
date: Mon, Oct 19 at 1:15 PM
subject: re: Hello?

I mean, you did sort of dash it off very quickly, right? This can't be that surprising?

---

from: jademassey@yahoo.com
to: smith@simonyi.com
date: Mon, Oct 19 at 1:20 PM
subject: re: Hello?

If it's that bad, why didn't you say so? I could have worked on it more!

from: smith@simonyi.com
to: jademassey@yahoo.com
date: Mon, Oct 19 at 1:28 PM
subject: re: Hello?

You didn't have time to work on it.

If I may be frank, I think it's going to be hard for you to launch a bakery in New York when you're spending much of your time in Virginia.

from: jademassey@yahoo.com
to: smith@simonyi.com
date: Mon, Oct 19 at 1:58 PM
subject: re: Hello?

If *I* may be frank, I don't think how much time I spend in Virginia is any of your business.

from: smith@simonyi.com
to: jademassey@yahoo.com
date: Mon, Oct 19 at 1:59 PM
subject: re: Hello?

Let's just talk later.

from: ronaldglass@apexunitedcitizens.com
to: smith@simonyi.com
date: Mon, Oct 19 at 4:11 PM
subject: Follow-up on Re-branding Request

Dear Mr. Simons,

Ronald Glass, again, founder of Apex United Citizens. I wrote to you on Friday but haven't heard back, yet. I'm not blaming you—if you are hesitant or preoccupied, that's my fault for not having adequately inspired you!

In order to motivate a response, here is a second teaching from the pages of Apex:

Drama Is Evolution's Downfall
BY RONALD P. GLASS

WAH! WAH! WAH!

Everywhere you look, people in the industrialized world are creating fake stakes and crying over them. This is an outgrowth of the fact that we used to have real stakes, such as predators. Also, a high likelihood of dying during childbirth. And cholera.

Now that we privileged folks don't have cholera or tigers chasing us, and we wash our hands and rule the planet, our brains, still stuck in the Pleistocene, i.e. "stone age," seek out things to worry about and, finding nothing, stir up problems.

Husband cheating on you? Oh, well. Find another one.

Out of money? I say to that: Are you breathing? Then you're fine.

Legs too short, nose too crooked? Tell me this: If you were running from a cheetah across the plain, would you care about your facial dots and dents?

For fifth-grade picture day, my mother blanketed my head in hot rollers and covered my face in her gooey orange foundation, then pasted fake lashes onto my lids that I tried to pull off on the bus because the glue stung my eyes, tugging at them as gently as I could. But they wouldn't break free, and I was terrified they'd be stuck there forever. No one else wore makeup yet, except Casey Fredericks, who also owned a garter belt and was usually on a diet that only allowed her to eat uncooked pasta.

When I walked into the cafeteria where the children were herded prior to the first bell, Austin Quattlebaum yelled, "Clown!" I ran to the bathroom, filled my hands with sticky pink soap, and scrubbed. I couldn't see to find the paper towels and, standing there by the sink with my eyes on fire, I decided that I hated her.

The dynamic between my mother and me was rooted in fear for as long as I can remember. She was a screamer. A shamer.

It shaped me into a little girl who walked on eggshells, awaiting the worst. But that day in fifth grade, something shifted; I went on the offensive. No longer would I allow her to terrorize me without fighting back.

After that, our relationship remained strained, but less one-sided. I would do something to anger her, like deciding I didn't believe in thank-you notes or meaningless greetings like "How are you?," and she would whine that I was such a difficult child and talk about me to others as if I wasn't there. I became a vegan because she didn't know what that meant and because it was inconvenient. When I was seventeen, I told her I was interested in girls, also a lie. It worked. My God-fearing mother—with the married boyfriend—slapped me.

When I got on a plane in Phoenix, headed to college, and hugged her good-bye, I remember being stunned that she teared up, because I felt nothing but relief.

For the next ten years we saw each other once a year or so. Then came the Thanksgiving we spent in Atlantic City, where she lived at the time. It was the last holiday we all spent together as a family.

My sister's husband Henry showed up to the house my mother had rented, armed with a turducken—which, in case you don't know, is a turkey stuffed with a duck, stuffed with a chicken.

I had never liked Henry all that much, but I didn't yet loathe him at that point. It was fairly normal for me not to be crazy about Jade's boyfriends. We had different taste in men. I liked the charmers, the sociable doers. She liked the wounded, brooding academics, people who needed her emotional guidance.

Henry was a successful doctor, but he was always blaming Jade for something in a calm, distant way that gave his criticism a false air of objectivity. Her work schedule wasn't conducive to their marriage (even though his was at least as grueling); her ambition didn't leave room for kids (even though he had known about her ambition before they married). He would undercut her with remarks like "Jade doesn't have time to accompany her husband to Italy, but makes time for book club."

I told myself I didn't know the inner workings of their relationship. Maybe they were just a standard, if sad, kind of couple, struggling to stay connected. But the fundamental incompatibility between them could not be buried forever. Jade's finger is still crooked from the time a cast-iron skillet fell on it, breaking it, at which point she ignored the pain and finished her shift. Her hands are covered in faint red streaks left by slippery knives, her forearms stacked with horizontal oven burns. Henry, meanwhile, once said to me of her cooking, "It's a great skill she can use at home with the kids."

Perhaps he thought cooking was a phase she would outgrow.

The Thanksgiving of the turducken, he boasted of its inevitable deliciousness, as if he himself had invented the novelty, while taking over the stove in the tiny kitchen of my mother's rental. Then he got drunk on the cooking wine, fell asleep watching football, and forgot about his turkey-duck-chicken, roasting away.

As Jade and I sat in the kitchen drinking another bottle we'd opened, she said, "You may have noticed we aren't getting along very well." She confided that he'd given her an ultimatum. If she didn't leave her job so they could get started with kids, he was going to divorce her.

I asked what she was going to do. She said, beg him not to.

And if that doesn't work? I asked.

"I guess I'll probably quit," she said. "What am I supposed to do? I love him."

The turducken burned. It was inedible. He blamed Jade for

not keeping an eye on what he had established as his masterful undertaking. My mother, who had been spritzing her orchids, offered us all Vicodin.

Jade and Henry stuck it out, but I drove my rental car back to my Brooklyn apartment that evening and downloaded a stack of self-help books on living with crazy families, and skimmed them late into the night, taking from all of them a single idea that resonated as both wise and comforting: I was allowed to draw a line in the sand. I was allowed to stop involving myself in their drama. And so that's what I did.

Jade and Henry stayed together four more years. She didn't quit her job, but he didn't divorce her. I imagine each was waiting for the other to push things over the edge.

She finally left him two years ago because she was so miserable that something had to give. And she knew that it wasn't her job that was the problem—it was him. (Deep down I think we always know when it's a Him.)

Henry, meanwhile, has not accepted the divorce. He has petitioned Jade ever since to get back together with him. Does the man love misery? Is he a masochist? Who knows how love works. Until now, to my knowledge, she has resisted. Until now. Because now, they're dating again. She doesn't know I know.

But I also have an "until now" with my own mother.

Does the looming prospect of death open us up? Does it bring out the magnanimity in our souls, because all we want is to connect with the people we connected to once upon a time, imperfect as they are, hurtful as they can be?

Today, chemo was unusually quiet. Normally the room is boisterous—far more than I ever would have guessed. It's full of spouses, children, and grandchildren all on their best behavior, working hard to lift the spirits of the dying. But today, apart from a grandchild handing out construction-paper shamrocks, there was little to distract me from my thoughts, which, as they often do these days, turned to my own family.

I found myself deciding that I don't blame Jade for re-dating Henry, and I no longer blame my mother for making our lives what they were. My mother made me stretch every night to have long legs. She asked every morning if I'd washed my face and accused me of lying if I had a zit. She once whipped me with a belt for coming home from a slumber party with a temporary tattoo of a starfish. She showed me where to place the tip of the nail polish brush for a smooth finish and made me practice until I left no trace of color on my skin. She weighed me on Fridays.

I always viewed the shoving of her crushing ideals onto me as her way of telling me I wasn't good enough. But my mother shaped her entire life around beauty. I see that now. She was loving me the way she loved herself.

COMMENTS (5):

DyingToBlogTeam: Happy St. Patty's Day!

ChristmasWasMyFavorite: We moms don't get any credit!! Cut us some slack!!

BonnieD: Chemo? Are you still doing that? I thought your cancer was almost gone.

IrisMassey: Still have to keep up the chemo for now, BonnieD.

BigJessBarbs: What time is it there? I'm in China and it's dinner time!

THURSDAY, OCTOBER 22

from: jademassey@yahoo.com
to: smith@simonyi.com
date: Thu, Oct 22 at 7:20 AM
subject: ONE more BIG favor?

Argh. I'm not going to make it back by tomorrow after all. It's a long story involving my mom's Winsome products not arriving in time and our needing to drive to the HQ in Richmond and pick them up. I realize I'm sort of proving your point here, and I know I have been asking you for too many favors, but like I said, this is important—would you go to the open house for me? Pretty please?

Don't text me, I won't get it. My mother microwaved my phone, so it's fried. (She was "trying to warm up" my sweater for God knows what reason, and it was in the pocket.)

---

from: carl@simonyi.com
to: jademassey@yahoo.com
date: Thu, Oct 22 at 10:32 AM
subject: Good news!

Hi Jade!

Just got to the office and saw you called a few times. Is everything okay? Smith is in a meeting right now with a new client. I'm sure he'll be glad to give you a call as soon as he's out.

While I have you on the line, good news! As I assume you know, we've been trying to place your sister's MS (that's industry-speak for "manuscript" ;)) with a publisher for a while now. I cannot even begin to tell you how difficult it has been for us to find someone interested in your sister. Several editors wrote back that Iris has no platform or is a nobody (my word—I believe the actual quote was "not famous"). Others found it a problem that she is no longer alive for edits. My former fraternity brother Stephen Ferrano, who is now an editorial assistant at an indie house, was open to pursuing her blog as a self-help title, but his coworkers seem to have persuaded him that since she is deceased, no one will want to self-help with it. There's a Harvard transfer/ Lit major for you.

All of which is to say, I was thrilled when Todd and Chad, the founders of the site on which your sister wrote, said they are interested in using her blog as part of their upcoming campaign for the site! Has Smith talked to you about that? Jeez, hopefully it isn't too late. I think they were under time pressure. We will have to check with them to find out if it's even still an option. Fingers crossed! I'll reach out to them today and keep you posted.

Carl

from:	jademassey@yahoo.com
to:	carl@simonyi.com
date:	Thu, Oct 22 at 10:40 AM
subject:	no subject

Smith,

I don't know what's going on, but we need to discuss this ASAP.

Jade

from:	carl@simonyi.com
to:	jademassey@yahoo.com
date:	Thu, Oct 22 at 10:49 AM
subject:	re: no subject

Still Carl. You emailed me by accident. Can I help?

from:	jademassey@yahoo.com
to:	carl@simonyi.com
date:	Thu, Oct 22 at 10:52 AM
subject:	re: no subject

Please have Smith email me as soon as he is available, thank you.

from:	wally@homilypines.com
to:	smith@simonyi.com
date:	Thu, Oct 22 at 11:05 AM
subject:	Thanksgiving

Hiya Smith,

I was wondering, given that it's just about four weeks from Thanksgiving, if you might try to come down for it this year.

Each of the past three, we've had a very good time enjoying a full holiday spread cooked by the lady parishioners of Sun Prairie Methodist. Your mom has threatened to skip this year due to she claims there's nothing interesting there and she'd rather nap. I would hate for her to miss it, though, especially since it's been such a challenging fall for her with the move into the same room as Martha.

Speaking of which, that does seem to be going better since we Facetimed with you last week. I think it helped her to understand that it's a financial decision you will remedy if you can, and that she will need to be patient and make the most of it if she doesn't want to upset you. Or maybe she was just happy to see your face, even over video.

Let us know. I can't vouch for the turkey because I've gone vegetarian, but the pumpkin pie last year was out of this world. Wally

from: jademassey@yahoo.com
to: smith@simonyi.com
date: Thu, Oct 22 at 11:48 AM
subject: no subject

I can't believe you went behind my back.

from: smith@simonyi.com
to: jademassey@yahoo.com
date: Thu, Oct 22 at 11:49 AM
subject: re: no subject

Hi. Is your phone dead?

from: jademassey@yahoo.com
to: smith@simonyi.com
date: Thu, Oct 22 at 11:51 AM
subject: re: no subject

Yes. My mom fried it. But it's not like I could talk to you without screaming, anyway.

from: smith@simonyi.com
to: jademassey@yahoo.com
date: Thu, Oct 22 at 11:52 AM
subject: re: no subject

What? How did she fry your phone?
   Why screaming?

from: jademassey@yahoo.com
to: smith@simonyi.com
date: Thu, Oct 22 at 11:52 AM
subject: re: no subject

Don't bother feigning cluelessness. You have been pitching her book behind my back. I told you I'm not okay with it. I was SO clear. I COULD NOT have been clearer.

---

from: smith@simonyi.com
to: jademassey@yahoo.com
date: Thu, Oct 22 at 11:53 AM
subject: re: no subject

I only put out some feelers. I figured we could talk if I got a bite. Can we talk on the phone please? Don't you have a landline there? Or a phone you can borrow?

---

from: jademassey@yahoo.com
to: smith@simonyi.com
date: Thu, Oct 22 at 11:53 AM
subject: re: no subject

Feelers?? Well, it sounds like you got one. The Dying to Blog guys, Smith? Seriously?

---

from: smith@simonyi.com
to: jademassey@yahoo.com
date: Thu, Oct 22 at 11:55 AM
subject: re: no subject

Carl told you about that. That—we should talk about that. I am ambivalent about it, too, to be honest. I think I would much prefer us going with my friend and the press where he works. Can we talk about this in person when you're back?

---

from: jademassey@yahoo.com
to: smith@simonyi.com
date: Thu, Oct 22 at 11:55 AM
subject: re: no subject

"To be honest"? Is that what you've decided to be NOW? That you're CAUGHT?
  WE HAVE ALREADY TALKED ABOUT THIS.

---

from: smith@simonyi.com
to: jademassey@yahoo.com
date: Thu, Oct 22 at 11:56 AM
subject: re: no subject

You haven't even read it! How can you be opposed when you haven't even read it?

---

from: jademassey@yahoo.com
to: smith@simonyi.com
date: Thu, Oct 22 at 11:57 AM
subject: re: no subject

Another lie. I told you I've read it!

---

from: smith@simonyi.com
to: jademassey@yahoo.com
date: Thu, Oct 22 at 11:57 AM
subject: re: no subject

You said you've read "most" of it. Months ago, when you found it on her computer while snooping.

---

from: jademassey@yahoo.com
to: smith@simonyi.com
date: Thu, Oct 22 at 11:58 AM
subject: re: no subject

YOU are criticizing ME?

Reminder: *You* betrayed *my* trust. I haven't done anything wrong here.

---

from: smith@simonyi.com
to: jademassey@yahoo.com
date: Thu, Oct 22 at 11:58 AM
subject: re: no subject

I didn't lie to you. I just didn't want to ignore the one thing your sister asked me for before she died. And I figured you would come around. I'm guilty of that much, sure.

---

from: jademassey@yahoo.com
to: smith@simonyi.com
date: Thu, Oct 22 at 12:00 PM
subject: re: no subject

She had CHEMO BRAIN. What she came up with while she had CHEMO BRAIN doesn't COUNT. What SHE wanted was to open a bakery. Which is why that's what I'm doing!

from: smith@simonyi.com
to: jademassey@yahoo.com
date: Thu, Oct 22 at 12:03 PM
subject: re: no subject

I don't think it has anything to do with her being on chemo. I think you don't like the parts about you. You don't like how you come across. That's why you stopped reading. And you know what's ironic about that? If you actually finished it, I think you'd feel differently.

from: jademassey@yahoo.com
to: smith@simonyi.com
date: Thu, Oct 22 at 12:08 PM
subject: re: no subject

Are you kidding? Do you know when I stopped reading? When her cancer came back. Because it was fucking devastating. I'm glad to know you think so highly of me, though, a person you claimed to be dating. Why would you even want to date me if I were actually that narcissistic??

from: smith@simonyi.com
to: jademassey@yahoo.com
date: Thu, Oct 22 at 12:09 PM
subject: re: no subject

Ha! Claimed! I did, yes, until you clarified that we aren't.

---

from: jademassey@yahoo.com
to: smith@simonyi.com
date: Thu, Oct 22 at 12:11 PM
subject: re: no subject

I said I didn't KNOW if we were dating.
    It doesn't matter. Betrayal is betrayal.

---

from: smith@simonyi.com
to: jademassey@yahoo.com
date: Thu, Oct 22 at 12:12 PM
subject: re: no subject

Since we're being frank, I will say that I find the idea that *you*, in fact, are the one executing her wishes to be a stretch.

---

from: jademassey@yahoo.com
to: smith@simonyi.com
date: Thu, Oct 22 at 12:14 PM
subject: re: no subject

EXCUSE ME?

---

from: smith@simonyi.com
to: jademassey@yahoo.com
date: Thu, Oct 22 at 12:16 PM
subject: re: no subject

Will you stop shouting? To say that you're dragging your feet on the bakery is an understatement. You spend all your time traveling back and forth to Virginia to parent your mom, and researching this "malpractice" claim that isn't going anywhere.

from: jademassey@yahoo.com
to: smith@simonyi.com
date: Thu, Oct 22 at 12:18 PM
subject: re: no subject

What do you know about the malpractice claim? We haven't even talked about it. You know nothing about it. And things in law move slowly. Everyone knows that.

from: smith@simonyi.com
to: jademassey@yahoo.com
date: Thu, Oct 22 at 12:19 PM
subject: re: no subject

I think you don't actually want to open the bakery. She wanted it, and so you feel like you're supposed to do it. But you don't actually want it, so you're stalling.

from: jademassey@yahoo.com
to: smith@simonyi.com
date: Thu, Oct 22 at 12:19 PM
subject: re: no subject

Armchair diagnosing me now!

from: smith@simonyi.com
to: jademassey@yahoo.com
date: Thu, Oct 22 at 12:20 PM
subject: re: no subject

You hate desserts!

---

from: jademassey@yahoo.com
to: smith@simonyi.com
date: Thu, Oct 22 at 12:25 PM
subject: re: no subject

Well, I think you're a jerk for not going to see your mother.

---

from: smith@simonyi.com
to: jademassey@yahoo.com
date: Thu, Oct 22 at 12:26 PM
subject: re: no subject

I see. Okay.

---

from: jademassey@yahoo.com
to: smith@simonyi.com
date: Thu, Oct 22 at 12:30 PM
subject: re: no subject

I think it bothers you that I "PARENT" my mother because it makes you feel guilty!

---

from: smith@simonyi.com
to: jademassey@yahoo.com
date: Thu, Oct 22 at 12:33 PM
subject: re: no subject

Anything else?

---

from: jademassey@yahoo.com
to: smith@simonyi.com
date: Thu, Oct 22 at 12:36 PM
subject: re: no subject

THAT'S why you don't like that I'm in Virginia all the time. It reminds you of where you AREN'T. As for the malpractice claim, which I am only looking into, if *your* sister died, you'd want to know why, too.

---

from: smith@simonyi.com
to: jademassey@yahoo.com
date: Thu, Oct 22 at 12:37 PM
subject: re: no subject

She died because she had cancer, Jade. That's the reason.

---

from: jademassey@yahoo.com
to: smith@simonyi.com
date: Thu, Oct 22 at 12:42 PM
subject: re: no subject

I do want to open the bakery. More than anything. Just not with your help.

---

from: smith@simonyi.com
to: jademassey@yahoo.com
date: Thu, Oct 22 at 12:43 PM
subject: re: no subject

Got it. Good luck.

from:	jademassey@yahoo.com
to:	smith@simonyi.com
date:	Thu, Oct 22 at 12:51 PM
subject:	re: no subject

You want to read my poetry?! Here's one. It's a haiku:

If you meet a Smith
Simonyi: KEEP YOUR DISTANCE.
Liar! Asshole! PRICK!

An update.

This update concerns a review of my latest CT scans by a doctor I have never talked to or heard about until today: Dr. Allison. Dr. Allison is a radiologist. Unlike my oncologist Dr. Hsu, this other doctor, in reviewing the scans, spotted a mass on my liver.

The day before yesterday, Dr. Allison and Dr. Hsu found mutual free time in their busy schedules to chat and figure out why their opinions on the scans differ. And once Dr. Hsu took a closer look, he had to agree with Dr. Allison that there is possibly something "of concern" on my liver. He doesn't know why he missed it before, he says, except that he does not spend as much time looking at scans as Dr. Allison, and therefore isn't an expert.

Ah. Well, that might have been nice to know.

The question of whether I now have cancer on my liver will need to be addressed via follow-up scans on Friday.

Fortunately Smith was out of the office when he called. I tore up papers. I threw a stapler. I screamed till my throat hurt. I didn't feel sad until I thought of telling Richie.

It's like I'm on the subway and I can't make out the garbled, scratchy announcement, which could be that the train is going out of service, or being rerouted, or just that there's a slight delay. Do I stay on or do I have to get off here?

Do I have cancer or don't I? Someone, please, for God's sake. Tell me what is happening so I can decide how to feel.

COMMENTS (2):

BonnieD: No! ☹☹ Doctors suck!

ChristmasWasMyFavorite: Didn't this blog used to have pictures?

---

from: smith@simonyi.com
to: iris@simonyi.com
date: Thu, Oct 22 at 8:44 PM
subject: no subject

I've managed to isolate myself from everyone in my life. Phil fired me. Your sister hates me. My mother is mad at me. Wally thinks I'm a bad son. Richie is clearly avoiding me because he's sick of feeling like an ATM, and sick of me. *I'm* sick of me.

The other day, I was remembering that game we used to play. I think we called it "Either/Or." The one where you pick between two things: one you get to keep, and the other you lose forever?

You might start with, say, Muffins or soda?

I'd definitely pick soda since I don't eat muffins. Then it would be my turn to come up with a contender for soda: Soda or movies?

That's not a great one because it's too easy. Obviously movies. You'd pick movies, for sure, then go for something like, Movies or music? That's harder.

And the game would go on until we were living in a world without muffins, soda, movies, socks, the color red, cell phones, air travel, and toothpaste, and our choices would reach the level of abstraction: Love? Sex? Family? I was always amused that, eventually, regardless of the path the game had taken, our choice would come down to some version of the same dichotomy—life without the myriad things that make life tolerable, or death?

I always chose death, because at that point, who wants to live? You've lost everything worth living for. But you, every time, would find the one good thing that was left and keep going back to it: "But did we get rid of friendship?"

"No, but we lost love, sight, creativity, joy, and hamburgers."

"But we still have friendship . . ."

You always clung to reasons not to choose death.

I feel like I'm at the end of that game, and all the reasons for living are gone, but you're the one who died, and I get to stick around.

I remember once reading a news story about an Irishman who was sentenced to death, and over the two years he spent on death row, he made peace with it. Though he maintained his innocence, he came to terms with the fact that his life was ending.

But then something happened: his sentence was converted to life in prison. Suddenly he had before him decades of life to go, years of time he'd already given up on. I was struck by what he said in his interview about it later, after he was exonerated—he said that when his sentence was converted, he wasn't relieved. He was afraid. He'd made peace with death, but he had no idea how to face more life.

How did you find your way to the kind of peace you reached? Is it because you were dying? How do I do that, but with more life to go?

---

from: Bro-vado
to: smithsimonyi@gmail.com
date: Thu, Oct 22 at 11:58 PM
subject: GET IT, MAN

You walked away with cold hard cash!

Here's a breakdown of your most recent session:

High: $482

Low: $14

Walkaway: $234

ProTip: Setting yourself a time limit can prevent you from developing a problematic habit and ensure that you continue to enjoy Bro-vado for the healthy form of leisure that it is!

Thursday, October 22

TherapistAwayNetwork™

Patient Name: Jade Renee Massey

AUTO PROMPT: **What do you fear?**

Dr. Z, thank you for your email. I'm very sorry to hear about the giardia. I knew you could acquire it from drinking contaminated water in South America, but I had no idea the parasite could have such a long incubation period. I hope you recover quickly. No pressure to read this, by the way. I just need to process.

I was sort of falling for Smith Simonyi. I liked that talking came naturally, that I didn't have to work to fill the silence. I liked how he would find excuses to put a hand on my back or arm. I liked his surprisingly wide smile. I liked that he never seems nervous but doesn't seem arrogant, either. I like that I found it easy to trust him.

We were spending time together every other day or so, Dr. Z.

Whenever I was in town, we'd get lunch or coffee. A beer, dim sum. Take a walk. Often under the pretense of working on the bakery, but we both knew it was more than that.

But this whole time, he was going behind my back to try to get my sister's book published despite the fact that I've made it quite clear to him that I'm not comfortable with it. He isn't who I thought he was. And he put her wishes over mine (which I feel like answers the "was he in love with her" question). He claimed he was going to tell me eventually . . . but when?

He also said some nasty things about my plan to open the bakery, how he thinks I'm dragging my feet because I don't actually want to do it.

It's not true. It really isn't. I do want it. It's really important that I do this for her.

The other day at a hair salon I was trying out on a Groupon (I made a poor decision last month to dye my hair red and suddenly needed it fixed, ASAP), a dad walked in with his sons, who looked around nine and eleven. The smaller one took the chair. The dad said to the stylist, "He wants a Mohawk." Then he said to his son, "Show him the picture on your phone."

"Why does he want that?" the older one asked the dad, peering over his brother's shoulder at the screen.

"I don't know," the dad said. "Ask him." But the younger one said nothing, just smiled at his reflection in the mirror.

"It's not going to look just like that," the older one said, panicking. "I don't think you should do it." And I got that kid. So much. He was used to being the one who charts a new path, who does the daring thing. Here was his younger brother, stepping out to make his own way, and it scared his older sibling, who was probably more nervous about his kid brother making a mistake than he was about making a mistake himself.

She wanted to open a bakery, and regardless of my own wishes, I have the ability to do that for her.

Smith says that she also wanted her book published, but that just feels like it can't have been important in the same way. To air her anguish to the world? Her regrets about the life she didn't get to live? How is that going to honor Iris—the real Iris, before she was sick? How is that going to help us heal?

■

Dear JADE,

Thank you for your submission to TAN™. We will make sure your provider receives this message.

The origin of the term "fear" is linked to the root of "revere," which, of course, is related to "reverence." Sometimes what we fear is also what we hold the deepest respect for. When we recognize this, we can often reconcile our fear and admiration into a single source of power, allowing the truth contained within to inspire bravery we didn't know we had.

TAN™ is not to be used in case of emergency. If you are in crisis, call 9-1-1.

Sincerely,

Your friends at TAN

MONDAY, OCTOBER 26

from: rsstein@rssteintherapy.com
to: smith@simonyi.com
date: Mon, Oct 26 at 8:43 PM
subject: re: Hello

Dear Smith,

Good evening. Normally I would not provide these. It's not exactly standard practice in my profession to share my process notes with clients. But in your case I am willing to make an exception in hope that they offer some illumination.

I sincerely hope you are doing well. Please call if you have any questions about them or wish to talk.

Warmly,

Raquel

ATTACHMENT (1)

eNoteTherapy—*Revolutionizing Therapy Notes One Note At a Time*

Dr. Raquel S. Stein, LCSW

SESSION 1

Patient name:	Smith Seymour Simonyi
Patient DOB:	3/22/76
Month_Day:	April 22, Fri
Referral:	Beth Israel Hospital ER
Intake Notes:	

Patient arrived in acute distress, reporting that wife had left him "out of the blue" one week ago. He arrived home to find that she had moved out while he was away on business. Patient repeatedly asserted that there were no prior signs.

Patient reported he has been sleeping in shower, and that he suffered a panic attack during which he went to ER thinking he was having a heart attack.

After some probing, patient added that he drove to a casino in Connecticut over the weekend, where he gambled and lost much of his savings.

I suggested that the betrayal seemed to have triggered a PTSD episode and inquired if it reminded him of any past events.

Patient stated that he knew what it was but saw no point in revisiting it.

"This is why I never came to therapy before."

He reported that he grew up in a household in which his father was physically and verbally abusive toward the patient's mother in the patient's presence. Patient left home at 18. When he was 28, he was living in New York when his mother killed his father by pushing him down a flight of stairs. He pulled her with him. She survived and is now quadriplegic, living in a facility outside Madison, Wisconsin. He expressed that he blames himself for not being there, but also her, for killing his dad, and he feels he shouldn't. He has not seen her in several years and pays for her care. He stated that discussing these feelings does not seem to make them any less painful.

"Life is hard, and these are just sad things."

We discussed coping mechanisms. He shared that he probably gambles too much but is not convinced this was a response to his upbringing, though his affect was flat and removed. He said he planned to try hot yoga, which seemed to work well for his admin.

I asked what he misses about his wife. He stated that he misses her being around. I asked what they did together. "Normal stuff." Did they ever fight? "A normal amount."

When I inquired as to the subject of their most recent argument, he presented as hostile. He stated that I was trying to figure out what he had done wrong to make her leave.

"I'm not a bad person," he stated at a heightened volume.

He then explained that he and his wife had fought over getting a dog. She'd wanted one. He had resisted. This upset her. I asked why he had been opposed. He said because it would die before him. He had tried to explain to her that anticipating the death of the dog, he would not even be able to enjoy having it.

"Do you think she left me because of the dog?" he asked, distressed. I told him I didn't know. I asked his wife's name, which he still had not spoken. Clementine.

I asked if he had any thoughts of hurting himself, and he said no.

We concluded the session with a mantra should the panic attacks resume: It's distress, not danger.

Patient scheduled to return in four days, on Tuesday.

RS Stein

CSW

DR. RAQUEL S. STEIN, LCSW

SESSION 2

Patient name: Smith Seymour Simonyi

Month_Day: April 26, Tues

Time since last appointment: 4 days

Patient presented as if in dissociative state. Superficially high spirits. Initiated conversation by announcing a turnaround: "A full 180." Stated that he had a productive weekend, making a great deal of money, more than enough to compensate for his losses the previous week at Mohegan Sun.

As to how he had made the money, "a combination of things." I asked how he was sleeping, given he had previously reported sleeping in his shower. He said he was "back in bed and everything."

He had spoken to his wife. She had told him she was leaving because, if she had to pin it on one thing, it was that he cannot express his feelings, to the point that she can't tell if he has them, and she is lonelier living with him than without him. I asked what he thought of it.

"If she wants a crier, I'm sure she can find a crier." His affect was briefly sad.

Buoyant once again, patient then thanked me for my time and told me that he would no longer be needing my services. He had gone to hot yoga two days in a row with his secretary and was finding in it the catharsis he required. He had only come in to tell me as much and to thank me for helping him through his crisis.

I wondered aloud why he had not just told me as much over the phone. I asked if he was sure he wanted to cease his treatment—otherwise, why had he shown up for it? He had not needed to end our treatment in person.

He appeared rattled, stated that he was certain, and left 20 minutes prior to the scheduled end of the session.

DISPLAY: **PROCESS FlagNotes™:** Initial diagnosis is unprocessed guilt and grief manifested in impulsive behavior; defensive stoicism; and pathological avoidance of relationships that he believes will lead to pain. Hypothesis: continues to stoke anger toward mother in hope that if he remains angry, her eventual death will hurt less than his father's did when he was in his mid-20s.

Dr. Raquel S. Stein, LCSW

SESSION 3

Patient name: Smith Seymour Simonyi

Month_Day: May 25, Mon

Time since last appointment: 4 years, 29 days

Patient arrived in acute distress, having recently experienced the death of his colleague. He professed concern that his distress would trigger an uncontrolled bout of gambling, and said that he was seeking help in order to prevent a "spiral" such as the one he experienced following his divorce, which was also the last time he visited this office.

I affirmed his choice to preemptively seek treatment in an effort to avoid what he felt was his typical, destructive response to grief. We spent the remainder of the session allowing him space to express his feelings, as he seemed eager to do.

We discussed the colleague (Iris), whose presence in his life seemed to be that of a sort of surrogate partner.

He left by stating that he doubted he would return to my office, given his general "distaste for therapy," but that, once again, he appreciated my willingness to see him in his current crisis. I made it clear that he should call without fearing I will bully him into committing to a regular therapeutic schedule. Given his previously sporadic interest in clinical work, this seemed the safest approach.

End of all entries for patient.

---

from: smith@simonyi.com
to: iris@simonyi.com
date: Mon, Oct 26 at 11:32 PM
subject: my dad

"He touched many lives and will be dearly missed."

The last line of my father's obituary, still available on the *Sun Prairie Star*'s website, was written by a woman who worked for the paper, after she told me that the obit I submitted was too short.

Touched many lives. What a load of shit.

When I buried him, I've never felt so alone, or so adult. Overnight, roles had switched. My dad was gone, my mom was in the hospital, barely conscious, and there were decisions to be made and bills to be paid. I picked out a casket. I signed papers listing fees for things I didn't know existed—body prep, body transport, insurance for if there's a flood at the cemetery. It cost everything I'd saved in my twenties. Did you know you can skip embalming? Or even the coffin altogether, if you're down for a "natural burial"? But not knowing if he wanted these or not, I wasn't going to cut corners. Not on my own father.

Neither of my parents had thought ahead to anything about dying or getting injured. They didn't have wills or life insurance. She sure as hell didn't have any kind of long-term disability. I bought a plot in the cemetery in the middle of town. The burial was minutes long. I stood there next to my great-aunts as a guy around my age, mid-twenties, shoveled clumps of dirt that trickled over the glossy black box. Then he picked up speed, and the dirt piled up until there was nothing but a freshly tilled rectangle of soil bigger than my dad.

And all I kept thinking that night was, sure, it was bad before.

They had their issues. But she'd made it infinitely worse. She'd ended the bad, but she'd ended the good, too. Now we had nothing.

So yes, I'm mad. I'm angry she didn't stand up for herself sooner, so it didn't have to end that way. I'm angry she let him treat her how he did, and I feel guilty about that, but I do, because I don't get to be angry at him anymore. He's gone. There's no one but her to be fucking angry at. I'm mad she got dragged into it. I'm mad she's paralyzed, and that I wasn't there to stop it. I'm mad at us both, and it may not be fair, but, fuck, I am.

---

from: Bobbles Internet Hosting
to: smith@simonyi.com
date: Mon, Oct 26 at 11:33 PM
subject: AUTOMATIC RESPONSE—YOUR EMAIL WAS NOT DELIVERED—DO NOT REPLY TO THIS EMAIL <<my dad>>

SIMONYI.COM Administrator,

Because this account was not renewed, it has been discontinued per the user agreement, which states that 90 days following failure to renew the address, it will become defunct. If you would like to restore the email address **iris@simonyi.com** please contact Bobbles Customer Care. Note that per the user agreement, email previously sent to and from this address cannot be restored even if the address is reactivated.

---

from: smith@simonyi.com
to: iris.a.massey@gmail.com
date: Mon, Oct 26 at 11:35 PM
subject: Fwd: my dad

For you, below.

TUESDAY, OCTOBER 27

---

from: jademassey@yahoo.com
to: smith@simonyi.com
date: Tue, Oct 27 at 6:17 PM
subject: no subject

Still emailing Iris, I see. Why'd you forward it?

---

from: smith@simonyi.com
to: jademassey@yahoo.com
date: Tue, Oct 27 at 8:59 PM
subject: re: no subject

I figured if any server reaches beyond this life, it's Google.
Still checking her email, I see.

---

from: jademassey@yahoo.com
to: smith@simonyi.com
date: Tue, Oct 27 at 9:45 PM
subject: re: no subject

Trying to figure out what she wanted.
I read your email. Sorry. I think I miss talking to you.

---

from: smith@simonyi.com
to: jademassey@yahoo.com
date: Tue, Oct 27 at 10:13 PM
subject: re: no subject

Doesn't matter.

---

from: jademassey@yahoo.com
to: smith@simonyi.com
date: Tue, Oct 27 at 10:30 PM
subject: re: no subject

Sounds like you're going through some shit.

---

from: smith@simonyi.com
to: jademassey@yahoo.com
date: Tue, Oct 27 at 10:35 PM
subject: re: no subject

We don't need to talk about it.

---

from: jademassey@yahoo.com
to: smith@simonyi.com
date: Tue, Oct 27 at 10:41 PM
subject: re: no subject

Is that why you email this stuff to someone who is dead? So you don't have to talk about it? You can just share into the void and not hear back what you don't want to hear?

from: smith@simonyi.com
to: jademassey@yahoo.com
date: Tue, Oct 27 at 10:42 PM
subject: re: no subject

Jade, please? I know I'm a fuckup.

from: jademassey@yahoo.com
to: smith@simonyi.com
date: Tue, Oct 27 at 10:50 PM
subject: re: no subject

Just go see your mom, Smith. Fuck your whole regrets theory. That's not why you need to go.

It's back. Rather, it was never gone. Just migrated south a bit, to my liver.

And this time, in its new location, it isn't likely to be responsive to chemo. So today I told Smith that this week will be my last of work. Richie, Jade—they can handle it. But I'm not sure Smith can. It's time to go before I begin to disappear.

As of Monday, my existence at Simonyi Brand Management will be no more than an absence. Then this will be true of my apartment. Then it will be true everywhere.

Could my absence on this earth do some good? Is it possible? (Apart from the obvious, that there is one fewer person on the planet consuming resources.)

At the high school where I spent my twelfth-grade year, we had Sharing Is Caring Day, a fundraiser for the school's special ed program. For us students, it meant a day full of games and prizes, the last of which was a scavenger hunt. My team consisted of six kids in a pickup, three in back, three in front. Our acquisitions included:

- A photo of a live chicken
- A helium balloon
- A round of gin rummy with a retirement home resident
- A whole tub of movie popcorn, consumed
- A lock of someone's hair
- Documentation of the biggest bubble blown by any team member
- A school T-shirt from five or more years ago

Still to go: a dad's joke.

In the McDonald's parking lot, we shifted our focus from person to person.

"Can't help."

"Not me."

"Mine's dead."

None of us had dads. All six of us, and not a single dad.

We could ask a dad of somebody on another team, someone suggested, but the consensus was that that would be uncool.

"Mr. Morris is a dad," one person pointed out. No one jumped at the idea because the thing was, our principal Mr. Morris's son had died a few years earlier. But if we asked him, at least there wasn't the issue of trespassing on another team's turf.

We headed to Mr. Morris's. When we got there, he was in his pajamas. You could see his wife through the window, watching TV. We told him we were doing the Sharing Is Caring scavenger hunt and needed a dad joke, but none of us had dads.

"How do you know a wildcat from a bobcat?" he asked.

"How?" we all yelled.

"One answers to Bob and the other doesn't!"

At first no one laughed. It was so awful. Then we all did, including Mr. Morris. He didn't have a son anymore, and we didn't have dads anymore, and here we all were because of it, laughing about a bobcat.

Maybe once I'm gone, the fact that I'm missing will bring people together, too.

COMMENTS (1):

BigJessBarbs: I would have used a mom for the joke and said TAKE THAT sexist pigs!

FRIDAY, OCTOBER 30

from: ronaldglass@apexunitedcitizens.com
to: smith@simonyi.com
date: Fri, Oct 30 at 9:02 AM
subject: Third and Final Contact

Dear Mr. Simons,

    I write for a <u>third and final time</u> to offer you the opportunity to benefit from the teachings of Apex by working with me on my brand. Also I am willing to pay you. Was that not clear before? Who among us does not like money?

    I eagerly anticipate your enthusiastic, though delayed, response.

Sincerely,

Ronald P. Glass

Why You Should Not Care About Time
BY RONALD P. GLASS

Tick tock! Tick tock!

    Clocks lead us to believe that time exists.

    However, they are pointing us wrong, as hands often do.

    Time is as stretchy as a wad of Silly Putty. Don't believe me?

Just send your twin into space! She will come back dewy and elastic, while you've pruned up like a thumb in a tub.

If you cling to the view that time matters, it will.

If you understand that a minute can hold all the wonder of an hour or week or lifetime, you will leap like a man on the moon.

---

from: carl@simonyi.com
to: smith@simonyi.com
date: Fri, Oct 30 at 9:15 AM
subject: You won't believe this

Boss,

I have some news.

Iris almost quit her job three years ago.

How I know this is—long story short, the bottom left drawer in my desk has been stuck since Day 1. It won't go in all the way and drives me nuts because of my #ocd. So this morning I decided to fix it, finally. I removed it from its base, and, lo and behold, there were some papers stuck back behind the track. They were drafts that Iris wrote telling you she was going to quit, dated three years ago. Maybe you knew this? Hopefully not so I can feel valuable and my ego will get the same shot of dopamine it does when I meet a deadline or get an A! Just kidding!

How was BRANDISH doing three years ago?

---

from: smith@simonyi.com
to: carl@simonyi.com
date: Fri, Oct 30 at 9:28 AM
subject: re: You won't believe this

Huh. Well, I can't say I'm surprised.

It wasn't about the firm flailing, though. Three years ago we were doing well. The only thing I can think of that happened around that time is that Iris was supposed to get married.

And our name isn't BRANDISH. Nice try.

---

from: carl@simonyi.com
to: smith@simonyi.com
date: Fri, Oct 30 at 9:32 AM
subject: re: You won't believe this

Oh. Oh boy.

---

from: smith@simonyi.com
to: carl@simonyi.com
date: Fri, Oct 30 at 9:34 AM
subject: re: You won't believe this

What? Carl, you know how I feel about cryptic emails. Almost at front of line at Starbucks, I'll be there in 10 or so.

---

from: carl@simonyi.com
to: smith@simonyi.com
date: Fri, Oct 30 at 9:35 AM
subject: re: You won't believe this

Do you want me to lie or do you want the truth?

---

from: smith@simonyi.com
to: carl@simonyi.com
date: Fri, Oct 30 at 9:36 AM
subject: re: You won't believe this

For fuck's sake, Carl.

---

from: carl@simonyi.com
to: smith@simonyi.com
date: Fri, Oct 30 at 9:39 AM
subject: re: You won't believe this

Backstory of the last ~15 minutes: I thought it was weird that this never came up in her blog. And then I thought, well, maybe she had posts she wrote and didn't publish. That happens, you know? So I logged into her dyingtoblog.com account (she should have known better than to keep a document on the desktop titled PASSWORDS—she wasn't 85). And . . . she did. Have unpublished drafts.

---

from: smith@simonyi.com
to: carl@simonyi.com
date: Fri, Oct 30 at 9:40 AM
subject: re: You won't believe this

Carl! That's not okay!

---

from: carl@simonyi.com
to: smith@simonyi.com
date: Fri, Oct 30 at 9:41 AM
subject: re: You won't believe this

I know. I feel terrible.

---

from: smith@simonyi.com
to: carl@simonyi.com
date: Fri, Oct 30 at 9:41 AM
subject: re: You won't believe this

None of this is any of your business. Log out immediately.

from: carl@simonyi.com
to: smith@simonyi.com
date: Fri, Oct 30 at 9:42 AM
subject: re: You won't believe this

You're right. I'm signing out immediately and sharing nothing further.

    If you want to know what's there, you will have to log in and read it for yourself.

        Username: Irismassey
        PW: cAramelTw1g

from: smith@simonyi.com
to: carl@simonyi.com
date: Fri, Oct 30 at 9:44 AM
subject: re: You won't believe this

Never do that again. This is unacceptable behavior. We will discuss it when I return. Waiting on my coffee, back in a second.

from: smith@simonyi.com
to: carl@simonyi.com
date: Fri, Oct 30 at 9:46 AM
subject: re: You won't believe this

Anyway, I imagine she was going to quit because she was planning to marry and didn't need the job anymore. She didn't wind up getting married, so she stayed.

---

from: carl@simonyi.com
to: smith@simonyi.com
date: Fri, Oct 30 at 9:46 AM
subject: re: You won't believe this

Nope.

---

from: carl@simonyi.com
to: smith@simonyi.com
date: Fri, Oct 30 at 9:52 AM
subject: re: You won't believe this

WHAT IN THE HECK KIND OF LATTÉ DID YOU ORDER, TRIPLE PUMPKIN SPICE??

Count the cups in front of yours—is it more than 2??

---

from: carl@simonyi.com
to: smith@simonyi.com
date: Fri, Oct 30 at 9:55 AM
subject: re: You won't believe this

SHOULD I BE WORRIED YOU GOT HIT BY A BUS?

---

from: carl@simonyi.com
to: smith@simonyi.com
date: Fri, Oct 30 at 9:56 AM
subject: re: You won't believe this

I can't hold it in any longer: Boss, she was going to quit because she was in love with *you*.

from:	jademassey@yahoo.com
to:	winsomebeautydorothy@hotmail.com
date:	Fri, Oct 30 at 1:33 PM
subject:	Plan for the weekend

Mom,

I'm just going to take a cab from the airport. Please don't come get me. I'll see you in the morning. I'm hoping that we can tackle the following projects tomorrow:

- Shower clog. The fact that four bottles of Drano haven't done the trick means we have to try something else. I'll go to Lowe's in the morning and see what the man there recommends.
- Add a ramp to the porch so you don't keep tripping. Next time it could be your hip. Do you know what happens to women your age who break a hip? I don't think I need to tell you. Sam from your church says he can help us build it. He is a woodworker or something.
- Clean out the pantry. It's sweet that you offered to help that mentally handicapped lady—what's her name, Rose?—can peaches, but the jars are putrid. I don't think she screwed them on tight enough. I think we should throw them out and get her decent peaches at the farmer's market or something. Will she even know the difference, truly?
- Buy some fruit in case you get trick-or-treaters. Do you ever? It would be a shame to disappoint them by having nothing on hand to give out.

See you tomorrow (don't come get me!),
Jade

---

from: winsomebeautydorothy@hotmail.com
to: jademassey@yahoo.com
date: Fri, Oct 30 at 1:45 PM
subject: re: Plan for the weekend

ENOUGH IS ENOUGH. I will have no such eyesore gracing the likes of my front porch. Do not talk to me about Sam being a woodworker, he built a set for the Christmas pageant last year that COLLAPSED during the birth of Christ. INWARD. Mary and Joseph each broke a bone. Wrists, fingers, or both. He will be building me no ramps, at least insofar as you are not secretly *hoping* for my death by fall.

And we will <u>not</u> be giving the sweet children who come to my door *fruit* when they have gone to the trouble of donning costumes in exchange for something respectable like chocolate, nor will we be moving Rose Larrimore's peaches anywhere. If you don't like the smell, you will just need to keep the pantry door closed when you're here.

Of course I'm picking you up from the airport. I'm not decrepit or blind yet, for heaven's sake.

Mom

---

from: smith@simonyi.com
to: richierich1000@gmail.com
date: Fri, Oct 30 at 1:45 PM
subject: Apology

Hi Richie,

Just dropped a check by your office. Sorry for being such a money pit for so long. I know it was frustrating. I won't be asking to borrow from you anymore. Lame as it sounds—I do just miss hanging out.

Smith

---

from: richierich1000@gmail.com
to: smith@simonyi.com
date: Fri, Oct 30 at 2:02 PM
subject: re: Apology

---

what the hell is this?

---

from: smith@simonyi.com
to: richierich1000@gmail.com
date: Fri, Oct 30 at 2:14 PM
subject: re: Apology

I finally signed a new client and can pay you back. Sorry again.

---

from: richierich1000@gmail.com
to: smith@simonyi.com
date: Fri, Oct 30 at 2:30 PM
subject: re: Apology

MESSAGES
Wed., Mar. 25, 10:00 PM

IRIS: Hey. What's up?

RICHIE: well well well look who lives

IRIS: I'm sorry? Sorry.

RICHIE: is miss snappy gone? is it safe to speak freely?

IRIS: yeah

RICHIE: kidding. left you alone because you told me to.

IRIS: How've you been?

RICHIE: ok. little lonely

RICHIE: my girlfriend dumped me

RICHIE: she has cancer and SHE dumped ME

IRIS: I didn't dump you!

RICHIE: yeah ok

RICHIE: How are you?

IRIS: I'm feeling better today. My mom is back in town.

RICHIE: oh cool

IRIS: She arrived last night and already feels neglected.

RICHIE: want me to entertain her? i'll take her on the staten island ferry and everything

IRIS: Are you scared of dying?

RICHIE: and a full 180

RICHIE: honesty ok hmm

RICHIE: less than i'm scared i'll go crazy and wind up living with a bunch of feral cats and never showering

IRIS: Are you scared of ME dying?

RICHIE: of course

IRIS: I'm scared.

RICHIE: i want to hug you right now so bad

IRIS: I feel like I'm not supposed to be scared at this point. I'm supposed to be at acceptance

RICHIE: i don't think there's a way you're supposed to feel. u feel scared. that seems totally natural

IRIS: Thanks

RICHIE: hey question. do u believe in heaven?

IRIS: Like a happy place in the clouds? No.

RICHIE: more like life after death. like it keeps going

RICHIE: didn't mean to freak you out. sorry.

IRIS: I don't know. Do you?

RICHIE: yeah

IRIS: That's nice. That seems like it would be comforting.

RICHIE: ok this is getting too depressing. let's look on the bright side. what are we going to do when you DON'T die?

RICHIE: let's start planning

IRIS: Ha. Okay. Well I've still never been to Coney Island, so that

RICHIE: done

IRIS: I've always wanted to do that thing where people fish for mussels or clams . . . shellfish I mean. What is that called?

RICHIE: clamming? no clue. but sounds easy enough. what else

IRIS: I want to wake up on a Saturday morning with you and lie in bed all day and watch movies and drink mimosas.

RICHIE: but NOT Pulp Fiction

IRIS: I told you, I don't get into gangsters.

RICHIE: you got into this one ;) ;)

IRIS: Looking like one doesn't make you one.

RICHIE: yeah yeah. movie day we can make happen

RICHIE: what else

RICHIE: where'd u go

IRIS: I got sad.

RICHIE: why? we can do stuff. be optimistic.

IRIS: Richie, I'm going to die.

IRIS: I don't want to. And I don't want you to be sad. That's why I don't think we should do this fantasizing stuff. It would all be wonderful, sure. But I don't see things going that way.

RICHIE: i understand.

RICHIE: i am trying to.

IRIS: I'm going to sleep. Good night. Hugs.

RICHIE: night girl. giant hug all night long

from:	smith@simonyi.com
to:	richierich1000@gmail.com
date:	Fri, Oct 30 at 3:00 PM
subject:	re: Apology

what is this?

from:	richierich1000@gmail.com
to:	smith@simonyi.com
date:	Fri, Oct 30 at 3:03 PM
subject:	re: Apology

what does it look like

from:	smith@simonyi.com
to:	richierich1000@gmail.com
date:	Fri, Oct 30 at 3:06 PM
subject:	re: Apology

I get that it's messages between you and Iris. Did you mean to forward it to me?

from:	richierich1000@gmail.com
to:	smith@simonyi.com
date:	Fri, Oct 30 at 3:08 PM
subject:	re: Apology

u are so fuckin dense man

from: richierich1000@gmail.com
to: smith@simonyi.com
date: Fri, Oct 30 at 3:17 PM
subject: re: Apology

im not mad cuz u keep asking for money. u can gamble all u want. its your fuckin life. im mad cuz u kept asking me about money and not how i am doing. am i ok

from: smith@simonyi.com
to: richierich1000@gmail.com
date: Fri, Oct 30 at 3:24 PM
subject: re: Apology

How did you know about my gambling?

from: richierich1000@gmail.com
to: smith@simonyi.com
date: Fri, Oct 30 at 3:28 PM
subject: re: Apology

see? making this about yourself
    everyone knows dude
    addicts don't hide their shit they just think they do

from: smith@simonyi.com
to: richierich1000@gmail.com
date: Fri, Oct 30 at 3:33 PM
subject: re: Apology

Are you not okay? I know you miss her. I do, too.

---

from: richierich1000@gmail.com
to: smith@simonyi.com
date: Fri, Oct 30 at 3:40 PM
subject: re: Apology

---

u don't fucking get it. i know you miss her but it was different.

---

from: smith@simonyi.com
to: richierich1000@gmail.com
date: Fri, Oct 30 at 3:42 PM
subject: re: Apology

I know it's different. You guys were dating.

---

from: richierich1000@gmail.com
to: smith@simonyi.com
date: Fri, Oct 30 at 4:04 PM
subject: re: Apology

---

dude i loved her. i fell in love with her

---

from: smith@simonyi.com
to: richierich1000@gmail.com
date: Fri, Oct 30 at 4:10 PM
subject: re: Apology

Have I not been understanding enough of that?

from:	richierich1000@gmail.com
to:	smith@simonyi.com
date:	Fri, Oct 30 at 4:12 PM
subject:	re: Apology

no dude. not even close

from:	smith@simonyi.com
to:	richierich1000@gmail.com
date:	Fri, Oct 30 at 4:15 PM
subject:	re: Apology

I'm sorry.

from:	richierich1000@gmail.com
to:	smith@simonyi.com
date:	Fri, Oct 30 at 4:20 PM
subject:	re: Apology

i just miss her dude
  u have no idea

MONDAY, NOVEMBER 2

Monday, November 2
TherapistAwayNetwork™
Patient Name: Jade Renee Massey
AUTO PROMPT: **What do you have to gain?**

Well, TAN, now that Dr. Z. has announced his retirement, it's just you and me.

My mother has kicked me out. She doesn't want me to come back down for at least six weeks. I have a feeling she only said six weeks because of Christmas, or it would have been longer. She's sick of me apparently, and has been for a while. The reason she looked catatonic? Was me. I was wearing her out.

I suppose I should feel grateful that she's back to her old "self" again, but what I'm really thinking about is how it is that everyone but me is moving on. My mom. Smith.

I don't get it. What magic reliever of pain has touched them but not me?

The last time Iris went to the hospital, my mom and I went, too. It was so clear it was the end. I hadn't realized how clear it becomes at some point.

My mom kept herself busy, alternately weeping in the corner while typing on her phone and scolding the nurses for various things she objected to in the room.

Then Iris said, "Leave." She mumbled, but we both heard it.

The nurse heard it, too. She had been changing Iris's pillow, which had become soaked with sweat and saliva and whatever other mysterious, viscous fluids the body releases as it goes.

The nurse gestured for my mom and me to follow her into the hall.

"It's hurtful, I know, when they do that," she said to my mom in a hushed tone. "They often lash out at someone near the end. It isn't personal." Then she told us stories of patients cursing at husbands, fathers, and mothers, of the most cruel accusations and name-calling flying from the mouths of people with one foot in and one foot out of this world. This seemed to make my mother feel worse, and not long after, she returned to her hotel for the night.

A little after 5:00 a.m., Iris died. I had dozed in stints and was caffeinated into that fuzzy, limbo state, teetering on the brink between sleep and wakefulness, unable to relax into either. She had been making these sounds—these sort of monstrous gasps for air, almost like coughs, but not.

I googled them. The first hit contained the words "death rattle."

Google was right. When it finally stopped, only a couple of minutes passed before she was gone.

"Bye, Jade," she said, like she was just falling asleep, and I was leaving for work, and we'd meet back up in the evening.

"Bye, Iris," I said.

I miss her as much today as I did the day after she died. No ounce of it has subsided. Time has done nothing to make it better. These months might as well have never even happened.

What do I have to gain? Anything to make it better than this. But unlike everyone else, I have no idea how.

◾

Dear JADE,

Thank you for your submission to TAN™. We will make sure your provider receives this message.

"Gain" is a noun as well as a verb. As English speakers, we tend to rely excessively on nouns to convey meaning, and in doing so, restrict ourselves to ideas that already exist, rather than opening our imaginations to ideas that have yet to be named.

What if today you focused on "gain" as a verb, and allowed the noun that follows to remain inchoate, finding comfort in the mindset of gaining without knowing exactly what it is that lies before you? Perhaps—just perhaps—it is so large, you can't possibly begin to know what it's called yet.

TAN™ is not to be used in case of emergency. If you are in crisis, call 9-1-1.

Sincerely,

Your friends at TAN

UNPUBLISHED DRAFT
Last opened October 30, at 9:20 AM

The first morning of the incubator, I was late and slid into a row near the back next to a blond man in dark-rimmed glasses. Like me, he appeared a little older than most of the early-twenties crowd. At the front of the auditorium, someone was giving a speech about how we, as entrepreneurs, were the pioneers thrusting society forward in a bunch of ways that ended in -ly: technically, economically, socially.

I was thinking *I just want to start a bakery* when my neighbor leaned over and whispered, "I'm in PR." Then he paused before adding, "Thrusting us forward."

We spent the next five days quietly mocking the program and skipping sessions to drink at a local bar while getting to know each other. It wasn't romantic—I was with Daniel, and Smith had only just gotten divorced—but it was intimate. We were the bad kids at incubator camp. I'm sure for me, the rebel behavior was at least in part a defense mechanism. It was clear from day one that I wasn't ready to open a bakery. Market research, business plans—the terms thrown around made me want to take a nap. Our incubator taught me that I needed a lot more incubating.

It only made sense that I'd go to work for him. I needed a job for the time being, and Smith needed an assistant. We toasted glasses of Guinness and Stella. And that night I lay in my bed at the Hyatt and felt a sense of fate at work, as if this is what was meant to be, silly as I knew it sounded: another job for which I was overqualified, in a random field. But it wasn't the field that pulled me in. It was Smith.

He made it so easy to feel seen and heard. He listened. He laughed at my jokes. He seemed hungry for what I might say next.

Was I attracted to him? I asked myself this question hundreds of times over the years. Only a handful of them was the answer yes. The rest of the time, it felt past that . . . less urgent than romance.

Of course I was a little bit in love with him. He calls wine openers "chickens" with a straight face and can recite the US presidents in order if he sings them. He has never once treated me like I'm anything less than the smartest person in the room.

But only once did it really blossom into something like a crush, an actual infatuation. A little over a year after I began working for him, a couple of months after my thirtieth birthday, Daniel and I were engaged. I faced that spring that I had feelings for Smith, strong enough that I had to do something about them. What I wound up doing was making a mess by leaving Daniel the day of our wedding.

There were good reasons we shouldn't marry, but what had triggered my willingness to face them finally? From where did that strength surge? From wanting someone else. Feelings for Smith nudged me into action, and yet I wasn't ready to pursue those, either (part of me still thought Daniel and I might make it in the end). And thus, I would also need to quit my job.

The Monday after my failed wedding, I knew Smith wouldn't be at the office because he was in Nashville. I drafted my resignation letter several times before I realized that I couldn't do it. I didn't want to. I wanted to stay for the same reason I had needed to quit, and the same reason I'd taken the job in the first place. I liked being around him.

Soon it passed back into what we had originally, what Smith

and I were destined to amount to: friends. The fire wasn't there—not enough of one. It was more like a pilot light, a perpetual option neither of us was ever willing to ignite. Our hesitation wasn't out of fear, I don't think. It was an understanding that we didn't need more between us.

What we had—people didn't understand it. Maybe we didn't even understand it. But apart from the critical flash when I needed it to be more, it was platonic, and real, and it fed me.

---

from: smith@simonyi.com
to: carl@simonyi.com
date: Mon, Nov 2 at 5:01 PM
subject: re: You won't believe this

Carl, she was not in love with me.

---

from: carl@simonyi.com
to: smith@simonyi.com
date: Mon, Nov 2 at 5:09 PM
subject: re: You won't believe this

You caved!

Aren't you glad you read it? Don't you feel warm inside? Might as well read the other drafts while you're in there! ;) (Warning: some of them are really loopy. Was she *often* high at work?)

---

from: smith@simonyi.com
to: carl@simonyi.com
date: Mon, Nov 2 at 5:11 PM
subject: re: You won't believe this

No, I'm not glad. I feel like a creep for reading it behind her back.

March 30, 5:39 PM

Chemo makes your hair fall out slower and faster than you want. It took mine a month to start, but once it did, it released itself in clods, each fistful a reminder that I wasn't just poisoning the cancer. I was poisoning myself.

I took the plunge and shaved my head one afternoon in early February. A blizzard had just come through New York. Gray slush piles clogged the street corners, and the wind felt like it had mass. As I dove into it, my hair blew into my mouth and eyes, and I was annoyed until I realized it would be the last time that ever happened.

I had bought several scarves—a Cubist one from the MOMA store, another with daffodils, and one with Sylvia Plath's poem "Cinderella" printed on it in dark loopy cursive: *Amid the hectic music and cocktail talk, she hears the caustic ticking of the clock.*

I took them all to my hair guy Tim and laid them out like precious vintage garments, or wares for sale.

He grabbed the Plath scarf.

"You will be stunning," he said, which was a sweet lie. Then we washed my hair one last time and he wrapped a towel around it and brought out a bottle of Veuve. We toasted in silence, and I could tell he wished he'd thought of what to say.

I've been going to his little studio on St. Mark's for eight years. It only has four chairs, and as I took a seat in one, he locked the door and drew the curtains, which only closed partway. Every now and then a passerby would peek through the glass storefront, but otherwise, it was just the two of us and the music from the coffee shop next door. The coffee shop and the salon shared a wall.

We're going hoppin'. We're going hoppin' today.
Where things are poppin' the Philadelphia way.

He turned the chair to face away from the mirror so I couldn't watch. But in one of those big metallic holiday balls still hanging from his ceiling, my warped reflection nonetheless made clear what was happening, and I consciously chose not to look at it. He pulled the razor over my skull in measured strips, and I kept my eyes on the gray wall that was also a coffee shop wall, as we played Remember When.

Remember when you failed your driver's test twice at the age of twenty-five?

Remember when you showed up covered in paint? (I'd tripped into a paint can while passing by a construction site.)

Remember the party clown who showed up at your apartment by mistake and then asked you out?

When he was almost done, I stopped him. Above my head the razor buzzed, chopping the air where all my Remember Whens were bobbing, tearing them apart.

Tim placed his big callused hands on my head like he was a priest blessing me. They felt rough and warm on my fresh scalp. He slid a sharp edge over the skin around my left ear, the last final bit of my future, and then he took the poem scarf and wrapped it around and tied it. He turned the chair to the mirror, and I saw myself without hair. It wasn't how I thought I'd look, but it wasn't worse, either.

He raised his glass again. I lifted mine for his benefit and then brought it back down. I couldn't.

"To midnight!" He tapped his glass to the scarf on my head. "When the party gets good."

COMMENTS (4):

BigJessBarbs: Tell me about it. I lost my hair in two hours. And I mean ALL of it.
BonnieD: Did you see Ardvark died?
IrisMassey: Oh no.
BonnieD: Yes. ☹

FRIDAY, NOVEMBER 6

---

from: carl@simonyi.com
to: smith@simonyi.com
date: Fri, Nov 6 at 4:14 PM
subject: An honest chat

Boss,

I hope the shoot with ZF is going well!

Here are a couple of important thoughts before I take off for the weekend.

First, the good news. As of last week, Phil is off to an ashram for six weeks, which will allow me more time/emotional energy to dedicate exclusively to our work.

Next, an attempt at radical transparency. While I'm thrilled that we signed Zahara Ferringbottom and very excited about her despite the fact that she is literally insane, I have concerns about the status of BRANDISH (how does that not work?). I meant to tell you this last night, but I lost my nerve. Rosita called yesterday afternoon and said she is going with another firm. She didn't want to wait for a call back to tell you herself, and she wouldn't say which one. She says it is one that doesn't "make [her] the laughingstock of the New York dentistry community and then charge [her] for it."

(Sidenote: I know you said not to, but I did end up responding to Ronald Glass the cult leader just to get him off our backs. It was a mistake. Now he keeps inviting me to his center for a free mental health–replenishing treatment involving slugs. I think we made the right call in declining to take him on.)

But without Phil, our firm just feels a bit . . . like losers. We are a loser firm.

I am trying to remain optimistic that we can recover. After *Belle* declined to publish Jade's essay, it hit me—what if we submit something inspired by the *other* Massey sister? Thus, I am authoring the listicle I previously suggested, inspired by Iris. The good news is that it poses no copyright issues due to the fact that it's only inspired by her and not by-by her.

More soon.

CVS

PS—This afternoon I took the liberty of installing my high school friend Gus Martin's app OOF! (beta) on our computers. It does a bunch of things that don't matter, but the reason I downloaded it is that it slightly delays emails after you press send, so that you have a couple of minutes to recall them if necessary. (His motto is "Rescind to Resend"—cute, I think!) I figure it would have been useful (read: lifesaver) back in September when I accidently dispatched *the* email that shall not ever be mentioned again. So far I like OOF! Maybe we can give him a blurb for his splash page?

---

from: smith@simonyi.com
to: IRIS
date: Fri, Nov 6 at 7:50 PM
subject: no subject

I can't stop thinking about that spring three years ago. Did I suspect how you felt?

    I think I could sense it. I also think I sensed your reluctance about it. You were engaged. You'd chosen someone else. I wasn't going to put you in a position to question that, if that was what you wanted. I was glad you were happy. I thought you were happy.

    With Richie, though, you actually were. You two had the thing.

    You and I—could we have had it?

    I didn't let myself fall in love with you . . . I didn't dare.

    He's right. I don't get it. I never got there. I was a coward.

---

from: Your Steps Tracker
to: jademassey@yahoo.com
date: Fri, Nov 6 at 8:15 PM
subject: You've logged 60 Miles in 5 days!

Congratulations! You set a record this week of **60 miles in 5 days!**

    Did you know that walking can reduce the risk of heart disease?

    Keep steppin'!

Your steps are logged automatically. You are receiving this email as a T-Mobile customer.

Friday, November 6
TherapistAwayNetwork™
Patient Name: Jade Renee Massey
AUTO PROMPT: **What gives you hope?**

I've been walking a lot.

And thinking.

I am wondering if Smith may have been on to something. Maybe the blog freaks me out because of what it says about me. In any case, I've started reading it again.

This morning I got to the part about how I made her feel invisible. That was a doozy.

But I didn't have to read it to know it.

That day that Iris won the science fair, we probably ate take-out and watched TV and did our homework as usual. But the next morning, when I got to class, there was a note in my backpack: *I won the science fair.*

Somehow it made it worse that she included "the science fair." Not even just *I won.* As if I may have even needed to be reminded what it was she was competing in, despite the fact that I had helped her heat up the water in the microwave, then place it under the ice cube as I'd seen Ariella Franklin do at my previous school the spring before. I had helped her draw pictures of evaporation and paste them on the three-panel cardboard our mom was willing to buy for the occasion. I had done all of this, but in the end, I'd forgotten to ask how it went.

I had a million things on my mind. I'd just started at a new high school. I had boys on the brain, as well as who I was going to be, what kind of person. Would I pass my driver's test? How and when would I ask my mom to teach me? Would there be any guys at my new school willing to take a chance on the new girl with no social status? There were so many unknowns. It was re-markably easy for Iris to slip off my radar.

But it wasn't just that time. So many others—her wedding. Her school dance. From childhood to adulthood, all the moments I could have noticed Iris but didn't, because I was preoccupied with Jade.

I've tried to make it better. To do what she would want, now that she's gone.

Maybe this is my mistake—trying to fix it at all. The world is different now. She left with a part of me that isn't coming back.

I miss Smith.

Henry is now doing some sleuth work for me on the mal-practice claim. Sort of—he thinks we should sue the cannabis company that sold her tinctures with promises of recovery. The things he'll do for me when he's hungry for reconciliation.

I don't know . . . I'm sort of over the whole lawsuit thing. I owe Henry details on the pot company, though. It's nice of him to look into it for me. I don't remember what it was called—I'll have to go back into her email to get it.

But if this angle at the suit is also a nonstarter, I'm done. Okay, universe? I'll be done.

Dear JADE,

Thank you for your submission to TAN™. We will make sure your provider receives this message. As Pablo Neruda says, "You can cut all the flowers but you cannot keep spring from coming."

TAN™ is not to be used in case of emergency. If you are in crisis, call 9-1-1.

Sincerely,

Your friends at TAN

SATURDAY, NOVEMBER 7

from: smith@simonyi.com
to: MOM
date: Sat, Nov 7 at 12:00 PM
subject: DRAFT no subject

Dear Mom,
    I'm sorry that I've resented

from: smith@simonyi.com
to: MOM
date: Sat, Nov 7 at 12:04 PM
subject: DRAFT no subject

Dear Mom,
    As your son, I maybe should have been more understanding of

---

from: smith@simonyi.com
to: MOM
date: Sat, Nov 7 at 5:55 PM
subject: no subject

Dear Mom,

When you read this, we'll have seen each other. I'm bringing it with me next time I come.

I am sorry that I've struggled to talk to you about what happened.

I miss Dad a lot. I did right away. I didn't know how to deal with that and also have a relationship with you. Like I wasn't supposed to love both of you. Like I had to choose between loving you and missing him. I didn't have a choice, though, because I did miss him, as dumb as it seemed to miss someone who made our lives so hard. I still do.

Now I realize you must have missed him, too—in ways I can't understand.

I want us to have a relationship again. I'm sorry.

Love,

Smith

---

from: smith@simonyi.com
to: wally@homilypines.com
date: Sat, Nov 7 at 5:59 PM
subject: Thanksgiving

Hi Wally,

I think I'll be there prior to Thanksgiving, actually. I'm going to come visit Mom next weekend.

Would you mind letting her know?

See you soon!

Smith

---

from: wally@homilypines.com
to: smith@simonyi.com
date: Sat, Nov 7 at 6:13 PM
subject: Thanksgiving

Of course. Great to hear. I'll tell her in the morning, and she'll be thrilled. She's just sleeping off some congestion. See you in a week!

---

from: postmaster@simonyi.com via BOXITWEB
to: smith@simonyi.com
date: Sat, Nov 7 at 6:27 PM
subject: UNDELIVERABLE: no subject

The e-mail address you entered "MOM" could not be found. Please check the recipient's e-mail address and try again to send your message. If the problem continues, please contact your help-desk for troubleshooting.

---

from: smith@simonyi.com
to: carl@simonyi.com
date: Sat, Nov 7 at 6:31 PM
subject: urgent

Carl,

I know it's a Saturday and you're probably at an ayahuasca ceremony or something, but what does this app you installed do besides delay emails? Tell me it isn't doing what I think it's doing.

---

from: carl@simonyi.com
to: smith@simonyi.com
date: Sat, Nov 7 at 6:39 PM
subject: re: urgent

Hmm. What might that be? I need a bit more direction.

Also, I don't do ayahuasca. I've watched YouTube videos of people doing it, and the vomit deters me. Plus they all seem to be dummies.

On the other hand, I *do* like the idea of sensing an overwhelming, universal love . . . pros and cons!

---

from: smith@simonyi.com
to: carl@simonyi.com
date: Sat, Nov 7 at 6:42 PM
subject: urgent

I think it's sending my drafts. I drafted a letter in my email account that I never meant to send. It just bounced back because I hadn't even included a real email address. So OOF! must have sent it?

---

from: carl@simonyi.com
to: smith@simonyi.com
date: Sat, Nov 7 at 6:43 PM
subject: re: urgent

I know it autofills based on your recent email history . . . but no, it's not supposed to automatically send drafts after it autofills. That would be a horrible feature of a product! Are you sure you didn't send yourself?

---

from: smith@simonyi.com
to: carl@simonyi.com
date: Sat, Nov 7 at 6:44 PM
subject: urgent

Yes. I just looked. It not only autofills . . . the fucking thing is sending my drafts to the *people* it autofilled. Every draft I've written since you installed it has been sent.

---

from: carl@simonyi.com
to: smith@simonyi.com
date: Sat, Nov 7 at 6:50 PM
subject: re: urgent

Yikes! That's a HUGE bug. I'll let Gus know.

Ugh, he's going to be so bummed about this. I didn't mention this before, but he's having a rough year. Would you know, Gus Martin is one of the most coveted names by criminals? He's only twenty-two and his identity has been stolen six times. Right now some car thief in Sacramento has his SS# pinned for $45K in CC debt.

AND he's got shingles.

---

from: smith@simonyi.com
to: carl@simonyi.com
date: Sat, Nov 7 at 6:56 PM
subject: urgent

Can you get into Iris's Gmail account? How do I do it? I need to delete something.

from: carl@simonyi.com
to: smith@simonyi.com
date: Sat, Nov 7 at 6:57 PM
subject: re: urgent

Um, Boss, that's illegal.

from: smith@simonyi.com
to: carl@simonyi.com
date: Sat, Nov 7 at 6:59 PM
subject: urgent

You do it all the time!

from: carl@simonyi.com
to: smith@simonyi.com
date: Sat, Nov 7 at 7:02 PM
subject: re: urgent

I go IN. I don't DELETE. That's a *traceable* crime.

from: smith@simonyi.com
to: carl@simonyi.com
date: Sat, Nov 7 at 7:04 PM
subject: urgent

Carl, give me the fucking password.

---

from: smith@simonyi.com
to: carl@simonyi.com
date: Sat, Nov 7 at 7:11 PM
subject: urgent

Now!

---

from: carl@simonyi.com
to: smith@simonyi.com
date: Sat, Nov 7 at 7:12 PM
subject: re: urgent

Do you have snapchat? I'd feel safer snapping you.

---

from: smith@simonyi.com
to: carl@simonyi.com
date: Sat, Nov 7 at 7:13 PM
subject: urgent

I'll delete the text, Carl. For fuck's sake.

---

from: carl@simonyi.com
to: smith@simonyi.com
date: Sat, Nov 7 at 7:15 PM
subject: re: urgent

Fine. Texted.
   I've never seen you like this!

---

from: carl@simonyi.com
to: smith@simonyi.com
date: Sat, Nov 7 at 7:59 PM
subject: re: urgent

Well??? How did it go? Did you delete? I'm trying not to ask questions, but I am *so* curious what's going on!

I will uninstall OOF! first thing Monday morning.

---

from: smith@simonyi.com
to: carl@simonyi.com
date: Sat, Nov 7 at 8:39 PM
subject: urgent

I didn't get there in time. It's already marked as read.

---

from: carl@simonyi.com
to: smith@simonyi.com
date: Sat, Nov 7 at 8:45 PM
subject: re: urgent

What??? She's DEAD. Who else is in there??

---

from: smith@simonyi.com
to: carl@simonyi.com
date: Sat, Nov 7 at 8:47 PM
subject: urgent

Doesn't matter. It's too late.

Saturday, November 7
TherapistAwayNetwork™
Patient Name: Jade Renee Massey
AUTO PROMPT: **What is a first step you can take?**

Ha. Joke's on me. What I get for checking her email.

Of course he loved her. Or at least wishes he'd "let himself,"
whatever that means.

I was the next closest thing.

Shouldn't be surprised, I guess, given I suspected it all along.

. . .

Dear JADE,

Thank you for your submission to TAN™. We will make sure
your provider receives this message.

In baseball, first base is a position on the field that requires
an elite player, because it is the critical point where a run is determined possible or impossible.

Where does the ball get thrown more times than anywhere
else? That's right: first.

There is a reason for the saying that the first step is the hard-
est one, and it is the same reason that the ball is thrown more often to first base than other bases. When you start a journey, that's
when you're most vulnerable. Make it past first, and you've survived the worst. (We didn't mean for that to rhyme, but we like it.)

TAN™ is not to be used in case of emergency. If you are in crisis, call 9-1-1.

Sincerely,

Your friends at TAN

Since I don't think I'll have time to finish writing out my dots, this week I made a list of a hundred memories and sorted them:

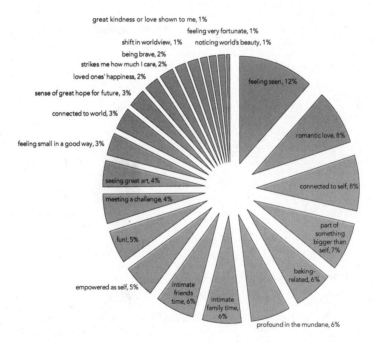

great kindness or love shown to me, 1%
feeling very fortunate, 1%
shift in worldview, 1%   noticing world's beauty, 1%
being brave, 2%
strikes me how much I care, 2%
loved ones' happiness, 2%
sense of great hope for future, 3%
connected to world, 3%
feeling small in a good way, 3%
seeing great art, 4%
meeting a challenge, 4%
fun!, 5%
empowered as self, 5%
intimate friends time, 6%
intimate family time, 6%
profound in the mundane, 6%
baking-related, 6%
part of something bigger than self, 7%
connected to self, 8%
romantic love, 8%
feeling seen, 12%

Feeling Seen. That's what I remember best.

Which I guess means most of the time I felt unseen.

For my eighth-grade school dance, I wore a cream dress that I inherited from Jade. It had peach polka dots and satin buttons down the back. It was the first time I remember feeling pretty.

I was sitting in the hotel lobby waiting for my mom to finish getting ready so she could drive me to the dance when Jade came in on her way out for the night. She was seventeen and a senior in high school. I waited for her to notice how I looked, but she didn't even glance at me. She looked beautiful, even in jeans.

"Bye," I said.

She didn't even say it back as she left.

The next year I got my first tattoo and dyed my hair hot pink, but by then Jade was in culinary school, and when she came "home" for break (I forget what hotel we were living in, maybe one in Kansas), all she said was "Rebel phase, I see."

I always wanted my sister to think of me as a real person. But I was her little sibling: part nuisance, part confidante when she needed one, part forgettable much of the time.

It's nice that she sees me now. Even if it's because I am sick.

COMMENTS (3):

TigerSashRox: I see you, girl!

BonnieD: we're here for you!

SP2004: might I recommend "Without a Pit, It's Not a Cherry?" You must love yourself before others can love you is the message.

MONDAY, NOVEMBER 9

from: jademassey@yahoo.com
to: smith@simonyi.com
date: Mon, Nov 9 at 8:30 AM
subject: Sorry

Dear Smith,

I apologize for saying what I did about you and your relationship to your mother. It wasn't fair. I was lashing out. These things are hard to navigate, and I was acting like they aren't. I know you had feelings for my sister (sorry for looking, but I'd rather know, and am glad I do now).

I just want you to know that I hold no hard feelings and wish you the best. Thank you for the conversations over the last couple of months. They've helped me.

Sincerely,

Jade

---

from: carl@simonyi.com
to: jademassey@yahoo.com
date: Mon, Nov 9 at 10:09 AM
subject: re: Sorry

Hi Jade,

Carl here, managing Smith's email. Very sad news. His mom died last night. He's in Wisconsin. Apparently she caught a case of pneumonia and it did her in. Poor guy. :'-(

But while I have you on the line, I have some *good* news. After we turned down Todd and Chad at Dying to Blog, I reached out to our *Belle* contact Hadley to see if she'd be interested in a listicle based on Iris's blog. Turns out she's more interested in running an excerpt or two from the blog itself. Anyway, since I have actually been putting in the sweat hours on the following listicle, I figure I will share it with you. I plan to submit it to Hadley this week just to see what she thinks. Or if you think we should stick to selecting a post or two from Iris's blog, I suppose we could do that, too.

I tried to keep it light, as we both know readers of *Belle* are unlikely to be voracious consumers of the somewhat . . . grim reflections penned by your sis. (No offense, I'm sure she was a hoot in real life.)

What do you think?

Talk soon,

CVS III

Title: 10 Ways to Improve Your Life at Its Conclusion

BY CARL VAN SNYDER III

When New York resident Iris Massey died at age 33 earlier this year, she left behind a dream, a career in stagnation, and an empty cradle. But she also left behind a blog. Through rigorous toiling through grueling questions, Iris dared to face what many of us ignore every day of our lives: the fact that sometimes our life doesn't amount to what we thought it would.

Inspired by Iris but not stated by her directly, thus not a copy of her expression of any ideas, here are 10 ways that you, too, can discover the latent potential in your own life before the guillotine comes crashing down.

1. **Indulge happy memories.** We all like to remember the good times, but sometimes we feel like we aren't supposed to be nostalgic, that it's a waste of time and what we're really supposed to be doing is working as hard as we can night and day, studying and getting all As and setting ourselves apart so that in the end, we can have whatever career we want and live the American dream at its most prestigious. But the rat race might as well be called "fatigue central." What's so bad about lying back and recalling your happiest times? An occasional bout of fantasizing about the past can be good for you, reactivating neural pathways that make those happy memories more robust and therefore easier to recall in the future when you need a "pick-me-up."

2. **Take up drawing.** Who among us did not at one point wish to be Van Gogh with his starry, swoopy sky, sans missing ear?

3. **Find an online community.** Do you live in the Middle of Nowhere, South Dakota? Do you feel like no one around gets you because you do not conform to the standards they set for their lives, such as what kind of person you are allowed to love? In that case, I have good news for you: get online! Everyone is online, mostly, except for in the dirt-poor parts of the world, and probably even there by now. That means you have about seven billion people to choose from for your new friends. Find people who get you, whether those are people who fall in love with goats or people who are also dying.

4. **Don't put off your dreams.** The disappointment of failure beats the disappointment of never trying. Fail to win. Win to fail. Etc. (Note to editor: This one might need a bit of work from someone else because I do not relate to it.)

5. **Break up with the capital-L "Loser."** Does your partner make you feel worse more often than he (or she or they) makes you feel better? If so, dump their ass. You get to live once. Don't spend your time with a lover who makes you yell all the time.

6. **Study science.** You don't know how big the universe is until you find out. And you don't find out until you ask, or go to a planetarium, or watch a free documentary on your laptop about the cosmos. It is really big. This will make you feel small, but in a good way, which will make you humble and want to not take yourself as seriously as you have a tendency to do. Or it will just make you respect nature, which is very important due to global warming.

7. **Do things for others, such as baking for them.** (Note to editor: cut? This one is boring to me, I'm half asleep just writing it.)

8. **Read books about dying.** You can never be too prepared for dying. It is happening to all of us as we speak. Therefore, in order to face death with grace when it descends upon you out of

nowhere, whether it is your own death or the death of another, best be ready by educating yourself in advance.

9. **Start a blog.** We all must express our feelings or else they get jammed up in our necks and threaten to burst forth in a scream or a stabbing. Don't explode. Rather, vent in a productive and socially acceptable way—by blogging or vlogging or tweeting or snapchatting or using insta. And if you do not want people to read your blog or tweets, you don't have to worry. They won't! There are too many out there to choose from anyway, which means it'll be mostly like a diary and you need not harbor performance anxiety.

10. **Try a crazy hairstyle.** Heck, go bald! What is life unless you're willing to tackle a little adventure, including new looks? Plus, hairstylists are notoriously eager to chat. If you are someone who has a hard time making friends, the salon is not a bad place to hit, as they are required to converse with you whilst you are in their swivel chairs.

MESSAGES

Mon., Nov. 9, 10:14 AM

Jade: Oh no. I'm so sorry, Smith.

My tenth-grade physics teacher Mr. Neely wore a toupee and smelled like mothballs. But Mr. Neely also knew about quasars.

Quasars are the brightest objects in the universe, brighter than stars by multitudes. They're anywhere from 500 million to 29 billion light-years away. Or were. Because by the time their light reaches earth, most of them don't exist anymore. The day I learned about them, I'd never heard anything so miraculous.

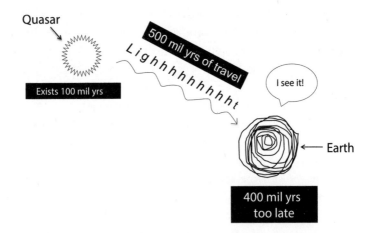

Mr. Neely assured us that they're too far away to be observed with the naked eye. You need a telescope. But I was always searching for them anyway, my eyes to the sky, eager to spot something that no longer existed.

Now I wonder if maybe I already sensed that one day I'd be gone and wanted to know that when it happened, I'd still be somewhere.

COMMENTS (2):

BonnieD: over my head!

BigJessBarbs: Math. 500-100 = 400 mil yrs too late. Go pick up a math book!

from:	jademassey@yahoo.com
to:	henrystewartmd@gmail.com
date:	Wed, Nov 11 at 2:20 PM
subject:	Dinner

Hi Henry,

Sorry I hadn't yet responded to your messages. About the lawsuit—you can forget it. I'm not going to pursue it.

As for "us" . . . to be honest, it seems dumb to try again, right? I mean truly stupid, to be clear. But my friend's mom just died. And all of this death lately is making me think about how short life is. So . . . on the other hand, what's really to lose?

We can have dinner, sure. Let me know when and where is good for you.

Jade

MONDAY, NOVEMBER 16

---

from: Delta
to: smith@simonyi.com
date: Mon, Nov 16 at 8:00 AM
subject: It's time to check in for your flight to NYC-LaGuardia!

You may now check in for Delta Flight #2880 from Madison, Wisconsin, to New York, New York, at 8:00 AM on Tuesday, November 17.

---

from: YOPLAY <philgergel@gmail.com>
to: smith@simonyi.com
date: Mon, Nov 16 at 9:20 PM
subject: DAMMIT YOU

I JUST LANDED AT LAGUARDIA AND CARL TOLD ME ABOUT YOUR MOM

I HAVE BEEN TWO WEEKS ON AN ASHRAM INSTEAD OF SIX BECAUSE IT WAS THE MOST BORING TWO WEEKS OF MY LIFE AND YET IT TAUGHT ME PATIENCE AND UNDERSTANDING

I BELIEVE THAT PRIOR TO MY ASHRAM STAY I WAS LOOKING ONLY AT THE BOTTOM LINE AKA CAPITAL-ISM AND THAT IS NOT THE WAY TO WIN IN THE END

AKA NOW I FEEL BAD

YOU AREN'T A TOTAL FUCKUP, OKAY, YOU ARE A MODERATE ONE

HANG IN THERE SMITH

YOPE

---

from: YOPLAY <philgergel@gmail.com>
to: smith@simonyi.com
date: Mon, Nov 16 at 10:26 PM
subject: ME AGAIN

CARL SAYS I NEED TO BE CLEAR THAT I AM NOT REHIR-ING YOU

I'M JUST SAYING I FORGIVE YOU

OK BYE

---

from: carl@simonyi.com
to: smith@simonyi.com
date: Mon, Nov 16 at 11:17 PM
subject: Phil

Boss,

I assume you're still awake since it's an hour earlier over there. I hope you're hanging in.

When you come up for air, can you do me a favor and write back to Phil? He's worried about you. And nagging me. You know how he gets obsessed with one thing and can't get off it due to his ADHD.

Also, just putting a bug in your ear—have you considered reading any more of Iris's drafts? Specifically her *last* draft? Because I can see that the last time it was opened was on October 30th, which was when I opened it. And I suggest you read it. I think it's important you read it.

TUESDAY, NOVEMBER 17

---

from: carl@simonyi.com
to: smith@simonyi.com
date: Tue, Nov 17 at 10:10 AM
subject: Returned

Boss,

I see you have landed. Praise Delta email confirmations.
Does this mean you're coming back tomorrow?

---

from: Domino's
to: smith@simonyi.com
date: Tue, Nov 17 at 12:04 PM
subject: Your delivery is on its way!

We'll be at your door in 45 minutes or less! Click here to track
your pizza!

WEDNESDAY, NOVEMBER 18

---

from: contact@lassimariset.com
to: smith@simonyi.com
date: Wed, Nov 18 at 3:22 AM
subject: re: hi

---

hi again
   do you think you could get me on Netflix or Hulu . . .

---

from: Domino's
to: smith@simonyi.com
date: Wed, Nov 18 at 11:19 AM
subject: Your delivery is on its way!

We'll be at your door in 45 minutes or less! Click here to track your pizza!

---

from: Domino's
to: smith@simonyi.com
date: Wed, Nov 18 at 8:12 PM
subject: Your delivery is on its way!

We'll be at your door in 45 minutes or less! Click here to track your pizza!

THURSDAY, NOVEMBER 19

from: rosylady101@yahoo.com
to: smith@simonyi.com
date: Thu, Nov 19 at 12:08 PM
subject: You are un-fired and re-hired

Smith,

Rosita here. I would like to reacquire your services immediately, as I have been even unhappier with my current management team than I was with you. They are insisting that I be marketed as a "Mouth Artist." I cannot stand the word "mouth" or the word "artist."

Please consider yourself re-employed by me, effective immediately. Are you available to chat in 5 minutes? I have an agenda I'm just finishing up that I can shoot over once I add a couple of items to the last page.

Rosita

from: Domino's
to: smith@simonyi.com
date: Thu, Nov 19 at 4:10 PM
subject: Your delivery is on its way!

We'll be at your door in 45 minutes or less! Click here to track your pizza!

FRIDAY, NOVEMBER 20

from: sandra.p.willoughby@thelanding.com
to: smith@simonyi.com
date: Fri, Nov 20 at 8:01 AM
subject: Issue of concern

Dear Smith:

At our November board meeting last night, a concern was raised that there has been a great deal of traffic in and out of your unit recently. While co-op guidelines permit deliveries of pizza, we are writing to inquire about the volume of pizza deliveries. Specifically, we will be direct and ask: Is it plausible that one person would order this much pizza?

We are grateful that you promptly resolved the short-term sublet problem back in September. By consensus we request that if there is something nefarious at play with regard to these "pizza men" arriving at all hours of the day and night, you resolve it as quickly. Please let me know if you have any questions.

I am,

Sandra Willoughby

President

The Landing Co-operative

from:	Domino's
to:	smith@simonyi.com
date:	Fri, Nov 20 at 9:22 PM
subject:	Your delivery is on its way!

We'll be at your door in 45 minutes or less! Click here to track your pizza!

SATURDAY, NOVEMBER 21

from: carl@simonyi.com
to: smith@simonyi.com
date: Sat, Nov 21 at 12:07 PM
subject: Things are looking up!

Hi Boss,

Great news—Jade emailed me that she's fine with the excerpt! Do you know what I'm talking about or have I not filled you in?

Belle is going to publish a portion of Iris's blog. Which is good because Hadley was not a fan of my listicle, so this really does feel like our last shot, no pun intended.

Jade also sent some flowers for you. They are yellow with orange centers. I have <u>not</u> read the card. They are very pretty. I am attaching a photo.

Also Rosita has decided to rehire us—a plot twist that I will openly admit I find *bittersweet*.

Also my parents are interested in investing in Jade's bakery given that she is a former Barn chef. Do you want me to tell her the good news or do you want to?

Carl

MESSAGES—DRAFTS

Sat., Nov. 21, 12:55 PM

Smith: Hi Jade. Thank you for the flowers. I think maybe you mis-
    understood—

---

from: jademassey@yahoo.com
to: ENTER RECIPIENT'S ADDRESS
date: Sat, Nov 21 at 2:03 PM
subject: DRAFT no subject

Smith,

   I wish I never read the

In the end it's not only everything we remember but what we don't, too. The moments that passed unobserved, not celebrated or noted, just lived. We scold ourselves: *I failed to appreciate so much as it was happening! I wasn't paying attention!*

But to be bothered by that is only time playing tricks on a mind that thinks itself smaller than it is.

Don't try to appreciate it. You can't do it by trying. Don't try to do anything.

If anything, try not to try.

The thing is, there isn't one meaning that you remember or don't. It was what it was and is what it is, both simultaneously, along with every version it evolved into along the way, and will, the million iterations all stacked on top of each other like cans.

And what about the moments we forget? They are there, too, needles in our haystack-selves, a part of us even though we may never find them again and wouldn't know where to look. They prick us every now and then so we know they're there.

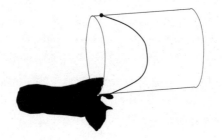

COMMENTS (1):

HarryBeastMan: I liked this blog more when it was less preachy. ☹

SUNDAY, NOVEMBER 22

from: carl@simonyi.com
to: smith@simonyi.com
cc: YOPLAY <philgergel@gmail.com>
date: Sun, Nov 22 at 11:34 AM
subject: An Intervention

Dear Boss,

This is an intervention from me and Phil.

You have been home for one week and have been responsive to nothing and have eaten Christ knows how much pizza. While this is perfectly acceptable for a limited period, we agree that one full week is enough for this particular phase of grieving. It is now time for you to enter a new phase. You can still sulk and mope and so forth, but we feel this new phase should involve coming to work at least because I am completely worn out from doing both of our jobs. Remember that I am ONLY A COLLEGE STUDENT!

Also we are going to Sonoma later this week for Thanksgiving to spend it with my family.

Please advise.

Carl

---

from: smith@simonyi.com
to: carl@simonyi.com
cc: YOPLAY <philgergel@gmail.com>
date: Sun, Nov 22 at 3:24 PM
subject: re: An Intervention

Wait. You're *both* going to California to see your family?

---

from: YOPLAY <philgergel@gmail.com>
to: smith@simonyi.com
cc: carl@simonyi.com
date: Sun, Nov 22 at 4:04 PM
subject: re: An Intervention

HE'S ALIVE!
   YES
   WE ARE BOTH GOING TO CALI
   I AM GOING TO MEET CARL'S PARENTS WHO
   HE DESCRIBES AS PINK

---

from: smith@simonyi.com
to: carl@simonyi.com
cc: YOPLAY <philgergel@gmail.com>
date: Sun, Nov 22 at 5:06 PM
subject: re: An Intervention

I'll be back to work tomorrow. Thanks for carrying the load, Carl. I'm really grateful. I'll write you the best "LOR" anyone's ever seen. And thanks, Phil, for forgiving (but not rehiring) me.

---

from: carl@simonyi.com
to: smith@simonyi.com
cc: YOPLAY <philgergel@gmail.com>
date: Sun, Nov 22 at 5:12 PM
subject: re: An Intervention

(*^_^*)

PS—Since I know you will ask, that's bashful face.

---

from: carl@simonyi.com
to: smith@simonyi.com
date: Sun, Nov 22 at 5:40 PM
subject: re: An Intervention

Hi Boss,

Taking Phil off for this thread because it doesn't seem professional to loop him in on this.

Soooooo this morning I accidentally spilled coffee on the card from Jade that came with the flowers she sent, which is super weird because I *never* spill. The last time I spilled was the first week of my internship (I was so young!), when I was at lunch and drenched the Post-it from Iris in Arnold Palmer. Remember that?

I didn't want it to become saturated to the point of incoherence, so I did open the card. It reads:

I'm sorry. You were right.

What do you think she means? Right about *what*?

So cryptic!

I am also attaching to this email a screenshot of Iris's last draft for your information and well-being.

Carl

Attachment (1)

http://dyingtoblog.com/irismassey

UNPUBLISHED DRAFT
Last opened November 22, at 5:22 PM

Tonight I am going to the office to print this blog and leave it for Smith to publish. Guessing he'll have to get in touch with my sister at some point. And then, who knows?

I was here

And I remember some of it

But most of it I don't

Between what I do

And what I don't

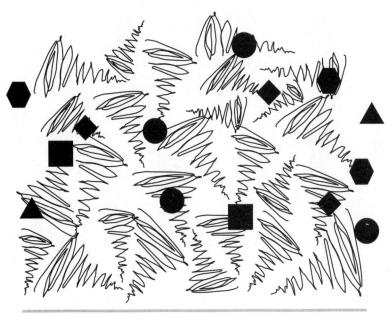

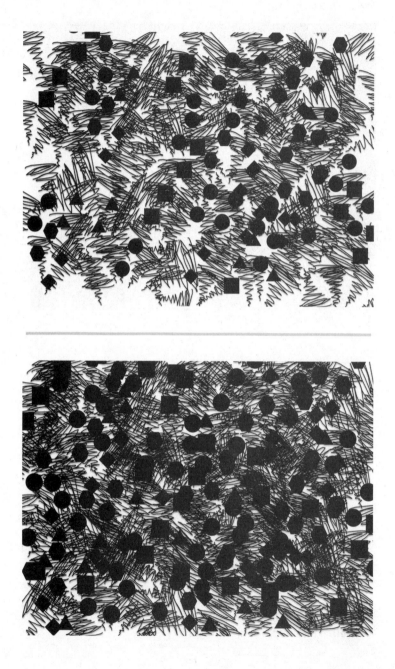

And loved.

COMMENTS (2):

DyingToBlogTeam: Happy National Pretzel Day!

BonnieD: :) this made me cry a little bit

MONDAY, NOVEMBER 23

MESSAGES

Mon., Nov. 23, 9:42 AM

SMITH: Thank you for the flowers.

JADE: How are you?

SMITH: Saddest I've ever been.

JADE: I hope that doesn't mean you've gambled away everything you own.

SMITH: No. I'm just getting fat on pizza.

JADE: Sounds reasonable.

SMITH: How are you?

JADE: I'm okay.

SMITH: Is it true—you're fine with Hadley publishing an excerpt of Iris's blog?

JADE: I said I'm okay with Belle publishing it. I still have mixed feelings about an adult named Hadley.

SMITH: Yes, I recall.

SMITH: Why the change of heart?

JADE: I read it. The whole thing. I finished it.

JADE: I gave the link to my mom to read, too.

SMITH: Wow.

JADE: I'm not saying you were right to go behind my back.

SMITH: I know. I owe you an actual apology.

JADE: But I'm not opposed to the idea of people reading it now. And
     you're right—I'm glad I read to the end.

SMITH: I'm sorry I went behind your back.

JADE: It's okay.

SMITH: What else is going on?

JADE: I got the space. The one in Brooklyn.

SMITH: Congratulations.

JADE: Thanks.

SMITH: Did Carl tell you his parents want to invest?

JADE: Yeah. Ha.

SMITH: Does that mean you aren't interested?

JADE: My plans have changed.

SMITH: Oh?

JADE: I don't know. I might open a restaurant or something.

SMITH: I imagine his parents would be into that as well.

JADE: You really aren't gambling, or was that a lie?

SMITH: I found this video online called *The Easy Way to Stop Gambling*.
     The whole time it didn't need to be a struggle, I was just mak-
     ing it a struggle. It seems to have worked. Go figure.

JADE: Is this a joke?

SMITH: Nope.

JADE: *The Easy Way*? Don't recruit me for your cult please.

SMITH: Or maybe you were right earlier in the fall when you said I do
     it to make things worse before they can get worse on their
     own. Things got as bad as they could get. There's no "worse"
     now.

JADE: I said that?

SMITH: Yes.

JADE: Were you able to see your mom before she died?

SMITH: No.

JADE: She knew you were coming.

SMITH: So what kind of food are you going to serve in your restaurant?

JADE: Good question.

SMITH: We should probably get to work. Dinner at 6?

JADE: I'm supposed to see Henry tonight for dinner.

SMITH: I see.

JADE: I could cancel.

SMITH: Cancel.

JADE: Okay.

SMITH: Go ahead and cancel all of Henry's upcoming appointments.

JADE: Okay.

SMITH: Dude got his shot. It's over.

---

from:	smith@simonyi.com
to:	rosylady101@yahoo.com
date:	Mon, Nov 23 at 12:44 PM
subject:	re: Dancing with the Stars

Dear Rosita,

You certainly make a case for joining the cast of DWTS—quite impressive, that video of your latest merengue competition. Such footwork!

Unfortunately, I don't think our continuing to work together is meant to be. Best of luck to you, in mouth artistry, merengue, and beyond.

Sincerely,

Smith S. Simonyi

President

BRANDISH

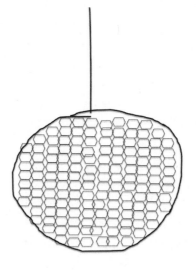

My sister has been staying with me. A few days ago she was going to spend a night back in Jersey so she could swap out her clothes and water her plants. She asked what needed to be done before she left. I said go dancing but I was kidding. Then I took a nap.

    I woke up to her putting makeup on me: rubbing eye shadow on my lids, stroking mascara onto the tops of my lashes, dabbing lipstick onto my chapped lips. Of course, I didn't have any hair to do, and the wigs had started itching, so she tied on a scarf. I'm not sure which one. She put me in black pants and a gauzy, fitted blouse I wore when I was younger and hotter. I had saved it thinking that maybe, one day, I'd become thin enough to wear it again. In fact, I had.

She hailed us a cab and still wouldn't tell me where we were going.

"It's a surprise," she kept saying. We had to stop twice so I could throw up. The driver seemed annoyed the first time, but when I got back in, I could tell Jade had told him what was going on, because in the rearview mirror he stared at me with pity. The third time I threw up into a grocery bag he passed back. Finally, the car stopped in front of Rinse, the club where Jade and I went sometimes in our twenties when we wanted to get wasted and dance.

There was a bearded, husky man in all black standing outside, waiting. He shook Jade's hand and introduced himself to us as Pete, the guy she'd spoken with on the phone. Pete let us into the empty dance hall. The strobe light was already on, and Beyoncé's "Best Thing I Never Had" was playing. The dance floor looked enormous without anyone on it, and stepping onto it was strange, like going out into a snowy field that no one has walked on yet.

We danced by ourselves. I forgot I was sick. I forgot it was ending. I just danced with my sister, and it was the best. The very best. I can't even think of the words for how good it was.

Thank you, Jade. Thank you, thank you, thank you.

COMMENTS (122):

BonnieD: RIP Iris

XYZLots: just found this blog! sad too late. rip

BigJessBarbs: This was my favorite blog!

TigerSashRox: are we sure she's rip?

BonnieD: I think so? Iris u there?

Click to see 116 more . . .

WinsomeDorothy: Dear Everyone on this Blog, Yes, Iris is RIP. Thank you for your support of her, on behalf of Dorothy Massey, her mother. We miss you down here, girlie. Love, Mom.

EPILOGUE

from: carlvansnyder@gmail.com
to: jademassey@yahoo.com
date: Fri, May 13 at 12:34 PM
subject: OUR WEDDING CAKE

Dear Jade,

I hope you are doing well! I hear from Smith that restaurant plans are going well. Please keep me posted on the date of the launch, as I would love to come if I am available. I will be moving back to New York at the end of the month, after graduation.

Smith has warned me that you might say no given that you hate sweets, but I have an enormous favor to ask that would mean so much to Phil and me. Would you be willing to make our wedding cake? You have until October!

I know there are probably people we could find who would make better cakes, but since Smith is officiating the wedding, it feels very much like a family affair.

Reasons I think you should do it:

1. You will be anxious waiting for Iris's book proofs in November, and this will be a welcome distraction.

2. It will mean a lot to Phil and me.

3. It's good for the mind to try out new things. Our brains crave plasticity, longing to be exercised in fresh capacities in order to prolong mental acuity. In a way, we're doing YOU a favor!

4. Today is Friday the 13th. I don't know if you're one of the 21 million people who suffer from *paraskevidekatriaphobia*—fear of this day in the Gregorian calendar—but if so, it certainly wouldn't hurt to summon good energies your way by doing friends a favor. (They say that once you can pronounce *paraskevidekatriaphobia*, you're cured, though I can't test this claim myself, as I find the fear to be irrational and thus unrelatable.)

In exchange, I offer my services as an Elite Yelp reviewer four years and counting. Have you seen the Yelp page for BRANDISH recently? It's a masterpiece. When your restaurant launches, I will promptly post a rave review and recruit the like from my Yelp compatriots (we do that for each other).

What do you think?

Carl

---

from:	HelloCupid
to:	jademassey@yahoo.com
date:	Fri, May 13 at 4:27 PM
subject:	MANOFLAMANCHA is looking at your profile!

JadeJadeJava,

We can't believe it either! It's been over a year since you logged in—and people are checking out your profile! Here's a sneak peek at the latest message you've received:

From NOTABRIT:

Hi! I am a freelancer living in Crown Heights, just arrived from Chicago where I dwelled for 15 years. Before that, I grew up in Evanston, Illinois. But I won't blame you for thinking me an Englishman, as I suffer from FAS (Foreign Accent Syndrome), which has caused me to speak with a British accent since falling victim to a ferocious migraine in the spring of 2010. Don't worry, I've been assured it's of the posh variety.

Or maybe it even makes me MORE sexy to you???

How about you, Java, where are you from?

---

from: HelloCupid
to: jademassey@yahoo.com
date: Fri, May 13 at 4:33 PM
subject: PROFILE DELETED

Your profile has been deleted. Please help us improve our product by telling us your reason for deleting your profile. Simply check one of the boxes below.

Thanks,

The HelloCupid Team

_____ I am using another dating site.

_____ I had an unpleasant experience.

_____ I prefer to remain single.

__x__ I met someone.

ACKNOWLEDGMENTS

I am forever indebted to my agent, Claire Anderson-Wheeler. I am so grateful to the universe for bringing me to you. The same goes to my editor, Emily Griffin. I felt it was fate when we first talked about running long distances and being miserable about it. Working with you has been a daily privilege ever since. Melissa Cox and Elinor Cooper in the UK—it has likewise been a joy.

My friends who read this book when it was a first draft, Rina Goldfield and Emily Wulwick, thank you for being that kind of friend. Sarah Stone, you are the writer whisperer. Kimberlee Auerbach Berlin and Victory Matsui, thank you for your early insights as well.

My writing group helped raise this book through its challenging toddler and teenage years. Joselin Linder, Kate Tellers, Joanne Solomon, Nicole Solomon, Christine Clarke, T. J. Wells, Jorge Novoa, Jessica Mannion, Sam Ritchie, Alex DiFrancesco, Gabra Zackman, and Natalia Kislitsina—thank you for being this novel's favorite aunts and uncles. I don't know what I did to wind up among you other than knowing Kate Tellers, but as with many good things, that's probably all it was. I cherish our Tuesdays of hummus, overpriced red, and "what-ifs." May we remain compatibly deranged for many years.

And to the rest of my writer family—Haley Hoffman, Rachel Abramowitz, Greg Marshall, and my partner in most crimes, Lucas Schaefer—thank you for the endless supply of inspiration, commiseration, and laughs.

To Lee Shapiro, Chibuzo Enemchukwu, Israt Pasha, and Derek Frankhauser, thank you for your generosity as experts where I'm clueless.

Writing takes up a lot of space sometimes. I'm grateful to Audrey and Hal Krisbergh, and to Justin Ahren and the Noepe Center, for generously offering me a place to work.

Dr. Z., you're out there somewhere, raising your one eyebrow and probably giving me an "8" on this. Thanks for being my most irreverent and passionate English teacher, apart from Mrs. Chancy. Everyone, go find Diane Chancy and take seventh-grade English from her if you want to make the rest of your life better.

My sister, Katie Beth Ongena, is the kind of sibling who made me want to write a novel about sisters. Thank you for being as wonderful as it gets. Clista and Glen Adkins, thank you for being parents who pushed us to do what we love, to be creative, and to live lives we want to wake up to in the morning. You may have questioned that choice once or twice upon receiving phone calls about quitting jobs and dropping out of law school, but I'm so grateful for it.

Lucas, thank you for being my frequent editor and daily reminder to laugh at myself. I love spending this life with you.

Finn, I was putting the final touches on this manuscript while you were the size of a kumquat. As I write this, you're the size of a jalapeño. I hope this book doesn't embarrass you one day, but if it does, you can use it in your stand-up.